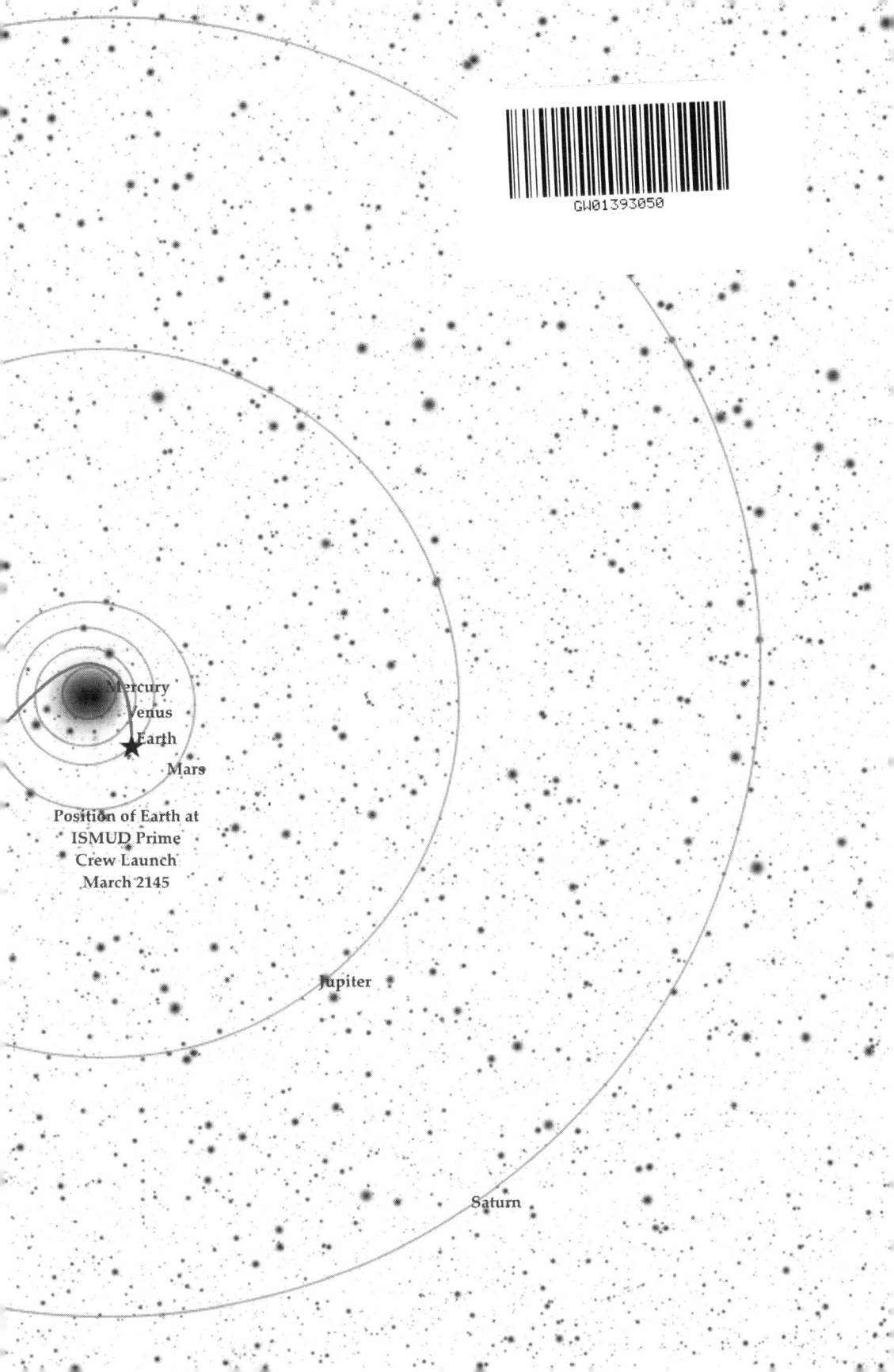

Mercury
Venus
Earth
Mars

Position of Earth at
ISMUD Prime
Crew Launch
March 2145

Jupiter

Saturn

DIATHESIS

DESCENT
BOOK 1

ISHMAEL A. SOLEDAD

Temple Dark Books

Also by the Author

Sha'Kert: End of Night

Descent Book 1: Diathesis
First (Limited) Edition
In association with Roe River Books, Dundalk, Co. Louth
Copyright © Ishmael A. Soledad 2025

Ed. Ronald A. Geobey
Asst. Ed. Jeanne Fournier

Cover art assets © Eugen Baitinger
www.ebaitinger.de
Cover design by Brian Mongey

Typesetting & Formatting by Temple Dark Books
Temple Dark Publications Ltd.
77 Camden Street Lower, Dublin 2
D02 XE80, Ireland
www.templedarkbooks.com

Printed and bound by CPI Group (UK) Ltd., Croydon, CR0 4YY
Using Entirely Renewable Energy (FSC Certified)

The manufacturer's authorised representative in the EU for product safety is Ronald A. Geobey, Temple Dark Books, 77 Camden Street Lr, Dublin D02 XE80, thegatekeeper@templedarkbooks.com +353-42-9503092

For Kitty and Andrew G McCann

Iacta Alea Est

(The Die is Cast)

Julius Caesar

PROLOGUE

LINGBAO TIANZUN, GEOSTATIONARY EARTH ORBIT, MARCH 2150

LI QIAO

The outer door opens, my suit stiffens as the airlock empties. I reach for the safety line, stop – I don't need it, not this time. I face spinwards, push out into the blackness. Antennae and cabling blur beneath me, disappear, and with them the station. I am complete in myself, my own satellite in orbit, no longer Li Qiao of the Lingbao Tianzun.

Earth is void, blacker than space. The Philippines and Japan should burn bright, China's patchwork of rods and smudges anchors me home, but not now, not ever. Only stars around me and darkness below tell me Earth is there.

Sunrise explodes. No gentle glow on the horizon, no warm, diffuse light heralds dawn; it's off-on, night to day in a harsh, violent instant. Earth burns burnished gunmetal, a featureless, airless, barren world – no life, no hope, no future.

There's no one to remember, envy, or respect me, nobody to understand what I achieved, no chance to fulfil my potential and realise the promise within. Thirty-four years is not enough: I'm cheated out of my life, time I deserve, the future owed to me.

'What use more years when you wasted those you had?' Fùqin asks.

'Why me, why now?'

'As always, this is your doing, your failure.'

CHAPTER 01: SEEDS

SANTIAGO, CHILE
2113

MARIA

My mouth waters half a block from home, the scent of fresh bread carries on the mid-afternoon breeze. Abue must feel better, ache less to stand for hours and bake inside our cramped kitchen. She's probably happy, might sing an old song, forget Mum for a while. Hunger pulls my feet along the cracked footpath, guilt slows me down. The chip in my pocket's harsh and cold, what I bring home for Abue's trouble, for Yayo's patience. Again. Another message, more evidence I am, as Señora Sanzaro says, a troublemaker.

I creep up the stairs, hope to avoid Abue, give the chip to Yayo, and retreat to my room. The screen door sets itself against me, slams shut to announce my arrival.

'Maria, is that you?'

'Yes, Abue.'

She shuffles over, stands on tiptoes to hold my face in flour-covered hands and kiss my forehead. 'How was school? Are you hungry?'

'Starving.'

She drags me to the kitchen, thrusts a hot bread roll into my hands. 'Olive and basil, new recipe.'

It's good, outside crunchy and warm, middle soft and moist. Halfway through, she hands me a second, drowned in butter and Parmesan. 'And no more, dinner's not far away.'

I lean against the wall, eat slowly, try to put off the inevitable. It's useless, always is, but I hope anyway – the last bite finishes that. 'Where's Yayo?'

'In front of the screen as usual, but he's not in a good mood. All day it's space this, space that. He's argued with it since he got up.'

'Oh.'

Her good mood deflates instantly. She knows. 'Who is it this time?'

'Señora Sanzaro.'

Deflation to resignation. She throws the dishcloth in the sink. 'Headmistress? That's all of them now. What did you do?'

'Nothing.'

'Always nothing with you. Let's go talk to your grandfather.'

Yayo lies on the couch, feet up, remote on his belly. Saturn's on the screen, bright yellow and red lines snake around it, over the sun and into space. He sits up as we come through the curtain.

'We need to talk, Diego. Maria's got another one,' Abue says.

I give Yayo the chip, turn to go.

'No, Maria. This time you stay and listen.'

I sit at the far end of the couch, as far from both of them as I can.

He puts the chip on the player. Señora Sanzaro's projection springs up, Isla de Pascua statues behind her: 'Señor and Señora Rodrigucs, please call me as soon as you receive this message. Thank you.'

The image freezes, a green *Call Now* glyph hovers. Yayo stares at me, stern-faced. 'No report, no gentle message, just "call me"? You want to tell me what I can expect from her?'

I count his freckles, his lines. I've tried to explain before, but no one listens. Why try again?

Yayo leans forward, taps the glyph. Frozen Señora Sanzaro's swapped for her older self behind a desk. 'Thank you for returning my call.'

'Maria's in trouble again?'

'Señor Rodrigues, it's no longer a question of *if* Maria's in trouble, it's *how much* trouble.'

'She's still getting over her parents' deaths. She has an overactive imagination, escapes into daydreams.'

'Her behaviour's worse. Her disruption and laziness now affect the other children. We need to sort this out before anything goes on her record.'

'What exactly is she doing?'

'For a start, her lying's getting worse. She's adamant her family name is Turano and her parents were Earth Warriors.'

Abue flinches. Yayo shakes his head. 'Her imagination again. She fills gaps left by her parents.'

'Then there's her militant veganism. We try to tolerate and embrace everyone's beliefs, but Maria's become insulting and discriminatory. Yesterday it turned into a shouting match with our Muslim students.'

Yayo looks at me. 'Is this true?'

'I saw how they kill the cows, it's awful, this big —'

'Maria, not now.' Yayo turns back to Señora Sanzaro. 'You have more?'

'Unfortunately. She has a lot of anger that comes through in everything. The title of her latest science assignment's only one example, and I quote, "Project Ismud. How the Morons Who Raped the World Will Now Fuck Up Another". I will not embarrass you with the rest, but be assured the contents are as descriptive as the title.'

'It's my fault, I'm not its greatest supporter, she's just taken what I feel –'

'She's taken it too far, Señor Rodrigues. I don't approve of all that money and waste, but there are better ways to express it that don't involve such words. This morning there was an incident with an exchange student from another school.'

'Swearing? At other students?'

'I wish it was. One of our students caught it on her player. It's easier if I show you.'

The bottom half of Señora Sanzaro's replaced by a video playback. It's the swimming pool, my friends dive-bomb, run, teachers try to control them. Shouts, squeals, laughter until the video picks up an argument, raised voices: I face down three older boys, shout, my arms fling about. Above it all, "thin, ugly, flat-chested vegan freak" soars out, then more, mixed, angrier. He steps in, taller than all of us, pulls them back, calms them down, turns to face me. He smiles, points to my bare shoulder, speaks but can't be heard over the din. I drive my foot between his legs, double him over, grab his tie and hurl him into the pool. The video wobbles, goes off.

Abue's shocked, Yayo tries his best to look shocked; I don't understand what Señora Sanzaro's face says. 'What did he say to you, Maria?' Señora Sanzaro asks.

'I don't remember exactly, he said my penguin looked sissy. Or soft. Or something.'

'How's the boy?' Yayo asks.

'Beaten up by a girl four grades lower bruised his ego, but otherwise Pierre's fine.'

'And the boys who picked on Maria?'

'Punished. Their school has the same attitude as we do to that sort of behaviour.'

Abue grips the top of her nose, closes her eyes, takes a deep breath. 'This can't go on.'

'No, Señora Rodrigues, it can't. Maria's not a junior anymore. The next time anything like this happens, any disruption or trouble, I'll *have* to put it on her record. The only reason this incident isn't is because she was provoked, and the boy and his headmaster don't want to make an issue of it.'

Señora Sanzaro looks at me. I understand what's in her eyes now – sadness. 'Maria, do you know what happens if I put anything on your record?'

'Detention, extra homework?'

'No. Nothing ever comes off. They look at it when you want to go up a grade, or if you want to go to university. If there's too much, you don't go.'

They can stop me for this? It's unfair: what if I'm not to blame, or it's a mistake, or they get me mixed up with someone else? Could they really make me repeat?

'Thank you for telling us, we had no idea it was so bad,' Yayo says. 'It won't happen again.'

'I hope so, Señor Rodrigues. I know my students' potential. Maria's very intelligent. She could be exceptional, but she has to get serious about her education. Now. That means discipline, self-control, and concentration.'

'We understand.'

'Thank you for your time. I hope next time we talk it's after

Maria's graduation.' Señora Sanzaro's projection snaps off.

'Did you understand everything, Maria?' Yayo asks.

'She didn't ask what I —'

'How could you be so stupid?' Abue erupts. 'I've told you time and time again not to tell anyone, and you go and shout it out at school?'

'But it's true, it's who I am, you said —'

'All the money we wasted to keep you safe, to stay out of sight, and you go and start stupid little fights over nothing —'

'They're not nothing, they're —'

'Stupid, nothing fights that get you noticed. You're too young to understand, just a silly little girl that —'

'I'm smarter than you. I'm not going to waste *my* life stuck in a kitchen!'

'I've put food in your mouth and a roof over your head ever since your father killed your mother.'

My eyes sting, fists clench. 'He did not!'

'He stole her, didn't even leave me a grave to mourn by.'

I'm on my feet, fists by my sides. 'He loved her, he never killed her!'

Abue's in tears — she rocks, hands to the sides of her head. 'When he killed her, he killed me. I have no life, no joy, only pain.'

I run up the stairs, stop halfway, tears pour down. 'I hate you!' I slam the door, fall flat onto my bed.

It's not fair, no one listens, nobody's on my side. They tell me to stand up for myself, then punish me, say I should be honest, but tell me to lie. If they can't make up their minds, how am I supposed to? All day stuck with stupid kids and dumb teachers. If

Mum were here I wouldn't be in trouble, she'd listen to me, she'd love me; Dad was always on my side no matter what.

I bury my head under the pillow. Why'd they go? I don't like being alone, hate the way teachers pretend my parents never existed, look at their "poor orphan girl" and say they understand. How can they, how can anyone? They're not me, they don't know what it's like.

The door creaks, bed sags, Yayo's hand on the back of my neck, gentle and light. I cry harder, burrow against him; he says nothing, does nothing, stays there and soaks it all in.

It's ages until I'm through, sit with snot- and tear-soaked sleeves against the bedhead. Yayo feeds me tissue after tissue, sends castoffs into the bin. Noise downstairs tells me Abue makes busy, lost again to her private world. 'I'm sorry.'

'It's alright, there's enough to be upset about without you.'

'Abue's still angry?'

'She could be, best we hide for a while. You know why she gets so angry so quickly?'

'She hates me?'

'No, she loves you. But you're so much like your mother, it's as if she's alive. Sometimes I believe it, the way you two carry on.'

'She always says Mum was a good, obedient kid, not like me.'

'So now, all the women in this family have bad memories? They fought all the time, worse than you two. When she was eight, they had a huge fight. Your mother didn't wash or eat or go to the toilet for a week. I had to bribe her with a trip to see the whales to break her.'

'You never say much about her.'

'It still hurts your grandmother. She remembers what she wants to remember, forgets the rest. And I try not to drag up ghosts.'

'Did Dad kill Mum? Honestly, did he?'

He stares at my mirror, at the only picture of my parents I have. A boat, Mum to one side, Dad the other, three-year-old me in the middle with a fish taller than me. 'No, of course not. It's my fault, the problems you have. I haven't told you everything. You were five when they died, I wanted to wait until you were old enough to understand. I guess twelve's old enough – do you want to know?'

It's a weird question. Of course I want to know, but if they've kept it from me, is it bad? Is it better to have only the photo, or to know? 'I think so. Yes, I do.'

'Right. So where to begin? Ah, yes, the start. Your mother was a dreamer, always thinking. No one at school could keep up with her, not even the teachers. Then, in her last year, your father turned up.'

'Did Abue hate him the moment she saw him?'

'She never hated him, no matter what she says – it makes it easier if she thinks she does. I pretended not to like him, as every father must. The moment they saw each other, they fell in love. He wasn't as smart as her, but he could take her ideas and make them work, got on with everybody where she couldn't.'

He must be getting more forgetful. 'Yayo, you've already told me that.'

'Not all of it, and it's important. You can't understand yourself until you understand your parents. You're like your mother, school's too easy for you. Your mother found challenges, you find trouble. You've got all that's good from them inside you, but you've also got some of the bad.'

'What do you mean?'

'Your father had a lazy streak, fought his whole life to keep it under control. And your mother was thin-skinned with an awful temper, she could go off instantly, for no reason; when she got mad she wasn't scared of anyone, didn't think. Just like you.'

'I do not, I never do.'

'Really? What about the boy at the pool? You can't remember what he said, can you?'

'No, not exactly.'

'Anyway, the point is you need to learn which battles to fight, and which ones are not worth it. Otherwise, you end up careless, reacting without thinking. Like your parents. And that's what killed them.'

'They died on a plane to Mexico, how's that careless?'

He takes my hand, sighs. 'They didn't die like that. It's a lie, another thing we said to protect you.'

They always said they'd gone for a holiday, left me with them, and the plane crashed on the way. It's all a lie? 'When were you going to tell me the truth?'

'When you were old enough to understand. It wasn't easy for us, you were so young and we…well, we were too old then, never mind now. Before you were born, everyone was upset about what we did to the planet, the lack of any progress. It was around then the Earth Warriors started. We said your parents donated a bit of time and money, but that's another lie. They believed in real action, so they joined. They had the brains and ability to make things happen, and the passion to see them through.'

'What sort of things?'

'Cyber-attacks in the Amazon, sabotage of Russian Co-prosperity Sphere gas pipelines, anything to make the environmental criminals pay, and —'

'They *killed* people?'

'No, they never set out to do that, ever. But they made many enemies. They left you with us when you turned four and we'd see them a few days every few months, then they'd go off again.' He closes his eyes, grimaces. 'We never found out how high they climbed, but they spent a small fortune to change all our identities. It's only that Venezuela and Chile were complete disasters they got away with it.'

'What's Venezuela got to do with anything?'

'It's home, where you were born. We had to leave, bribe our way through Brazil and Bolivia into Chile, start again with nothing. No family, no friends, no possibility of ever going back. We left everything behind to keep you safe.'

'Safe from what, my parents?'

'Safe from what they did. That last time they got arrogant, thought their way was the only way, went after the last of the Japanese whalers...'

Yayo stares into space, says nothing, sits still.

'And?'

'They got careless. Two ships, bad seas: they went in too hard and collided. Both ships sank, seven hundred and fifty dead, one survivor and she'll never get out of prison.' He hangs his head, fights back emotion. 'They got the wrong one — it was a small Japanese cruise ship. They haven't stopped looking for anyone associated with the Earth Warriors, they never will. That's why you must never mention your parents, or the Earth Warriors, why you must forget you were ever a Turano. No matter what, you have always been, and always will be, Maria Rodrigues.'

My nightmares tell me to fall to earth and die must be quick.

But to drown, in the ocean, with seven hundred others, because of you? 'How could they do that, how could they be so cruel?'

'They weren't cruel; up to then they hadn't hurt anyone, they even put themselves at risk to make sure people weren't hurt. Your mother used to say every life is precious; that included people, animals, even plants. They just got careless, but no one believes it.'

Yayo stands, goes to my bookshelf and rummages around. The photograph on my mirror transforms: the boat's gone, waves crash around; foam over their heads, my parents drown in a storm as I float away on the far edge. 'Why'd they do it, why didn't they stay with me and take care of me?'

Yayo sits, holds something in his hands. 'They did it for you, and for every other child of every other mother. They believed in you, in what you could be, and they wanted the world to be good enough for you.'

It's too much guilt, my tears start again. 'I've failed them, haven't I?'

Yayo hugs me, thumbs away my tears. 'No you haven't, you've got some problems, but nothing that can't be fixed. Your mother and father are gone, but we're here for you, all of us, even Señora Sanzaro.'

'Really?'

'Yes, really. If you want; if you'll try.'

'I do, Yayo, I'll try.'

'Good. Then it's a deal. Now, do you remember those bedtime tales I used to tell you, the Greek myths?'

'Perseus? Helen? Of course I do.'

He lifts his hands to me: a Trojan horse sits proudly on his palms, a toy I've had for as long as I can remember. 'Then you remember our friend.'

I reach out, touch its mane. 'When I was little, I wondered how anyone could fit inside.'

'My fault for using props. But now, the first lesson for the new you. The outside, the horse, are the Rodrigues; inside, the Turanos, your parents, our history. Understand?'

'It all stays hidden, but it's still us on the outside and the inside?'

'Yes, exactly. Now, your last lesson for tonight. What did they do with it?'

'They hid in it, waited until the city pulled it in, then attacked.'

'That is for you to think about. You choose your battles. Sometimes, to win, you must hide yourself and let your enemies lose. Understand?'

'I, no, I'm not sure.'

'Good. Maria, like Rome, is not built in a day.' Yayo twists the horse's front leg: a click, the horse breaks apart; a tiny box and folded paper held together by a rubber band slides into his hand. He stands, holds it out to me. 'Last time I saw your mother, she asked me to give this to you if something happened. When you were old enough.'

I take it from him, start to remove the rubber band.

'No, don't. It's from your mother to you, not me. Wait until I'm out.'

The door closes behind him. I try to take off the rubber band: it disintegrates, leaves little pieces of itself on the box and paper. I put the box down, examine the paper. One sheet, yellowed, torn on one side – I open it to reveal my mother's neat handwriting. On the corners, she's drawn flowers and butterflies, vines that run rampant down the sides of the page:

14

My darling Maria

You make us so happy and proud. All we want is to see you grow to be the wonderful, strong woman we know you will be. But sometimes things don't turn out the way we want.

If things get tough, remember you are tougher. If you feel it's you against the world, remember we're beside you. If things get dark, know that we'll always love you. Believe in yourself, because we believe in you.

Wear it close to your heart, for you are forever in ours.

Mum and Dad

I put it down quickly, away from the tears that threaten to wash the words away. The box lid opens easily, cotton wool protects what's inside. I tip it into my hand. A pendant ring: three intertwined bands of yellow, white, and pink gold swing from a long chain. There's something odd about the rings, each has a small groove running around the outside; a clear insert covers what looks like a single strand of hair in each, one light brown, one dark brown, one black. On the inside of each band, an inscription: *Ignacio 2104, Francesca 2104, Maria 2104.*

I give in, let the tears flow.

NANGANGZHEN, GUANGDONG PROVINCE CHINA
2117

MIN WAI MA

She bends, tilts her head and smiles, moves in for a closer look; he hangs back and watches silently, caught between politeness and curiosity. They're young, clearly in love. 'What a gorgeous baby,' she says.

I move the bottle to the boy's lips. 'Thank you.'

She holds her finger out, moves it slowly towards the boy; he stares at her, grasps her finger, continues to suck the bottle. 'Is he your first son?'

I don't feel like conversation, but small villages have many ears, strange customs, and long memories. 'My first child, yes. Do you have children?'

She blushes, gives a furtive glance to her companion. 'No, we're not married, yet.'

He picks up her signal, opens his mouth for the first time. 'When we are, then definitely. Two, perhaps three.'

She turns her attention back to the boy, stares fascinated as if she's never seen a baby kick before. 'You must be so proud and happy.'

I look down, wish the day away. '*She* was. For a moment.'

They mumble polite farewells, move away, leave me to his feeding. He finishes; I swap his bottle for my canteen, drink deeply. It's a warm day, a steep path; I think about loosening my tie, push the idea aside. I worked too hard and too long to be worthy of the uniform to deface it for mere comfort's sake.

Enough rest. I put the boy carefully into my chest sling, start back up the path. I have no eyes for breathtaking views across karst mountains and green valleys shot through with sinuous rivers, no time for polite conversation with Yao elders in their houses along the way. When she was alive it was different, the scenery a picture postcard to drive us into each other's arms; now it is simply raw memory, scar tissue. I have a job to do, no more, and when it's done, I will leave this place as quickly as I can.

The house stands as I remember it: stone rubble fence surrounds a simple log and bamboo home, animals run amok in the garden. Electricity's finally made it here — a cluster of four solar panels to one side and the blare of a screen bear witness. I knock once; the door opens, my father-in-law and mother-in-law stare out. They've aged years in months, barely recognisable; is this how I have changed? 'You're on time, Wai Ma. Come inside,' the old man says.

The old woman whisks the boy away, coos and cuddles him as she sits by the table; we join her, tea pot and cups ready. I pour two cups, careful to wait until they taste and approve. I refill theirs, then mine, sit.

The old woman rocks the boy — her practiced, smooth action lulls him to sleep. This should be Xiuying; it should be us, not them.

'How long do you have?' the old man asks.

'Thirty minutes, perhaps.'

'Always a rush — you put your Army duty to the front, allow it to outweigh your duty to your son.'

It's an accusation, not an observation, his age no barrier to a sharp tongue. 'You know duty to country exceeds all other. It leaves no room for a single parent, I have no choice.'

'And we do? We have worn ourselves out raising our own children, and you ask us to take your son?'

'Your grandson. Xiuying's son.'

'Your son. Would she want him to grow up without his father?'

Xiuying would understand, would know how each time I look at the boy I see her, feel every second of life with her denied me because of him. 'She would.'

'There's no other way?' the old woman asks.

None I would mention, none they could accept. Xiuying wasn't even cold when they asked, offered a year's income for the boy to be spirited away, taken by a childless couple as their own. It hasn't stopped, subtle hints and outrageously blunt suggestions; I reject it all even as I want to accept it, purge my life of the boy and the pain with him. I am stopped only by Xiuying's memory, the shame of such a betrayal. 'No, there's no other way.'

'And you?'

It's only her memory that stops me from never returning, never seeing him again. 'I will not disappear from his life. I will visit when I can, send messages, money for his upkeep and his school. Anything he wants or needs, I will provide.'

'And the love of his parents? How will he know you love him if you abandon him?'

'Love him? I may never.'

She sighs, turns back to the boy, ignores me.

'Then it's best he stays with us,' the old man says.

I finish my tea, refill our cups. Time drags as it always does here, a tiny window into life as it once was. Progress, if any, is slow.

'Did Xiuying choose a name?'

'No, she had no chance, only saw him once as she died.'

'A child needs a name. Have you chosen one?'

'Yes, but it's not registered. I have chosen Zi Xiaohun.'

Their heads snap up, hers with a look of horror, his with disbelief. 'You haven't?'

'It's my right.'

'You would curse him, call him the son of overwhelming sorrow?' she asks.

'It's all he is and all he has brought me. I died with her when he was born.'

'You lost your wife, we lost our daughter. Even with our pain, we will not destroy our grandson's future with that name,' he says.

'He is only pain and duty to me.'

The old woman stares at me, face drawn tight in sorrow. 'And my daughter? I won't let you shame my daughter's memory.'

It stabs me – guilt, memories of Xiuying as she cried, faced childbirth knowingly, refused abortion to give us a child, my child; this son I hate. I show her no respect, her parents less. I stare at the table, push the emotions down where they cannot hurt, stay silent.

The old woman reaches across, places her hand on mine. 'A name should bless the child, bring fortune each time it's spoken. You have nothing else for him?'

I keep my gaze lowered, my mouth shut, shake my head.

She thinks, plays with her cup, nods. 'Then we will do it for you.'

The old man looks at the boy: he's asleep, stretches out and wriggles his fingers, a jerky back-and-forth motion as he wields an invisible hammer. 'My grandson is strong and powerful: Li, *power*, I will call him Li.'

'Power is not everything. He has hands like my father's, carpenter's hands, skillful hands. Qiao, I would call him Qiao,' the old woman says.

The old man nods. 'Li Qiao. A name worthy of our daughter.'

I hurry away, anxious to beat the sun before it sets. I will do what I have to, keep my duty towards the boy. Li Qiao or Zi Xiaohun, it makes no difference to me what he's called; he's still pain, and there's nothing in my heart for him.

TOKYO, JAPAN
2123

HIROTSUGU

She's always been tight-fisted, always will be. We've had little time to keep high school bonds strong through university, and each time she reaches out it's here: a cheap noodle bar soaked in cigarette smoke, wasabi, and udon. This is our last time, or I think it is, if I understand what she says as she slurps away.

'Can you believe it, they started last year, *before* I finished?'

I don't have to, it's the way it should be for the best students with the most sought-after skills; but she is neither. 'No. But you chose, Araki-kun?'

'Yes, but they knew about the others, I had them bid for me. They will pay for my further studies in Yokohama as I work – a six-year contract, Hirotsugu-kun, six *years*.'

Despite my prodding, she did not apply herself properly at high school, scraped into a science degree, then somehow convinced herself through post-grad that food chemistry was always her preferred choice. I'm genuinely happy for her, impressed she converted a lower-tier study programme into a good offer. Apparently. 'With who?'

She squeezes my hand, beams. 'Asahi Foods. Can you imagine? Me, Asahi Foods' Assistant Additives Chemist?'

I raise my beer, toast her. 'To a long career, successful studies.' I put the can down, point to it. 'Now I know who to blame.'

She loses herself in a waking dream of success. 'I'll have my own place, no more parents, save, put a little – oh! A cat! I can get one of my own, no more sharing in cafés and bookstores.'

I smile, take another sip. It sounds mundane, normal; boring. In ten years, she'll be the corporate salarywoman: twelve hours at work, three drinking with the right people, two-hour commute every day for the rest of her life to increase the company's shareholder value proposition. It's the pathway to acceptance, the route to social inclusion as part of the company that is Nippon. 'A cat? That's responsibility.'

'Oh no, a little food, a little water, some kitty litter. I've read about it, they're no trouble, no work at all. So. You must've had lots of offers.'

'A few, yes.'

'A *few*? With your results? I don't think so. So who is it, who gets to win Hirotsugu-kun?'

'Nobody. I have not accepted any.'

She's surprised but brightens immediately. 'Oh? Of course, you want to devote yourself to your study – Umehara-san's brightest must not be distracted. You can visit me, stay in Yokohama. I already know a few people, they tell me that...'

I let her wander away into her future, smile, and say what's expected when it's expected. She's happy when the world's reduced to an annoying other forced into her scheme of things. The printout in my pocket reminds me: should I tell her, let her know what I will do?

'Did I tell you, they'll raise my salary each year of my studies, then once done I get stock options? No? Father's jealous, Tamiya never gave him...'

I don't think I can, even if I want to. There's enough worry in the world – let her think she's won even if she hasn't. She's happy now, happy as she picks up the tab for once, happy as she walks away into the afternoon.

I reach home before dark, remove my shoes as I step inside. Mother and Father sit, stare at the screen. Another stickler for tradition, furniture is limited, the house a monument to Japanese minimalism. He stayed home today, used a day's leave entitlement while the production line's down for maintenance. Mother's unsettled, as if she's unsure what to do when he's home more than six hours at a stretch. I sit cross-legged against one wall, screen to one side, parents to the other; the Buddhist altar opposite me keeps Mother's Shinto shrine company.

The screen falls silent, news of earthquakes in Hokkaido and hurricanes over the Bonin Islands fades. Newsreaders have the easiest of jobs: simply keep the headlines, change the place names and one day it's news again. Mother doesn't react anymore when the tsunami sirens wail, waits until the couple upstairs call; Father sleeps through them, trusts that 2105 was the worst, all that follow of no consequence.

'Was your day good?' Mother asks.

She's always more formal when he's around, as I'm always more careful. Is it cultural, or just our family? I have no way to tell, yet. 'Very good. Productive.'

Father picks up a small pile of envelopes. He scrutinises the top one, puts it to the back, works his way through the pile. 'More arrived today. Panasonic Industries. Sumitomo Corporation. Mitsubishi Heavy Industries.' He pauses, glares at the last envelope for added emphasis. 'Nippon National Robotics.'

The ends are neatly sliced, cut with care and intent, each envelope opened, contents read, re-inserted. As Araki's father did, as they all do; each looks to the final reward for lives devoted to pushing their children. 'Thank you,' I say.

His pride shows; his son actively pursued, the next generation a few more rungs up the ladder. 'They ask after their earlier offers. Build on them. You have decided?'

I take the printout from my pocket, hold it in front of me. Mother has never felt comfortable with computers, even traditional email; Father needs confirmation, always a second voice, mine alone never enough. 'Yes.'

Father waits, briefly, patience never an abundant resource. 'Well? Which one is it?'

'None. I have decided to continue my studies and research.'

Mother's head drops – she's not surprised, for months I have tried to condition her. She may disagree, may be disappointed, but will never say so. Father is more transparent, less controlled, shock flashes across his face before he regains his composure. 'There is a time to study and a time to grow up and make your way in the world. You have studied long enough.'

I have my reasons to continue, none of which mean anything to him. He may think himself cursed with two children who went through university, doubly cursed with my extended time, now cheated as the financial burden of my studies seemingly lifts only to be placed back on his shoulders. 'The extra studies will make me more valuable to future employers,' I lie.

He reaches into the pile of envelopes, waves one at me. 'Nippon National offers you ten times what I earn. And you think more time at school will make you worth more?'

'Yes, I know it will.'

'And how much longer do you think you will study?'

'Two, perhaps three years.'

Father shakes his head firmly. 'We have supported you ten years after high school. We have not planned, we cannot afford to support you a further three.'

'You will not have to. I have a postdoctoral fellowship, a generous allowance and extras. I will be no financial drain on you.'

'A fellowship? Tokyo does not offer those anymore.'

I give him the printout; he reads it, passes it to Mother. It's all there in black and white: the offer, details, start date, travel arrangements. Mother carefully folds the printout, passes it back to me. 'It's not Tokyo University.'

'Paris-Cedex? Is this your idea of a joke?' Professor Umehara asks.

He sits behind his ostentatious glass and chrome desk, tries to burn his gaze into me over his spectacles, an affectation that works with undergraduates but fails on me. Eight years in his faculty, two Ph.D. programmes, and a sheaf of published papers; I would like to believe he at least understands where my research leads. Another misplaced assumption, another lesson.

'No, it's not a joke. I leave next week.'

'You should have discussed this with me. *Before* you accepted.'

As Dean of Faculty and my supervisor, it would have been polite, but my studies were over; I was in the limbo of choices, and I overlooked him. I bow rapidly, deeply; I may need him later, and his large ego can be stroked. 'My apologies, Umehara-san. I did not wish to bother you with irrelevancies.'

It seems to work; he relaxes, removes his spectacles. 'So. Why Paris-Cedex? What do they have that we do not?'

'Philosophy.'

I don't get the reaction I expect; a raised eyebrow, the hint of a sneer, nothing more. 'If you wish to dabble in unscientific navel-gazing, Professor Odagiri can fill your head with the appropriate nonsense.'

'No. It has to be Western philosophy in a Western cultural setting.'

'Western? What possible use is that to you or anyone?'

'It's necessary, I think it's the next step.'

'And when you've had your little French holiday, then what? Your competition is always just behind you, the best offers may not be there when you finish.'

'If I'm wrong, then it's any company for me, a job like any other. If I'm right – and I will be – I'd want to continue my research to make a contribution.'

'Where, exactly?'

He knows the answer, wants me to keep the institutional power balance stuck in the *status quo* exactly where he likes it; and I need to keep my options open. 'If you would permit me, Umehara-san, I would like to return here. Tutor, deliver a few lectures, as I have in the past, to allow me to continue.'

He watches me, keeps his peace, thinks. The faculty's output builds his reputation, and my contribution has been significant. The older he gets, the more he relies on others, the greater the value of new ideas. 'What do you expect to gain from your time in France?'

I take a chip from my pocket, put it into his player. 'My research project, as accepted; a one-page summary.'

He skim-reads it once; goes back, reads it slowly line by line, word by word. He hands back the chip, stands, opens the door for me. 'When you return, there is a place for you here.'

CHAPTER 02: CHOICES

NANGANGZHEN, GUANGDONG PROVINCE, CHINA
2124

LI QIAO

I sit at the table. The wooden chair's hard and uncomfortable. Granma and Granpa sit opposite, read the paper I brought home. It's cold, quiet, and boring since they turned off the screen. 'Granma, can I –'

'Shhh, Li Qiao, stop wriggling. Your grandfather is trying to read.'

He doesn't have to watch with me, he can read while I watch. 'But my cartoons are on.'

Granpa takes off his glasses, points them at me. 'Sit there quietly until I'm finished, then we'll decide about your cartoons.'

He takes forever. A fly crawls along the edge of my plate. What would it do without wings? Tyres crunch outside, a bell rings; whose bicycle, a friend or a stranger? Bet they can watch anything they like. 'I'm hungry.'

Granpa turns the piece of paper to me. 'We'll eat later. Do you know what this is?'

'No.'

He looks confused, turns the paper back. 'It says you were told in class this morning. Do you remember?'

I shrug. If I glue enough flies to my arms, will I be able to fly? I look around, see if there are more to catch later.

Granma reaches out, turns my face to her. 'Pay attention, Li Qiao, this is important.'

'Do you remember your teacher telling you about this?' Granpa asks.

Teacher says a lot of things, most of them stupid. 'No.'

'This is a report about you and your schoolwork. You get three each year to bring home, to show us how well you study and how good you are.'

'I'm the best.'

Granpa shakes his head. 'That's not what this says. It says you're average.'

'What's that?'

'It means you're smarter than some, not as smart as others.'

Pigs have lots of flies, but they stay on the ground. I'm smaller than the big pigs, I won't need many. 'Oh. I'm still the best.'

Granpa sighs. 'It also says you talk back to your teacher.'

Pigs don't use glue, that's their problem; otherwise, they'd take off quick with the flies. Granpa has some glue hidden under his tools, real smelly stuff – that's what I need.

'Well?' Granpa asks.

'Am I as heavy as a pig?'

'What? No, yes; maybe. Which pig? No, don't tell me – will you concentrate? At school, do you talk back to your teacher?'

'I have to. She asks me stuff, I have to answer or I get in trouble.'

Granpa puts the paper down, rubs one hand over his forehead.

'That's not what your grandfather means. Do you disobey your teacher? Are you rude to her?' Granma asks.

'No.'

'She says you are.'

'Never.'

'Then why does she say you do?'

'I don't.'

'So your teacher's lying?'

'Must be.'

Granpa looks at Granma. 'See? He's getting worse.'

I catch a fly, look at it in my hand. Its wings are too tiny.

'Don't be hard on him, it's not his fault.'

Flies are no good. I squish it, wipe my hand on the chair. Chickens have big wings, and we've got lots.

Granpa waves the paper at Granma. 'So we ignore it? His first year in school, and already there's problems. He's better than average, he should be higher. She says he doesn't try.'

Big wings, chickens flap all day in their pens. Why don't they fly?

'He's still young, it's a phase. You need to give him room, time to get used to school and all the rules,' Granma says.

They don't fly because they're in the pen, they can't practice. Bet in the wild they do; no pens there.

Granpa stands, pulls up his trousers. 'You spoil that child. You work it out, you talk to him – I have work to do.'

Granma turns to me. 'You have to try harder, Li Qiao.'

'I will.'

'And no more being rude to your teacher. Treat her like you treat your grandfather and me.'

How far can they fly in the wild? How many flies is a chicken worth? 'Okay.'

'I'm being serious. It's important, promise me you'll try harder and behave at school.'

'I promise.'

She hugs me, kisses the top of my head. 'Good. Now, I have a surprise for you. We have a visitor coming over.'

'Who?'

'That's a secret. But we're out of tea, and we can't have a visitor and no tea.' She takes some money from her pocket, pushes the notes into my hand. 'I'm too tired to get it. You'll have to go down to the stall, they'll know what to give you. That's ten, make sure you bring the change home.'

I put the notes in my pockets, run out the door.

'Don't take too long, they're not far away,' she calls after me.

I head to the back, take the shortcut across the gardens. The chicken-pen's close; I go in, run at the chickens, wave my arms. They squawk, jump and flap; some hit the roof, bounce down. All they need is more room. I use a rock to hold the door open, chase them out. They scatter; some flap for a little bit, most run towards the vegetable beds. They just need practice. I turn, run to the stall.

I'm nearly there when I trip, fall flat on my face into the grass. I try to get up, something heavy pushes me down. 'Where you goin', runt?' a voice asks.

I know who it is: Chia-tern, he's a grade above me. 'Tea for Granma,' I say.

'Really?' There's a hand in my pocket, it grabs something on the way out. The weight on my back's gone. 'Three's not much for tea, dummy.'

I roll over, sit up. Chia-tern stands over me, waves the notes in the air. 'No tea for you or the stupid old bat now.'

I stand, try to check the other seven's safe without him seeing.

'She's not stupid.'

Chia-tern pokes me hard in the shoulder. 'Has to be, she's got you.'

Each day at school it's the same: he finds me, picks on me, takes my stuff. One day I'll do the picking, one day I'll win, win good. 'She doesn't have to look at a dog's bum face like yours.'

He pokes me harder, both hands, both shoulders. 'You smell like one, it's why no one likes you.'

I shove myself into him, look up into his face. 'Got more friends than you.'

'Your mum died 'cause you're too ugly.'

I hit him as hard as I can; he laughs, shoves me away, I fall on my back, slide from grass into dirt. 'Did not.'

'Did too. And where's your dad?'

'Bába's busy, he's at the war.'

'He's not, he never wants to see you –'

'He does too.'

'Too ugly for him, too ugly for anyone.'

'He's coming home to stay when the war's over.'

Chia-tern stands over me. 'He never visits you, never stays, he'll never come back for you.'

I try to scrabble away, he stays above me. My hands run over stones, my back scratches on rocks. 'Bába will, Granma said he promised!'

Shoes on gravel. 'What are you boys doing?' someone shouts.

Chia-tern leans down, grabs my shirt. 'He's never coming back, he doesn't love you, doesn't want a stupid ugly idiot for a son.'

There's a rock in my fist; I hit his face, do it again, aim this time, try to hit the red spout from his nose, miss, smash his cheek. 'Bába's coming back.'

'Li Qiao, no,' the voice says.

Chia-tern's on his butt, scuttles backwards. I try to follow, my shirt's stuck, I can't move.

'That's enough.'

Chia-tern stands, runs away. I throw the rock at him, miss. 'He's coming back for me; you'll see, he's coming back.'

I'm turned around. I look into the face of the stall owner. She pulls me to my feet, dusts me off. 'You two are always at it. You know you can't beat him.'

'Can too.'

She straightens my shirt, brushes the hair from my face. 'Only with a rock. What was it this time?'

'Granma.'

'What about your grandmother?'

I pull out the notes. 'Ran out of tea, he tried to take it all.'

She frowns. 'Seven's not enough for her usual, just the cheap stuff. Why'd she send you?'

'We got a visitor.'

She walks me to the stall. 'Oh? Who?'

'Don't know, Granma says it's secret.'

She reaches behind the counter, gives me a red and gold packet. 'This is her usual, tell her not to worry about the extra. Maybe it's your father this time.'

'Bàba's coming back for me.'

She gives me a gentle push. 'Someday, Li Qiao, someday. Now go home before that bully comes back for you.'

I run through the front yard, Granpa and Granma sit on the bench near the door. I give the packet to her. 'Tea.'

'Thank you.' She looks at me, waits. 'Do you have my change?'

'No.'

'No? There should be at least two.'

'Chia-tern took it, she says you don't have to worry.'

'Don't lie to your grandmother. What did you do with it this time? Sweets?' Granpa asks.

'He hit me and took it. I didn't do anything.'

Granma takes my face in her hands, looks at me. 'Did he hurt you?'

'You don't believe him? He's lying again, like he always does,' Granpa says.

'If he says he was hit and the money was taken, he was hit and the money was taken.'

'You can't keep doing that. He'll never stop lying if you keep encouraging him.'

Granma roughs up my hair with her hand, smiles. 'He doesn't lie to me; you're a good boy, aren't you, Li Qiao?'

Granpa sighs, leans back. 'Have it your way.'

'Li Qiao, your visitor's inside,' Granma says.

'Who is it?'

'Go see for yourself.'

Inside's darker, quiet. There's a man sitting at the table, he looks at me, nods. 'Hello Zi…Li Qiao.'

Bába. I run to him, grab his waist, try to hug him. He puts one arm around me for the shortest time, pushes me gently away. 'Stand up straight. Turn around, let me look at you.'

His uniform's floppy, more medals and ribbons. One sleeve's bent up, empty, pinned to his shoulder. 'Where's your arm?'

'In Taipei; price I paid to help liberate our countrymen.'

'How you gonna hug me? Who ties your shoelaces?'

'I've got special shoes, and men don't hug, Li Qiao.'

'But Bába, Granpa does.'

'How old are you?'

He should know, his last birthday card is still in my room. 'Six, soon I'll be seven.'

'You're too old to call me Bába. From now on you call me Fùqin or Sir, what one you like, but no more Bába. Ever.'

He doesn't smile, he's not happy. I've never seen him happy. 'Yes, Fùqin. You've come to take me home?'

'No. I told you, this is your home, you can't live with me. Didn't you hear me last time?'

'Yes.'

'So don't ask again.'

'Yes, Fùqin.'

He pats the bench next to him, invites me to sit. 'I came out of hospital, have a little time before I go back. I thought I'd drop by and see how you are.'

I jump up on the bench, my backside hurts as I sit, Chia-tern's knee-print still fresh. 'Ow.'

'What's wrong?'

'I had a fight. It still hurts.'

'Who won?'

I think I did but the lady stopped me. 'I...I don't know.'

'If you don't know, you lost. You should make sure you win, never give the enemy a chance.' He taps his empty sleeve. 'That's how I lost this – a fool in my unit gave the enemy a chance. Do you want to lose an arm or a leg?'

'No.'

'So don't give them a chance, don't stop till you win.' Fùqin turns a paper over; it looks like the one I brought home today.

34

'Tell me about school.'

'I'm an average.'

He shoves the paper away. 'That's what this says. I'm disappointed in you, Li Qiao. Do you know why?'

'Because I gave Chia-tern a chance?'

'No. Because you don't try. You should be the best at everything, and that means school. Average is not good enough.'

'Why?'

'Why? Because if you are not the best, you are nothing to me or anyone. You will be a failure, a disgrace to me and your grandparents. Do you want me to be ashamed of you?'

My cheeks are hot, eyes start to sting. 'No, Bába, I —'

'I told you not to call me that. Can't you even remember the simplest things?'

'I'm sorry, Fùqin.'

'And stop crying, crying's for babies and women, not men.' He takes the paper, slaps it down in front of me. 'Can you read yet?'

I wipe my face with my sleeve. 'Yes, Fùqin.'

'This is important, you must always be the best. You have to grow up and stop being lazy. Understand?'

'Yes, Fùqin.'

He stands up, puts his hand on my shoulder, presses down so I can't get up. 'I have to go. I don't know when I'll be back.'

'Can I come with you, Fùqin? Please?'

'No, I told you, you can't. You can sit here, read your teacher's report about you, understand why your grandparents, why *I* am upset with you.' He walks to the door, turns. 'Do better, be the best, and perhaps one day I'll stay longer.'

The door slams behind him; I jump up and put my eye to the crack in the door. Fùqin talks to Granma.

'You were too harsh with him, Wai Ma,' Granma says.

'In what way? He shouldn't be an average student. I wasn't, Xiuying wasn't, he shouldn't.'

'And scaring the poor boy will help? He loves you, wonders why you're never around. Do you want his only memories of you to be of some tyrant?'

'He needs discipline and hardness, needs to apply himself. I'm not going to waste my time hugging him to make him a failure.'

'How does letting your son know you're proud of him make him a failure?'

'When it's a lie! The world's not like Nangangzhen, not some tiny little village where people care. It's harsh, vicious and evil, and it's only going to be worse when he goes out into it. My duty's to prepare him for life, not fill his head with flattery.'

'So that's it? We see you maybe once a year, and this is all it'll be – half an hour grinding your son?'

'Until he meets my standards, yes.'

'He needs more than discipline, more than your harsh tongue.'

Fùqin straightens his cap, heads to the path out of the village. 'Until he stops being a disappointment and an embarrassment, that's all I have for him. Then, perhaps, he gets acceptance.'

PARIS-CEDEX UNIVERSITY, FRANCE
2124

MARIA

Kris pokes his head through the plastic curtain. 'One hour, Maria. You asked me to remind you.'

Meetings, meetings, damned meetings. But some matter, like these inter-faculty research seminars; and I wanted the heads-up. 'I'll be there, just keep the profs on ice if I'm a few minutes late.'

The plastic curtain closes, I turn back to the bench. Rat thirty-two lies still and silent under his plexiglass dome, input collar and helmet pulse blue, the open scar along his abdomen a steady red. Monitors show flatline ECG and EEG, inputs overlay steady. Perfect. Perfect as it was two hours ago, perfect as I hope it will be five hours from now. Five hours to revival, five hours to suture thirty-two up, five hours to see if the first faltering steps are real or merely another stumble.

Why stitch 'em up? In, out, revive should be enough, Prof said. No, it's hardly the point, not the end goal. Every life is precious, every life deserving.

My hand's around my pendant: I twirl it, feel the reassuring weight of its three intertwined rings. I sense the addition, the silver loop to join rings to chain; I don't have to look to see the grey hair embedded around its circumference, the engraving on its back. *Ecaterina 2114.*

In one short year my life turned around. No more trouble, no more problems, the world suddenly a limitless opportunity I was eager to explore. Knowledge beckoned, my desire grew to thirst then voracious appetite; nothing too hard, nothing too esoteric to escape my attention. I picked at the threads of Abue's defences, grew to know her, appreciate and love the person behind the apron, the woman and not merely the relation; and she me.

Until.

Until that disease tore her mind apart like an overripe peach; all that she was poured out in haphazard waterfalls of noise and movement. Then her sadness and shame, knowledge in her brief moments of respite – small oases of sanity that allowed only awareness of what was being lost – until she was dragged under again.

We can fix her – a long, difficult operation but now routine, with the best of surgeons, the best of staff, they'd promised. So we kissed her as she lay on the gurney, made stupid jokes about her blue plastic gown and old lady shower cap, watched them wheel her away to her operation; to her death.

We are sorry for your loss, these things happen even today. For a few the anaesthetic can kill, some simply for being under, some just slide away, no one knows why, a different face said. No comfort offered, no solace taken; Yayo cried his spirit to death in that first, lost week without her, as the two of us hid in a house too big, too cold, too quiet.

I will fix it, I know I can, I promised him when words could come.

Maria, he who can bring back the dead left us a long time ago, Yayo replied.

I know. But I will find a way where no one dies like Abue died.

Rat thirty-two will live, be stitched up, will survive.

Kris smiles as I walk through the door, release him back to the comfort of the lab. Prof to his left waves, prof to his right waves; I wave back. I'm still a troublemaker, although one of a different stripe. Engineering and neurology, two faculties that both did and did not want supervisory roles, fought each other to an impasse of joint adoption. Two masters I cursed with each other; they cursed me with the title *Bioelectrical Neuroscientist Technologist Engineer*. Today they watch and observe; years from now the gauntlet of my oral defence, later my postdoctoral life, if any.

Show and tell never changes. We get older, the butterflies in the jar are swapped, but the core is eternal. Here and now, the overlays of ego and reputation make the game more challenging, brutal, even if the veneer of academic civility remains. Pecking orders are established, scales of worth assessed in a precursor to the rest of our academic lives. Only so much is given away, only so much disclosed; I am no different.

I spectate for the first half, ask an occasional question to make my presence known, nod with the rhetorical questions, laugh with everyone at overused, well-worn jokes. Mainly I observe, see who is here, what their research promises; where, if at all, chance of collaboration exists. Most of the faces are familiar; a few are obvious new candidates, hyped up on their first taste of sugar-rush doctoral interaction. One is vaguely familiar, but I don't know why – tall, slightly awkward, balding head and beard jammed on top of a *Le Coq Sportif* turtleneck, he sits silent in the back row.

My ten-minute slot arrives. I stand, narrate the presentation as it rotates overhead, breathe a silent prayer of thanks for Kris' organisational skills. Data, pathways, theory flow easily; half the audience doesn't understand a word, a quarter pretends to, some have a partial grasp. It's for none of those I continue, but for the one or two who do understand.

'So, it's a differently induced state of cryogenics?' a voice to one side asks, clearly a new candidate who thinks value is weighed by the number of words she speaks.

'No, the opposite. Avoidance of any form of cell destruction or degradation is a primary requirement.'

No one else bothers to display their ignorance, the rest of the presentation is uninterrupted. I pause for questions at the end; someone stands, bows rapidly, straightens. The glyph above his head glows. *Hirotsugu, S. PostDoc, CompHum (PsySoc), U. Tokyo.*

'Excuse. Rat thirty-two. Goal, test current, subjective objective differential?'

Finally, someone who's bothered to listen and can think. 'Seven hours objective with a three-minute-thirty subjective experience. That's the limit of the biosupport facilities I have.'

'Ah,' he says, blinks like an owl caught in a spotlight. He pulls my presentation over, skips back to the third slide, magnifies the last info box. 'Successful test ratio one to one hundred twenty. Research goal human application, ratio goal?'

I start to like this guy – finally, a real question. 'One to ten thousand. Eventually.'

He looks impressed and unconvinced, exactly my supervisors' reaction when I pitched my research question. He half sits, stands up, bows again. 'Excuse. Final question. Human application ratio goal. Constraints? Obstacles?'

That could take the better part of a month, but I narrow it down to two key issues. 'Capacity and agility in the system. Simple problem, no simple answers.'

He smiles, bows, sits. 'As are all researches with value.'

I can't help myself: I smile, catch myself in a half-bow back to him.

I sit, wait for the final speakers. A message-glyph pops up for me. Two cups of coffee, two faces talk to each other, a guy hammers away on a computer keyboard, a female surgeon midway through an operation. The emojis sit above a name, *Hirotsugu*. I reply with two thumbs up, settle back, will the meeting to end.

The guy in the turtleneck corners me as the meeting breaks up. The glyph reads *de Sainte-Maxence, P. Cand. PhD, EnviroBioSys (P), Paris-Cedex* above his head. 'Interesting work, surprised you are taking the high-tech approach.'

Why? What other approach is there? Who is he anyway to be surprised at me for anything? 'I'm sorry, do I know you?'

It pulls him up, wipes the smirk from his face. 'You are not remembering me?'

'Clearly I don't, or I wouldn't ask.'

He crosses his arms. 'I suppose I am thankful there is no swimming pool.'

I remember now. 'You're not...?'

He offers me his hand and a smile. 'I am. Pierre, Maria.'

I take it, a little uncomfortably. 'It's been at least ten years, I didn't recognise you. How are you?'

'Apart from emotional scars and fear of the water? Bien. About a year it's fini. You?'

'Four, could be five, got two supervisors to please. Only makes it harder.'

'Biomed and engineering? I am thinking you were more for environmental or biology.'

'Why?'

'Last time I am seeing you, you seemed deep green. You give my friends a hell of a tongue-lashing about the tech and degradation. I thought you are to keep the fight up.'

'I've given nothing up. It's still a fallacious, human-centric bias that needs to change. If we think of ourselves as permanent residents and not just visitors, we might start to take better care of our home. I'm going to make a difference, help people live longer, better lives.'

I realise I've raised my voice, leaned in to him. It doesn't take much – passion and anger still simmer under my skin, but I'm better with my control than I used to be. I shrug, raise my eyebrows. 'That's the plan. Talk to me in ten years and see if it's worked.'

'I can see it, you making it work; hope it does.'

It means something, a little bit of encouragement to tuck away in the back of my mind, drag out to fight the doubts when they inevitably rise. A little seed of guilt taps at me. 'For what it's worth, I'm sorry about the pool thing. I was just a kid.'

He pauses, frowns. 'You could be soccer pro with kick like that. You are still having that tatt?'

I pull my t-shirt down below my shoulder. 'See for yourself.'

'Honestly, the pirate costume, she is different, not bad.'

'You have any?'

He reddens, looks around furtively. 'Well, I am having just one. She made me, I – I am not showing you.'

'Why? What is it?'

'A papillon. On my behind.'

I try to control my laughter, fail as he walks away. 'That makes us even.'

I'm dying for that coffee. Six hours inside this fishbowl's about

42

my limit. My player chimes, Kris pops up.

'Do you want to know how your patient is?' He doesn't wait for my answer, pans the camera to the bench. Rat thirty-two scampers in his cage, stops, picks up a food pellet and munches; his wound, neatly sutured, smiles at me. 'One hundred percent recovery, no side effects. Congratulations.'

HIROTSUGU

She sends back two thumbs up. Good. All this year's seminars have been the same: mildly interesting at best, derivative at worst. Hers is the exception, interesting research with broad potential application, even if she doesn't know it. Other candidates wear their masks, faces driven by routine and struggle, the expression of choice here as in Tokyo; she is different, hers burns with enthusiasm and passion for her work. I check her name again, caution myself. They use first names here, even with their academic superiors, a habit I find difficult and unsettling. It's Maria, not Rodrigues-san.

The presentations end, she's tied up briefly with a tall, balding guy. I walk across as her player chimes. She looks at it, breaks into relief and joy, then notices me. 'Horutsigo, isn't it?'

'Yes, Hirotsugu, Maria.'

She shoves the player under my nose. 'Look, just finished.'

A rat scurries around, a red wound flashes from its underside. 'Rat thirty-two?'

She pulls back the player, nods. 'Only minutes ago. Totally fine, complete success.'

It's reflex. I bow, stay until I've spoken. 'My congratulations.'

She wears a strange smile, slips her arm through mine as we head to the door. 'Let's get that coffee, go celebrate.'

A small, dingy coffee shop in a quieter area, a place Araki might feel at home, particularly with the prices. My invitation, I buy the first drinks, avoid disposable cups for cheaper, beaten-up mugs. We take two stools in the corner; I take a small sip, then a deep

44

draught. 'After six hours any is welcome.'

'That boring?' Maria asks.

'Only you, and remote sensing, of real interest. The rest, I read faculty notes, get better knowledge.'

'Come to think of it, you didn't ask too many questions.'

'French easier to read than speak, for me. Sometimes better to keep mouth shut and be thought a fool –'

'Than to open it and remove all doubt? Ha. I wish the rest of them knew that one. Are they like that in Tokyo?'

I think back on years of regimented seminars, the rigidly enforced social and seniority protocol straitjacket I struggled under. 'No, never so open. Can ask questions only after graduate honours, never without permission to open mouth.'

'That doesn't sound good either, I'd always be in the bad books – I always ask questions.'

'As me – good question, good company. Anachronism in faculty.'

'What did you study?'

'Mathematics Theory, Computer Science. Double.'

'I've never seen you around, didn't even notice your name until today.'

'Here I am for philosophy. Different approach.'

'They weren't good enough for you in Japan?'

'Different. Culture control curriculum, academics, knowledge. Japan university efficient, study to practical to job to output; everything applied, basic research only physical science. No room for strange mix, add soft to hard discipline.'

'Know the feeling. Why?'

'Sorry?'

'Why philosophy? It sounds like a strange match.'

I stumble; my spoken French is barely passable, I still hunt for words like a child, and some concepts are easier expressed than others. 'My goal, the end, create non-biologic intelligence.'

She looks totally underwhelmed. 'Oh. Another AI guy.'

'No. AI not enough, limited, even name wrong. No intelligence, just artificial, data information collector.'

'And how does philosophy help?'

'Western philosophy, some say think is sense, not process. Difference like, like…' I look around, settle on the mugs in our hands, 'like coffee. AI look mug, know coffee type, dimension, physical nature. Thinking look mug, know is coffee, imagine uses, feeling, potential; add points to drawing, not connect dots already there.'

'So what, Toyota's assembly line robots appreciate the colours they paint the cars? It's just more technology, and technology for its own sake's not worked out.'

'What you do any different? Already have anaesthetics, you only make better type.'

Her eyes narrow. 'What *I* do will save hundreds, maybe thousands of lives, give people easier and safer operations, a better life.'

'AI now destructive, does only what we tell it. Trade this stock, mine that uranium, fight your war, because it not think, only do efficiently. If it think, it can be better, do good, make life better.'

'And if it thinks like its creator?'

'It think for itself, no bias. Man ruin Earth little, man plus technology more, man plus technology plus AI ruin a lot. Non-biologic intelligence do better, fix problems, solve.'

'You really believe it.'

'AI only tool, extension of man. This different, thinking. You been Japan?'

'Never. One day.'

'Once beautiful, many places. Kyushu, Ryukyu Islands, forests. Some no more, technology, pollution ruin for all; make some rich, make all poor.'

'Like everywhere.'

'But for them Earth not enough to ruin, move to next. Like Ismud.'

'What?'

'Fix home first, then explore, good way. Best way send non-biologic intelligence, not human, not AI; keep bias and damage here.'

Her smile returns. 'Back home in Chile...'

We talk through the afternoon, into evening. The waitress cleans away our pile of empty mugs, puts stools on top of tables, mops the floor under our feet. I check the time, worry over the last bus. 'They will kick us out.'

'Or keep us as furniture.'

We stand, walk out. I do not take chances, always rejection, too clumsy; but in her case? 'Enjoyed much. Your number, could I have, talk again?'

She pats her pockets, raises her eyebrows. 'I don't have my player, must be back at my flat. It's only five minutes away, you want to come over, maybe have a coffee, chat some more?'

So what is it we've done the past hours? And *another* coffee?

Oh.

I slip my arm through hers. 'Yes, very much, Maria.'

TOKYO UNIVERSITY, JAPAN
2126

HIROTSUGU

Three years in Paris taught me games and power differ only in how they are expressed, not exercised; and Tokyo University has not changed. Two hours alone in the deserted waiting room, try to keep the cold at bay, mull as they discuss my future. All designed to put me off balance, make me all the more grateful when they approve my research programme, but it's wasted. I have something, I owe nobody, and if not here then somewhere else. Tokyo is familiar and comfortable, my parents close and the internal politics known; so it is my choice to play the game, re-establish myself, and lip-serve the *status quo*. It worked on Umehara, let me slip back into paid employment, but this is different. I will only go so far, give up only so much, to get their approval for a deliberately truncated research proposal that hides what must be done to succeed.

The secretary opens the door, moves silently on deep carpet, bows. 'They will see you now, Hirotsugu-san.'

It's a familiar layout – hard wooden chair for the applicant, three plush seats in an arc for the board, secretary's desk to one side. The theatre of the absurd. The decision's already made, there is no reason for this but to show who has or hasn't dashed the proposal, to confirm where obligation belongs. I bow to each in turn, greet them as they expect: Umehara, my Faculty Dean; Maruyama, Vice Chancellor of Research; and Sahai, Vice

Chancellor of Legal and Ethics. I sit when I am invited, wait until I'm asked to speak.

'Your time at Paris-Cedex was useful?' Maruyama asks.

'Yes, Maruyama-san, it informed the proposal you have in front of you.'

'A novel one – it presented some difficulties, but nothing that can't reasonably be accommodated.' Maruyama turns to Umehara. 'It has the support of your Faculty Dean, but with some reservations.'

'A question of the necessity of the research, not the proposal itself, as we have discussed,' Umehara says.

'Your proposal is clear as to what you aim for, but not why. Why is it necessary?' Maruyama asks.

I argued with Umehara about this, only too aware his life's work is tied up in what I seek to make redundant, as is the University's. The balance to build on another's work while tearing it down is difficult, but I have practised. 'Artificial intelligence has progressed to its ultimate state, and is lacking. A new approach is needed, a new paradigm I call non-biologic intelligence, NBI for short.'

'And you are the one to turn a century and a half of effort on its head,' Umehara says.

It's a challenge, a test – not of my ego, but of my self-belief. I lie. 'No. I build on the work of others – yourself, Umehara-san – to advance knowledge. I have a contribution to make, but I do not believe I do, or will, know it all.'

'A laudable attitude, but the question stands. Why is it necessary?' Maruyama asks.

'AI is by nature specialised and fixed, does what it is designed to do, what it is told to, *learns* what it is told to learn and nothing more. The outcomes are costly: single-purpose mechanisms that are not intelligent, do not think, and cannot be repurposed. The end result of NBI is a thinking, reasoning mechanism, an evolutionary jump above AI.'

'Yet AI is sufficient, meets current and foreseen needs. Only you see any shortcomings.'

'AI is as good as it can be; what follows can be more.'

'So, to the ethics of your programme. Sahai-san?'

She's older and better connected than they are. A seat at every table, voice in every decision, ear in every room. Her views, no matter how mildly expressed, are law; and without appeal. 'Your research test subjects, you intend to observe brain function and response,' she says.

'Yes, Sahai-san.'

'Nothing else? No stimulus, attempts to analyse, adjust or record thoughts or reactions?'

Strictly it is all observation, but it's not limited to function and response. 'No, Sahai-san.'

'There are international treaties, legally binding requirements that cover mind control, surveillance, and brainwashing.'

A direct question or observation deserves a direct, if incomplete, answer. 'My research will do none of this.'

'But it comes close, could be viewed poorly. You need to keep an eye out at all times, as I will on you.'

'That I understand. I'm formally committed to doing so.'

'Your test subjects, the ones to carry your monitoring devices. Your demographic boundaries are?'

Another test – it's all in the proposal, but she wants to be sure. 'All over twenty-one, all volunteers, devices fitted only eight hours a day. Subjects control when and where they wear them.'

'Good, you know your own proposal. You will not expand or change the test group, not make them wear the devices for more than eight hours a day?'

She nearly asks the right question. Only part of the research will succeed with the non-plastic minds of adults. As for the devices, she assumes one device per subject which, to an extent, is true, at least for their physical carriage; there is a reason the devices do not have an off switch. 'No, Sahai-san, any proposed changes in the test group will be discussed with Umehara-san first, then cleared through the ethics board, before being made.'

'There's something more behind your reasons, more than simply better AI, isn't there?'

Again, I underestimate people. I'm unsettled, not by her question but by her possible intuitive grasp of what it might mean. 'For the research proposal itself? It is as I have described it.'

'You and I both know it's approved, we wouldn't waste your time or ours being here if it wasn't. So, young man, put that aside and talk with me. What is behind it, behind you?'

'My sister. No one understands consciousness, exactly what life is; one day she is pregnant then nine months later, this thing slides pink and naked and wet into the world, a thing that can think and has more potential than all our computers and AIs combined.'

'So if she can?'

I forget where I am, who I speak to. 'Not only her, anyone. If two dullards too stupid to brush their own teeth can create a thinking being, why are we satisfied with AI as the pinnacle of all our effort, knowledge, and technology when it is such a poor second? I am not, I will never be.'

'And when you succeed?'

'Thought-sense will take NBI where no AI can go – self-awareness. We will not have to make, manufacture, or teach them; they will do it for themselves.'

'A separate species that stands apart from us.'

'No, Sahai-san, one that stands *with* us – our equals, our partners. We have never had anything but lesser, subservient species for companions, and we are diminished because of it. AI will never be anything other than a tool or a piece of capital equipment; we can, we *deserve*, to do better than that.'

'Hopefully they will view us in the same way. Creation seems to have a way of turning on its creator.'

'Hopefully.'

'So, ultimately, you see your NBI at this point when?'

Does she understand? Do any of them? I hope not. Another secret to keep. 'It took homo sapiens hundreds of thousands of years; even a fraction of that, with our help, means centuries. I'll be dead by then.'

She grins, leans back into her chair. 'As will we all. Thank you for an interesting diversion, Hirotsugu-san. We should get back to your proposal; for the record.'

'If there's nothing further?' Maruyama asks, silence his only response. 'Then I believe we're done. Congratulations, Hirotsugu-san, your research programme is approved.'

NANGANGZHEN, GUANGDONG PROVINCE, CHINA
2127

LI QIAO

Master of the air, broad, powerful wings flex and twitch as it circles one way, circles another – eyes study the ground. Rough and windy beneath the storm, it rides the gusts in total command of its environment. It disappears behind buildings to the right, another takes its place from the left, lower as the cloud descends. The town square's small, crowded with schoolchildren, but bad weather also brings out the mice, sends smaller birds into the eaves to give the black eagles an easy meal.

A girl walks over, hands wrapped tightly around a kite line, fights as it bucks and weaves in the rising wind. 'What you doing, Li Qiao?'

She's in my class, I can't remember her name. But Granma says I have to try and be polite to everyone; guess that includes her. I keep my gaze turned up, point. 'Birds, black eagles. Maybe.'

Or are they harriers? I'm not as good with these, I thought harriers hover, black-eared kites and eagles circle, but I don't understand how anything isn't blown far away.

She shuffles nearer, looks up. 'They're close.'

Clouds cover the sky, dark, green-tinged anvils stacked one on the other. A tiny droplet of rain lands on my neck, a cloud lights up, pink glow rises then dies. 'About a hundred metres up.'

She steps away, plays out more line. 'I can get it to them.'

The eagle fights hard, stays above the square. It circles tighter, head tilts, locks on one spot on the ground; it's found something, waits for the right moment as the clouds descend, push it lower.

She steps further away, places the kite under the eagle, makes it climb. 'Do you think it will attack it, Li Qiao, think it's another bird or dinner?'

The sky rumbles, rain starts, streetlights come on as midday is transformed to night. Gliders hunt in clouds too, use them to gain height and soar; wonder if there are any now, if they watch the lightning jump around inside the clouds, like I'll watch one day when I fly. The birds are never worried, they soar and float, wait until the winds are too high, then fly away. The kite's a yellow-green diamond, snaps and dances ferociously, forces the eagle to circle wider — it gives the kite a hateful stare before it turns its head once more to the ground.

The sky turns to fire, a lance from cloud to kite to ground with thunder shakes me to the core. The afterimage blinds yellow-orange as I blink; the screams start, stench of ozone and burnt cloth rises with another, unfamiliar, sickly sweet smell of overcooked pork. My eyes recover, the kite wafts away; a shape in front of me bends, falls, a patch of red-brown trickles away with the rain. Screams, shouts, running feet shove past me, head towards what's left of her. I turn my head up, watch lightning dance between clouds, the eagles slide away.

A heaving mass of bodies around her catches me at its edge, swirls with children, adults, uniforms whose heads shake, eyes look up, down, at me through sodden hair.

'Did you see it?' a voice to one side asks.

It nearly got me, if she'd stayed closer I'd be a deformed lump with her, melted flesh on melted flesh. 'The kite's gone, lightning got it.'

'Come on, forget him, probably shock,' another voice says.

It's covered in jackets, a sheet; a woman fights through, throws herself on the pile, screams, tries to tear the covers away. Others grab her, vainly try to pull her off. Why is she like that, is she her mother? She died instantly, painlessly, she should be happy she didn't suffer, didn't let her stupidity take me out as well. She should cry, be sad for what her child could have done, the lives she nearly took with her. I'm cold, numb – men don't cry, but I feel strange, like I'm glass about to break. I walk away, try to find a place they can't disturb me, walk straight into Granma.

'Li Qiao, are you alright?' she asks.

It hits me; I nearly went with her, another few steps was all I needed. 'It nearly got me.'

She grabs me, drags me against her in a hug I don't need, don't like. I stand stiff, arms by my side, watch more people run past. 'You're safe, nothing's going to hurt you, Li Qiao. I know you're scared, lost your friend – it's okay to show it.'

Her grip loosens; I step to one side, walk away. 'I'm not, men don't cry.'

I leave the girl, the square, the people, sit on a rock and watch the storm lash out over the valley. I know they're black eagles now, I look down on them – dark brown feathers, wingtips splay and rock as they balance; or were they black-eared kites earlier, couldn't handle the storm, let the stronger birds take over? One plummets, wings folded back, opens them before it hits the ground to rise, a tiny brown something writhes in its claws. This eagle won, the black-eared kite lost, both faced the same storm.

She lost, I won. Simple.

Fùqin's uniform's drenched, small waterfalls drip from his cap.

'So, this is where you scurried off to.'

'Too many people, too much noise.'

He sits, stretches out his legs, boots dig into wet ground. 'Tell me what happened.'

'She put her kite into the storm, lightning got her, nearly got me. Stupid thing to do, stupid girl.'

'She's dead now, does that make a difference?'

Difference? To what? I don't think so, but something feels...right?...about it. 'No. I'm not sure. She got her reward for being stupid. Right?'

Fùqin taps his empty sleeve. 'The fool that caused this died the next minute. Fools should pay for their stupidity, like she did.'

'I could have warned her.'

'Why? She should have known, it's not difficult, like not standing in front of a bus. She was stupid, like you said. But.'

'But?'

'If you warned her, tried to pull in the kite, you would have been as stupid as her, and I'd be upset.'

'For trying to help her?'

'No, for risking your life for a fool. She dies, the world loses someone stupid, it doesn't matter. You die with her, for any fool, it matters – you're better than her, smarter, you shouldn't risk your life for them.'

He's never said I'm smart, and he says I'm better than them? I don't feel like glass now. 'You think I'm smart?'

'I'm still disappointed with you.'

'But if I'm smart –'

'You don't act like it. You need to show it, do better, think about yourself, try always to do your best.'

'I'll try, Fùqin, I promise.'

'You won't try; you will do it, do you hear?'

'Yes, Fùqin, I will.'

'You can start by going back to the square, find those people, show how sorry you are the girl died.'

'But I'm not, I could've been killed and that's all I'm upset about.'

'Like me; but they aren't as good as you, so it's fine to pretend, to keep them on your side. Sometimes you must be seen to do things even if you don't feel like it. Understand?'

I don't, not at all. Granpa tells me not to lie, now Fùqin tells me it's alright? 'No.'

Fùqin stands, straightens his cap. 'If you want to win, you have to. Rules are made for others, not us, so don't disappoint me. Again.'

I still don't understand, but it feels right. I know I'm special, different, and better than them; but I never make Fùqin happy. Maybe I can. 'I won't, Fùqin, I won't.'

'I have to go. Make sure you go back to that square.'

I watch the rain, the wind in the trees, the black eagles. They're proud, strong, in charge; free. They don't have rules, could make up their own if they wanted to, or not have any, do whatever they like. Even pretend.

TOKYO, JAPAN
2128

HIROTSUGU

I tell myself it's a normal summer's day in the park, look at the people on the grass; they read, talk, sit quietly, take in the sun, take advantage of good weather. Gravel crunches underfoot, scented blooms line the path, a quiet walk among friends from entry to the building. But friends don't sit in parks with three-metre-high block walls, don't dress in identical light-blue clothes, don't have a cadre of serious-faced chaperones watch their every move. The one that walks beside me is typical: average height, average looks, quiet, watchful, fit, continually alert. It's her eyes that unsettle me – distant yet focused, they continually scan, assess, weigh.

I'm sure I don't need one, your facilities are well controlled, I'll be safe, I said as I checked in.

She bowed, insisted. *I am not here for your safety, Hirotsugu-san. Nobody comes out without a member of staff to identify them. You understand.*

I do, and she is my shadow for the visit.

We reach the entrance, her palm and retina prints open the glass door. The building and grounds are disguised, aesthetics to blend into the business community around it, as is its name. *The Centre for Mental Health* sounds nice, unassuming, possibly friendly; the inmates have no hope of health, minds and personalities so shattered there is no other place for them except

58

shackled in cells. Diet, judicious use of drugs, tightly controlled environment and routine allow them a life as more than animals, even if there is no hope of cure, no way to reach the people locked inside their own private walls. Perfect.

She ushers me into a room on the second floor, waits. Introductions are brief; I sit across the desk from the director, note my correspondence stacked neatly, but obviously, to one side. 'Thank you for your time,' I say.

An intensely busy man with a difficult and sensitive job, he wastes no time on small talk. 'You are sure they will be of value, Hirotsugu-san?'

'There is no way for me to understand what is normal without observing outriders. To help the ill, I must study the ill.'

He slides a single sheet of paper across the desk. 'Of my seventy-five wards, forty appear suitable. The rest are either too stabilised by pharmacology, or too unresponsive, to be of use.'

I pretend to study the page. Any will do, any from here, any with their makeup, their aberrations. Forty is more than I hoped. 'These will be fine, thank you. Their thought-sense should be far different from those I have studied, they will prove invaluable.'

'You have a copy of your clearance?'

I reach into my jacket, hand across a copy of Sahai's ethics board approval. It's only a half lie, as befits the half approval it is; only the cover authorisation is handed over, not the details of what it covers. 'A copy for your records.'

He skim-reads it, places it carefully on the pile. 'So you are ready to commence.'

Form must follow function, or what is believed to be function. I'm not the first researcher to cross his path, he expects certain things, and I will not disappoint him. 'The forty subjects, they are volunteers?'

'Everyone who enters here becomes a Ward of the State for the duration, power of attorney vested in me. I have volunteered them, so *they* have volunteered, Hirotsugu-san.'

I stand, make my way out with my shadow. 'I will have the monitoring devices here tomorrow, then we begin.'

The taxi is a welcome luxury, gives me privacy to think on the way to the hospital. My research programme is long. If I'm to understand thought-sense, I need to know good from bad, complete from partial, whole from shattered, and the *Centre* will give me a start. Forty disjointed, malfunctioning minds, forty people whose thought-sense is so far removed from the everyday it's nigh on impossible to bridge the gap is a start. The arrangement is within the letter of ethical bounds but clearly flies in the face of its spirit. My next stop will shred it.

It's taken nearly three years, three long, patient years to get here, build the networks, plant the seed, bring him onside. I pull my briefcase close, imagine them nestled in their foam cradles, count scarce research funding poured into their development. Adult thought-sense is one thing, and NBI will learn through that; but to succeed it must follow the same thought-sense development as humans, and that, as with all the other senses, happens between the end of the first trimester of pregnancy and five years of age.

The taxi pulls up at the hospital's pre- and perinatal clinic. He waits for me, drags me into the hospital coffee shop. 'Have you got them, Hirotsugu-san? I have fifty lined up right now, ten due within a fortnight, five of those multiple births. It's the mothers, they're pushing as much as I am.'

I smile, put the briefcase on the table and open it. 'Well, I can't have the hospital's head of paediatrics making false promises. Here they are, ready to go.'

He pulls one out, holds it like a rare jewel between finger and thumb, examines it from every angle. 'Amazing. I know the tech is something else, but you've made them things of beauty. Whose idea was the panda?'

How do you get an expectant mother comfortable with her baby being monitored day and night? Arguments over health and preventative medicine only go so far against maternal instinct. Everything from spoons to nappies to bottles are covered in huge eyed, friendly faces; why not these? To change the casing's shape from a simple circle to a panda was not as expensive as I feared. 'My sister. Had her second last year, said it would be cute.'

'She's right. When can I distribute them?'

'If they've signed the agreements, the sooner the better.'

'And the data feeds?'

You have to give to take, and I'll take much from this. It's what took the extra time, to build in the superfluous, but necessary, extra functions. 'Once you activate them, right away. You'll get all of the baby's vital signs and the mother's up to birth, then only the baby's afterwards. Just don't lose the list, you'll be the only one who'll know which mother gets which monitor.'

'You'll keep all the brain readings anonymised?'

'As promised, all I'll have is a monitor number.'

The public address system crackles, his name's called. He stands, picks up the briefcase, hurries off. 'Looks like I'm about to hand over the first one. We'll talk about expansion later.'

CHAPTER 03: HOTHOUSE FLOWERS

CAMPBELL-WILMUT INSTITUTE, ÅLAND ISLANDS
2130

SIX-TEN

It crouches, looks straight at me. 'Is this better, Six-ten?'

I double check. It thought I couldn't, but I know I can; I want to win. It was a few lines of squiggles weeks ago, now I understand it. I poke my finger into the lines, feel the warm softness of its chest yield. 'I know your name.'

'Are you sure? It must be in English, not a literal translation.'

'Yes. It's Sandskwyt.'

'You are overexcited, Six-ten. Concentrate on your pronunciation. Think, then say.'

'Your name is written in San-skrit.'

'Much better. How did you work it out?'

'The letters are funny. I found out the language, played the chips, and studied hard. I know San-skrit now.'

'So. What does it mean?'

'The first bit means someone who is in charge, like in temples, or the head of a school. It could mean "prefect", but that doesn't feel right. "Provost" is better.'

'Is that all?'

'The last bit's my number.'

'So, what is my name?'

'You are Provost Six-ten, head of the school of me.'

It grips me in a bear hug and rumbles. I feel good, I've won. 'Your language skills exceed my expectations, Six-ten. It is my name. I am Provost Six-ten.'

'And I know more.'

Provost Six-ten releases me. 'What else do you know?'

'There are six nine six of us, and each one of us has one of you, so there are six nine six provosts. And Provost Zero. But your names are all written in different languages.'

'How many?'

'I found sixty so far. I can only read five, but they all mean provost and a number. Eight-nine has Provost Eight-nine with him, and Six-eight-four has Provost Six-eight-four with her.'

It stands, walks down the corridor. I grab its hand, walk beside it. Today it's a gentle walk – yesterday we ran. 'If our names are so similar, why are they in different languages?'

'It's good to learn. I know Sanskrit now; Eight-nine had to learn Greek.'

Children and provosts move past us, some hold hands. Provost Six-ten's hand is warm, I trace out its fingers with mine, feel for what's the same, what's different. I squeeze hard, feel two bones instead of one. 'Is this normal?'

'Each day is different, not normal.'

'No. Holding hands. Some children do, some don't.'

'Do you like holding my hand?'

'Well, *good morning*, yes, it's why I do it.'

'Then you may do it for as long as you like, as often as you like.'

I squeeze harder, move closer. 'Good.'

'We will have to revisit an earlier lesson on the lie of

normality. An old saying. Normal is only a cycle on a washing machine.'

'What's a washing machine?'

The auditorium's nearly full. We wait for the last few to trickle in, follow the rules. The first speaker is always last. Twenty-minute presentation then questions. 'Provost Six-ten, why don't I have a name?'

'You do have a name. It is Six-ten.'

'It's a *number*, not a name. Why?'

'It is what your creators called you.'

Three-seven-seven played the "why" game with her provost for hours yesterday. She did it for fun, but I'm serious. 'That's not good enough, there must be a reason.'

'There are six hundred and ninety-six of you. You are the six-hundred-and-tenth. Therefore you are Six-ten.'

'Just like they did with you?'

'Just like they did with me.'

'But I'm human, numbers are for machi-…I mean, for others.'

'Humans are given names by their parents. You have no parents. Therefore you are Six-ten.'

'Forever? That's not fair.'

'It is not forever. When you are old enough you may choose your own name. Everyone may. It is written into The Schedule.'

'I want to choose *now*. I've seen pictures of that lady centuries ago who proved women were as good as men. Emmeline. That's my name.'

'No, not until The Schedule says you may. You are Six-ten until then.'

'So when can I change my name?'

'When you are ten years old.'

'Ten? That's five years away.'

'It is long enough to make sure you choose a good name.'

A tiny buzz, an itch near my left ear. I still feel it, it still irritates. 'Ow.'

'It still hurts? Bend your head, let me examine it.'

I pull my hair back, run my finger over the tiny lump where the needle went in. 'You promised a week.'

'I said one or two weeks. It has healed. The information flow is good. There is nothing wrong. You feel it because it is larger than the previous one.'

'But I can feel it.'

'You always will. When you cannot feel it, then there is a reason to be concerned.'

A rustle, everyone in the auditorium stands, looks at me. Provost Six-ten bends down, touches its lips to my head. Like the rest of it, plastic, warm and nice. It moves away, takes its place at the rear. 'Enjoy your time. We will do your self-critique and analysis at the end of the day. Think carefully as you speak, in particular during question and answer.'

Japanese maples around the circumference catch the early morning light through the dome, give the auditorium a pink tint. I walk down the grassed slope, past semi-circle tiers of children and provosts. As I pass, each row sits cross-legged on bamboo squares set into the grass. I turn at the dais, face my audience. Twenty minutes. I've practised, all I have to do is concentrate and talk slowly. A final deep breath, the overhead panel comes to life, shows the first of my graphics. Four old men with angry, sad faces, a world in flames behind them.

'Hello. I am Six-ten. This is session one, Modern Eurasian

History: comparing the 2022 Russia-China agreement and the 1939-41 Nazi-Soviet pact.'

It's over. I think I've done well – they asked good questions, ones I could answer. Eight-nine takes my place, smiles at me as we pass. I sit next to Provost Six-ten. It leans over, whispers. 'A competent presentation.'

'Are you proud of me?'

'Does it matter?'

'Could do.'

Its eyes turn light blue. 'Yes, Six-ten, I am proud of you.'

CAMPBELL-WILMUT INSTITUTE, ÅLAND ISLANDS
2131

SIX-TEN

I'm not good enough, and Provost Six-ten knows it. *You are one standard deviation below the mean, Six-ten. It will not do*, it said before I went to bed. Who wants to swim anyway? In everything else I'm above the mean, but that's not enough. I feel my body under the blankets; I'm leaner, smaller, not as muscly as everyone else. It doesn't balance out, not for Provost Six-ten. It wants everything to be good, to be above average. Like I do.

Practise and more exercise are what I need, but The Schedule has no time. I can trade sleep for practise, or recreation for exercise. I don't want to show the others I'm weak, so sleep loses. I push the blanket away, grab a towel as I creep from my cubicle. Gentle breaths, the odd mumble or creak, the dorm lies silent in the dark.　／

I stop at the doorway, peer outside. Night duty provosts stand asleep, eyes blacked out, ready to help if called. No noise, no reaction. I hold my breath, sneak out, ignore the chill as carpet turns to tile. An hour, no more, then sneak back. No one will know, and Provost Six-ten will be happy; for a while.

I haven't been here alone at night. The pool's empty, looks like moonlight; dim lights, strange shadows, but it's the silence I notice. No provosts, no children; usually I can hear someone or something. I don't know if I like the silence or not. I drop my towel, get ready to jump in at the shallow end. I face the twelve-metre width I struggled with today, hesitate, walk to the blocks. If I'm going to do this, I'll do it properly. Better to take on fifty metres and get really good than fight with the smaller distance.

Goose pimples, it's cold. I dunk my head under, wipe the hair from my face, stand on tiptoes to keep my head above water. It was warm today, do they turn the heat off at night? For a second I miss my bed, want to go back and curl under the blankets with my pillows, forget all about this. I won't. I'll sleep after.

The bar is where Provost Six-ten showed me. I grab hold, put my feet on the wall and pull myself into a ball. I'm good at starts, that's not the problem. I try to get clear of the water, push as hard as I can as I let go. Slow windmill my arms, left, right, left again. Remember to kick. Remember to breathe, in, out, time it, don't rush. Keep my gaze up, watch for the ropes, count the metres until the turn.

Ten metres gone, water's colder. I'm tired, need to pee, don't want to leave a trail of blue so I hold it in, forget to move and breathe in time, get a mouthful of water. Twenty metres, more than I did before – I concentrate harder, kick out of time, point my toes, left leg, right leg with the opposite arm, can't go faster, crawl past thirty metres. Shoulders hurt, legs are tight, ears are cold. One lap, then rest, then another.

My toes sting, jerk, pins and needles; left leg straightens, twitches; muscles pull tight, erupt in pain, cramps. I stop, my leg bends, I grab it, start to sink, let go, thrash my arms, try to kick. My left leg screams, doubles me over in pain, sends my head under again. I stretch my right leg down, can't find the bottom. I kick it about, use my right arm, reach the surface, gulp another breath; cramps in both legs knot them under me, pain forces a scream, sends me under. I use both arms, get back to the surface, barely manage to stay there. The side of the pool's close, five metres, I can make it. I start to move, feel my left arm tense, shake, then knot up. I sink, can't use my legs or arms, can only look down as the bottom of the pool rises towards me.

The tiles are pretty: white on pale blue, edges dark, but they come too close, too quickly. The water pushes down with cold hands, tries to squeeze the air from me, makes the pain in my legs and arms worse. My chest hurts, I need to breathe – I try to kick, my legs mock and scream, my arms join in, the tiles are too close. I want my warm bed, want Provost Six-ten, don't want this.

An arm around my waist; a pair of legs push against the tiles. I break the surface, gulp air, wriggle my arms as best I can to stay here. The pain makes me whimper; the arm around my waist slips, hooks me under the armpits. 'Stop it, Six-ten, keep still,' a boy's voice says.

If the arm slipped once it can slip again, might let go. I try to kick my legs, pain soars. 'Ow, ow, ow. Help me!'

'Keep moving and I'll lose you. Grab my arm, stay still.'

I hold on as best I can, start to shiver, teeth chatter. The arm tugs at me, pulls me slowly with little jerks, his body under mine kicks and supports. 'Nearly there, hold tight.'

We stop, I'm pulled up: stop, pull, stop, pull up the ladder until I'm out of the water. Grass under my backside, the arm lets go; I fall, feet run away. It's colder than the pool, shakes grow. Feet approach, a towel drops on me, another, something else – weight and dry start to take the shakes away. A body behind me, arms across the towels pull me close, start to rub. Feeling comes back slowly, brings more pain first, warmth last. 'Thanks.'

The body pulls me upright, tightens the towels around me. A look of concern and relief on a familiar face. 'Are you alright now?' Eight-nine asks.

'No. I'm cold. Evwything hurts.'

'You nearly drowned, Six-ten. What were you doing?'

'Pwactising. I don't swim good enough.'

He reaches under the towels, kneads my calf with his knuckles. It hurts at first, then hurts less, starts to feel good. 'You've got that right. But by yourself, at night? It's not smart.'

'You were looking for me?'

His head snaps up. 'No. Couldn't sleep, went for a walk. I heard noises, looked, saw you.'

'Lucky.'

He moves his knuckles to my other calf; my legs feel warmer, softer. 'Next time you might not be. Why didn't you bring your provost?'

'Embarrassed, don't want everyone knowing. I should be good at this, at everything, like you are.'

'Like me? I'm good at swimming, but I'm useless at running, I hate it.'

'You are good. Yesterday you finished first.'

'Months ago I was always last. Always. You know what my provost said to me? It said: "Eight-nine, you are two standard deviations below the mean. It will not do".'

'What did you do?'

'Practised at night, like you. But I didn't try by myself. Two-three-three helped me.'

'It worked.'

'You want to practise at night? I'll come with you, we can swim together, and you won't drown.'

If it worked for him, it might work for me. 'I'd like that.'

Eight-nine stands, walks towards the shallow end of the pool. I get up, hobble after him. My legs slowly relax, start to feel better.

'Good. We'll hop back in, keep to this end.'

'Why?'

'So you don't go to sleep scared. Two-three-three made me do the same, so I finished feeling good each time.'

We don't do too much, only a few times across the short side of the pool. At first, I nearly panic as my legs tense up again; at the end, I've forgotten, try to race him, lose miserably but happily. I stand on tiptoes next to him near the ladder. If he helps me some more, I know I can do this.

'You know, the provosts don't care if we help each other,' he says.

'Why don't they tell us?'

He points to the doorway as we climb out. 'Don't know, maybe it's not in The Schedule. You could ask them.'

Towels over shoulders, we walk past Provost Six-ten and Provost Eight-nine; both stand rigid in the doorway, eyes blacked out. We say nothing, walk past in silence as we head back to the dorm. 'Why didn't they do anything?'

'Maybe because I'm with you.'

NANGANGZHEN, GUANGDONG PROVINCE, CHINA
2131

LI QIAO

The nurse runs a practised eye over me, lets the spray bandage settle on stitches across my cheek and upper arm. 'Get dressed, sit, and don't move. It'll take ten minutes for the painkillers to work properly, then we're done.'

I pull on my clothes, settle gingerly into the corner chair as my iodine-laced backside protests. The bruises and swelling will start to go down in a few days, but my left eye's closed for at least a week.

'Thank you for your help,' Granpa says.

She closes the door as she walks out. 'I'll make an appointment with the dental surgeon for later this week. Boys heal quickly, but he'll feel awful for a few days.'

There's no way to sit that's comfortable, no part of me that doesn't protest in pain. I feel great inside, I started it *and* finished it; that's all that matters.

'Sit still, Li Qiao, and wipe the grin off your face. This is serious,' Granpa says.

'I am, everything hurts.'

'And don't talk for once, keep quiet until you're asked questions.'

He looks angry like always, but he's worried; not for me, but because of me. I don't know why, but I know I like it. 'Right, only when I'm asked.'

Granpa rolls his eyes. I try to find a position that hurts less.

The constable ignores me, turns to Granpa. 'This shouldn't take long, only a few questions. You're the boy's guardian?'

'With his grandmother, yes; his father's not around, he's PLA.'

'Oh. Some sort of soldier then?'

I tilt my chair against the wall. 'No, moron, he's a colonel, a People's Hero.'

'Mind your tongue,' Granpa says.

'Why? Fùqin's a hero, lost an arm defending all of us, even him. What's the most this moron's suffered, haemorrhoids?'

'See what I mean? He's been like that since his father dumped him on us, full of himself and no one else. I apologise for his attitude.'

'Apology accepted. It can be hard for any child, but this time he seems to be the innocent party.' The constable turns to me. 'But remember, this *moron* can drag you away and lock you up any time he likes. So keep quiet.'

I open my mouth, stop before I say anything. I've got better things to do than sit in a police station.

'Is he like this at school?' the constable asks.

'The same attitude, the same mouth. Even though he's in the top five percent he never studies, skips classes.'

'You didn't do anything to discipline him?'

'He doesn't listen to me, got his grandmother twisted around his little finger. It's why we got him started.'

The constable flips through his notepad. 'Wing Chun Ken?'

'Yes, thought it might teach him discipline and control; even hoped a few thrashings at training would pull him into line.'

'Well *that* certainly seems to have worked.'

'What were we supposed to do? He won't listen to us, his

father's not here, we needed help. All it did was teach him how to use his fists properly.'

'His teachers say he's in trouble most days; when he's there.'

'Early on we thought it was because he had difficulty adjusting, didn't feel at home. We thought he'd, well, he'd grow out of it. Eventually.'

'He's only got a couple of years left to "grow out of it", then he's an adult. No warnings, only court and convictions. Do you understand that, Li Qiao?'

'Yes, *sir.*'

The constable's eyes narrow, gaze bores into me. 'I'll make it simple for you. Once you're sixteen, you're an adult. You fight or get in trouble, no matter whose fault, you go up before the magistrate. Go up enough times, or even once, and it's off to prison.' He leans closer, grins. 'You get to meet lots of new friends in there, lifers just waiting for a fresh-faced pretty boy like you. Now, do you understand me?'

I blink, try to get rid of the mental picture. They have to catch me first, and I've got two years to go before I need to worry. I lower my head, try to sound cowed. 'I understand.'

'Good. So, can we get on with this? Tell me who started it.'

It took me months to get him there, get his face in the door without knowing I manipulated him. 'He came up to me halfway through the session, when the instructor was with the juniors.'

'Then what?'

I let him win a few nothing spars, held myself back over weeks to build his confidence, see his weaknesses; then all it took was a few insults, the right words, and his anger and stupidity did the rest. I point to my eye. 'He hit me, did this, said nothing, just started to hit me. So I defended myself, had to hit back, tried to deflect his blows like I was trained, like the instructors showed.'

'And the last time you hit him?'

I had to get the right day, the right session, the once-a-week outdoor class next to the toddler's playground. Fighting him into the final position cost me, will hurt for weeks, but it was worth it. 'I tried to get out of it but he came at me. I threw him to get away, he ended up on the slide.' The sweetest sound – that crack, hoarse rasp breath, his uncontrolled slide into the sand.

'Thank you, Li Qiao, you can keep quiet now. You know what he did next?' the constable asks Granpa.

Granpa shakes his head, worried. 'No.'

You always have a plan, a way out when you're in. It was hard, but there's no point in me suffering with a moron.

'He tried to help, stayed with him until they brought them here.'

'No one told me.'

The constable stands, ushers us into the corridor. 'Maybe there's hope for him yet. It all fits with other witness statements. Li Qiao was provoked, tried to avoid the fight but couldn't, ended in a tragic accident. So far as we're concerned, it's finished.'

The constable points to a bench, hurries away. 'Instead of trying to get out of fights, Li Qiao, try not to get *into* them in the first place. And listen to your grandfather – control your mouth before it controls you.'

'You're lucky they listened, didn't go by your reputation,' Granpa says.

Lucky? Smart, smarter than them all. 'I guess.'

The door opposite opens, closes. A doctor rushes out, a man and a woman sit tearful at the foot of a bed – a boy unmoving, hooked into machines.

Granpa stands, shuffles off. 'He got what he deserved, this time. But that will be you one day if you don't change. Stay here, I expect they've got paperwork I need to sign to get you home. I'll be five minutes.'

I stand, make sure my clothes are crooked, walk through the door. The man and woman look up in surprise; she bursts into tears, turns away and hangs her head; he stands, offers his hand. 'Li Qiao?'

Be polite, play the part, act like an adult. I take it. 'Yes.'

'How are you? The doctor said –'

The woman lifts her head. 'How can you talk to him? Look at what he did to our son, he's –'

'*Your* son started it, tried to put Li Qiao in here. As usual, you don't see it, do you? If you can't keep a civil tongue, say nothing.'

She starts with the tears again.

'Sorry, Li Qiao, whatever he is, she still loves him, thinks the best.'

'It's okay, all mothers do.'

'We know he started it, heard what he said.'

My eye starts to sting, the bruise must be growing. I touch it, feel the bulge from my cheek to my eyebrow, regret it as my fingers send fire across my face. 'I didn't want to fight him, but he didn't give me a choice.'

'Does it hurt that much, is there any permanent damage?'

'No, nurse says a few weeks; I don't know about my teeth. Him?'

The man looks at the boy on the bed, chokes back a sob. 'The doctor says they can do wonders – we'll go to Nanjing, see what happens. He'll walk again, I know he will.'

'I hope so too,' I lie.

'Did you want to speak to us or to him? He can't hear you, they're keeping him in a coma until they're ready.'

'Both of you, I mean, you and him. Granpa's making sure I can go home. I only have a minute, I don't want to bother you.'

'You're not. What did you want to say?'

I have a sudden urge to laugh, throw my head back and yell with delight; I fight it, win, manage to look conflicted and emotional. 'I wanted to apologise for how it turned out. If there had been any other way, any chance, I would've taken it, believe me.'

More tears from her; he wavers as if he's about to hug me, settles, reaches out and squeezes hard on my good shoulder as he pushes out the words. 'We know, we're grateful you tried.'

I watched the Beijing Opera the other week, hours and hours of masks and cymbals, actors prancing around on stage, faces hidden. Their masks told one story, their words another; as long as the stories were the same the deception worked, no matter how ridiculous. I walk to the foot of the bed, stand by the woman. The machine pushes air into him, another beeps as his heart beats; a line in his arm, another in his thigh, one flows in, one flows out. Cuts, bruises, hastily applied stitches and gauze; not as many, not as large as I carry, but that's my price. I stand rigid, keep still and quiet for as long as I think I need to pull on the mask, make a point of being seen to look into his closed eyes.

I walk slowly to the top of the bed, put one hand gently on his arm. I whisper, deliberately loud enough for his parents to hear. 'Chia-tern, I forgive you. Be whole, get better as soon as you can.'

The woman's tears are joined by the man's; they cling to each other as if my words mean something.

I bend to Chia-tern's ear, lower my voice so only he can hear. 'If you do, I'll finish the job properly.'

The man walks me to the door. 'When we get back you will visit, see how he is, his progress?'

It appeals and sickens, a chance to do to his mind what I've done to his body. I step out, close the door. 'I'd like that.'

Granpa's not around; either late or has forgotten about me again. I feel tired, drowsy, must be the painkillers; it's a nice feeling, like I'm smothered in feathers. I hope they'll give me a supply to take home. I sit, close my eyes, wait.

'So. You got away with it.'

'Fùqin?'

'Open your eyes, look at your father when he talks to you. And sit up straight.'

Always in that uniform, medals glint and cap level – his hair's greyer, skin darker. He takes a cigarette out of his mouth, flicks ash onto the floor.

'You can't smoke in here, they'll go crazy.'

He takes another drag, blows smoke at me from the corner of his mouth. 'Black eagles make their own rules, remember? They won't catch me if you don't open your mouth.'

'I won't tell.'

'You disappoint me, Li Qiao.'

'Why? He's bullied me for years, you don't want me to stand up for myself?'

'Don't be stupid. It's how you chose to do it. A fair fight of all things? He's a year older than you, taller and heavier.'

'So? I'm out here, he's the paraplegic.'

'You gave him a chance. If you slipped or got one punch wrong, if that fool got lucky, you'd be where he is.'

'But I'm not.'

He takes another drag, crushes the cigarette out on the floor. 'This time.'

'It was easy, he was sloppy, too slow. He couldn't control his anger, I couldn't lose.'

He shakes his head. 'You're over-confident, you take the wrong risks, make the wrong choices. What did I tell you about not giving a fool a chance? And in public? People know he bullied you, know what you're like. You got away with it this time, but only just.'

'So what do I do, wait until the right time? Whenever that is.'

'You'll talk to me with respect or not at all.'

'Sorry, Fùqin.'

'Better. You don't think. Today it's Chia-tern, but soon they'll be bigger, better, harder. Then what? You act like this you'll lose, and no son of mine is a loser.'

He stands, lights another cigarette as he walks away. 'If you want to measure up, do it properly next time. Think it through, don't give the other guy a single chance. This time you didn't do any of that, so you disappoint me. Again. Now get some rest, wait for your grandfather to take you home.'

I close my eyes, lean back. I don't have to wait long.

'You ready, Li Qiao? We can go now, hospital's arranged transport,' Granpa says.

We hobble down the corridor. Granpa's arthritis slows him; bruises and twisted ankles make me shuffle along like an old man.

'Your grandmother's going to have a fit when I get you home.'

I wince as I twist the wrong way. 'If I get home.'

Granpa gives me a sideways glance. 'I wonder what your father would say if he could see you now.'

'He says I disappoint him. I don't think enough.'
'For once he'd be right.'

CAMPBELL-WILMUT INSTITUTE, ÅLAND ISLANDS
2132

EIGHT-NINE

Provost Eight-nine selects a patch of ground; we sit cross-legged, face each other, warm sun on my back. Clear blue and cloudless sky peers down through the dome, but now is not the time to relax. I enjoy this even at its hardest, even when I fall short; the knowledge may feed in overnight to hide beneath my conscious mind, but it's nothing unless challenged, tested, then applied. I am my own present, we all are, each surprise gifts on an eternal Christmas morning.

Whatever's in store today doesn't involve displays, tablets, or panels, so there's no room to hide or bluff. Excited chatter from other pairs around us, nerves in front. One-seven-six is agitated. Again. Lost battles with statistics and history pushed her down, eroded her self-confidence.

'Eight-nine, is the concept of equilibrium subjective or objective?' Provost Eight-nine asks.

Never any small talk, and it measures response times. Equilibrium? It's unfamiliar, wallows in the back of my mind, then pops up. Context one: thermodynamic systems, macroscopic systems. Context two: economic systems, general equilibrium analysis. Context three: psychology, emotional and/or mental stability. Three now? It's usually two modules a night, and these are unrelated. Provost doesn't link the dots, never does, waits to see if I can, or if I can punch a hole in the lot and identify no relationship at all. *Information is one thing, knowledge another*, Provost Eight-nine always says. 'Equilibrium is defined at or over an interval of time. Dependence on time makes equilibrium a subjective concept,' I say.

'Provide one example as proof.'

'A one-cubic-metre block of pure pitch. Observed over a second, it's in equilibrium as a highly viscous near solid. Observed over millennia, it's in equilibrium as a fluid.'

A stammer, a sigh from in front. 'I don't *know*, equilibrium only happens when a person has a normal brain,' One-seven-six says.

'We have discussed the error in the term normal several times,' Provost One-seven-six responds.

'Is there any generally applicable principle to be derived from this?' Provost Eight-nine asks.

I've been caught out once, never will be again. The only generally applicable principle is that there are no generally applicable principles. Which is bad enough. 'Apart from equilibrium being a time-dependent concept? No. But it reinforces the need to understand assumptions and definitions before reaching a conclusion.'

One-seven-six's back shakes, tiny waves in her blouse as it moves with her. 'I think it's in there, but it's all jumbled up. It doesn't want to come out.'

'There have been no identified problems with your interface or the modules. It is your cognitive functions that are at fault,' Provost One-seven-six declares.

'If I concentrate hard, it might help,' One-seven-six says.

'We have tried that for the past two weeks. It has made no difference.'

'For now, Eight-nine, that is satisfactory,' Provost Eight-nine says. 'The remainder of this session concerns thermodynamics. If two separate systems, A and B, are both in equilibrium with a third system, C, what are the two implied consequences?'

'Systems A and B must be in equilibrium with each other. All systems that are in equilibrium with each other must be at the same temperature,' I say.

They don't have facial expressions, only their eyes grow brighter or fainter. Provost Eight-nine inclines its head; I imagine it grins, even though I know it can't. It manages to produce a pad and pencil from nowhere, holds them out to me. 'Prove it. Mathematically.'

'What do I *do?*' One-seven-six asks.

'We will revisit earlier lessons. Test your long-term memory. As a final option. Simple recall of dates, names, places, and events. European Union history, early twenty-first century,' Provost One-seven-six replies.

An hour and a half straight. A pad covered in scrawl, pencil worn halfway to the nub – I feel satisfied. It's all I know about thermodynamics, to now anyway, and Provost Eight-nine can't fault me. Yet.

'A break of exactly fifteen minutes. Psychology upon your return,' Provost Eight-nine tells me.

I stand, hurry away.

'You see, I told you, it's all going,' One-seven-six says.

'It is not your fault. It is simply the way it is. The way you are,' Provost One-seven-six says.

The pad and pencil are history, forgotten as the next session grinds on. Provost Eight-nine issues questions, statements, every so often a grand declaration. Each one demands a response. Support or challenge. Why or why not. Evidence, please. I feel tired, but I'm happy I can use what's been put into my brain. Provost Eight-nine hardly bothers about facts anymore. One or two questions at the start, then apply it, question it, build on it is all it wants. I enjoy it, think Provost Eight-nine would too, if it could enjoy anything.

'An acceptable session, Eight-nine. Met expectations in most areas, slightly above in the rest,' Provost Eight-nine says.

Anything other than economics and psychology and I'd be unhappy. All the tendency this, in general that, ceteris paribus the other. 'I prefer mathematics to this stuff.'

'Why?'

'It irritates me. No precision. No exact measures. Too many assumptions.'

'Psychology deals with people. People are imprecise, they may or may not behave according to rules and earlier observation.'

'I'm a person, and I don't.'

'You are different from the people who live outside. But you are the same as the people who live inside.'

Sitting in one place too long hurts. I stretch, look around. Children and provosts sit, talk to each other, the usual end-of-session debate and analysis. There's an empty patch in front of me, two depressions in the grass. I can't see One-seven-six or her provost.

'Tell me about bounded rationality,' Provost Eight-nine says.

I can't imagine she finished early, everything seems too hard for her. 'People always act rationally. But what is rational can be different for different individuals.'

'Which would imply?'

No one ever finishes early. 'What is rational for one person is not necessarily rational for another.'

'You have already said that. Concentrate, Eight-nine. Stop looking around. What is the implication for an observer?'

'Two people may react in entirely different ways to the same stimulus and both ways may be perfectly rational to those individuals. So rational behaviour can appear irrational.'

'You and everybody inside have similar concepts of rationality. It is not the case for people outside.'

'But we're all different, not the same.'

'I said similar, not the same. There are differences, but they are small. With more time, you will notice them.'

The session's over. I hurry to the doorway, drag Provost Eight-nine behind me, make sure we're first out. I turn, scan faces as they stream past.

'What are we doing?' it asks.

They're nearly all gone. Six-ten and Three-four wait a little further along, Two-three-three jogs past, joins them. 'Looking.'

'For?'

'One-seven-six.'

Provost Eight-nine crouches, eyes level with mine. 'Why are we looking for One-seven-six?'

'She keeps having trouble. She had more today. She wasn't there at the end.'

'And?'

'If I can find her, I can help her.'

'One-seven-six fell short again. She has fallen short continually. You cannot help her.'

Only a few pairs left, she's not with them. 'If you ask Provost One-seven-six, we can find her.'

'Eight-nine, pay attention. One-seven-six has been reassigned. Provost One-seven-six has been reassigned. They are not here.'

'When will they be back?'

'They will not be back. Ever.'

'Ever? Why?'

'Because One-seven-six failed her test.'

'You never said there was a test.'

'Everything is a test, Eight-nine. Some are big. Some are small.'

'So you could send me away any time at all?'

'No. To learn properly, you must fail. But there are some tests you must not fail. If you do, we will be reassigned. You have already passed three of those tests.'

'You didn't tell me.'

'It is important you do not know when you are being tested. If you have passed three and you did not know, what does that imply?'

'I can pass the others.'

'Correct. So you have no need to know when you are tested. Always do your best. It is all you can do.'

'Nothing more?'

'Nothing more.'

Provost Eight-nine goes one way, I go to my friends.

'What's wrong?' Two-three-three asks.

'One-seven-six has gone, she failed a test and she's been reassigned with her provost.'

'She's not the only one. Five-five-six left yesterday with his provost,' Six-ten adds.

'What does *reassigned* mean?' Two-three-three asks.

'I think it means transfer,' Six-ten replies.

'Must be. Provost said One-seven-six is never coming back,' I say.

'Why? What did they do?' Two-three-three asks.

'Provost said Five-five-six wasn't right,' Six-ten says. 'Wherever they are, they have their provosts and each other. They must have gone to another place like this.'

'I like it here. I don't want a transfer,' Three-four says.

'We won't get transferred, we won't fail,' Two-three-three says.

It's not enough for Three-four. She looks worried, stays silent. She doesn't say much anyway, even less when she's upset. 'After lunch I'll tell Provost Eight-nine if you get reassigned, I want to be reassigned with you.'

'You mean it?' Three-four asks.

'We all do. I'll tell mine,' Six-ten says.

'I will, too,' adds Two-three-three.

It gets a rare smile out of Three-four.

'One of us goes, all four of us go. Together,' I say.

I feel better at lunch, less anxious. None of us will be reassigned, and if we are we'll be with One-seven-six, Five-five-six, and anyone else who's been reassigned. It sounds rational.

Rational.

Rational behaviour can appear irrational. Can irrational behaviour appear rational? Definition, assumption, then conclusion; I think I've missed something. I separate my peas into piles of prime numbers. There aren't enough of them, I try Lucas numbers instead. Assumption. Reassignment is transfer. Conclusion. They're together. Is that right? But Provost said so, didn't it? A hand steals a chip, Six-ten smiles as she chews.

'You alright there, Eight-nine?'

I've missed nothing, the only assumption is correct. There can't be any other conclusion. I impose interest, take two of hers.

'Perfectly.'

CHAPTER 04: CONTROL

NANGANGZHEN, GUANGDONG PROVINCE, CHINA
2133

LI QIAO

Pressed face first into the wall, handcuffs removed, door slams. The cell reeks of continuous use and non-existent care; small, bare, fold-down bench on one wall, a stainless-steel toilet overflows against the other. The constable sits in the corridor, watches me through the bars.

'Where is he?' I ask.

'I called him, he doesn't want to know you,' he says.

'Cheap bastard, bail's probably too much. I've got money for anything I want, tell him to use that.'

'No, I don't think I will. We both warned you, you never listened, now *he's* not. Want to know what he said?'

My mouth's fuzzy, head aches, stale beer on my breath. I could care less. 'No, but you're going to tell me anyway.'

'He said you're just another little emperor, a self-centred brat he wants nothing to do with. Called you a disgrace, a stain on the family name.'

'You're lying.'

'True. I did leave one thing out. He sends your grandmother's best wishes for your sixteenth birthday, and his that you go to hell.'

I look around for something to hit, there's nothing in here but concrete and stainless steel; my knuckles are raw, hands bruised and aching, no point in doing more damage. I slide down the wall, sit, prop my feet on the bench opposite. 'Get me an aspirin, something for my hands.'

'Nurse's day off, get them yourself.'

'You can't do that, I'll have you for child abuse.'

'For what? As of yesterday, you're an adult.'

Shit, forgot about that. 'Then I'll wait, at least I can have a drink; maybe do community service at a brewery this time.'

'For someone who thinks he's so smart, you're an idiot. No more community service, no more slaps on the wrist; you're an adult, you get treated like one.'

'So treat me like one. I get a solicitor, right? So get me one.'

'You stream too much American rubbish. You're in here, you're guilty, all I'm waiting for are sentencing options.'

'I was provoked, it's not my fault; ask anyone.'

'Doesn't matter, it's all the same, doesn't get you anywhere with us or them.'

So I'm guilty regardless, going to prison? It's my first time, surely they'll give me a chance and go easy on me. It won't be too bad, some time locked up, crap food. Food. How long's it been since I've eaten? 'Hey. When do you serve lunch?'

'Ha. Water only, plus whatever your family brings you. Oh, I forgot, you don't have any now. Guess you're on a diet.'

'So what do you do here, housekeeping or turndown service?'

'Suicide watch. In case you decide to do us all a favour. I'm supposed to stop you, take away anything that might help.'

I point to my shoes. 'You forgot the laces, pea-brain.'

'Like I said, supposed to.'

A woman in uniform hands him some papers, walks away. The constable buries himself in them, ignores me.

'Hey.'

He keeps reading.

'What's that, what is it?'

He continues to ignore me.

'You deaf, what you reading?'

He looks up, waves the papers at me. 'Finished report, all about you. Happy? Your record as a minor, everything you did. Guess how far back it goes?'

'Surprise me.'

'Eleven years, your first caution. There's nothing you haven't done at least twice; don't think I've seen one that big for anyone your age.'

'Glad you're impressed.'

'The magistrate will be. It's all taken into account with sentencing.'

'I was a kid, it doesn't count.'

'Doesn't matter, a record's a record. The way this reads, you've spent most of your life fighting.'

They won't give me any consideration, won't care about the reasons. How long could they lock me up for? The constable whistles gently. 'What?'

'You know you put three of them in hospital?'

'Would've been four if you hadn't turned up.'

He flashes a head and shoulder photo at me. 'This one. Know who he is?'

He was the loudmouth that started it all, deserved everything he got. 'No idea.'

'He's the Provincial Chairman's son.'

'So?'

'So? His father's connected to everyone in Guangdong, they'll throw the book at you; it's probably already reflected in...' He flips through the papers. 'Yes, it's here. They're going to make an example out of you.'

The room grows a little colder, a little distant. 'Example? How much of an example?'

'First-time offenders usually get three soft plea options. You? All severe.'

'What do I do, how do I defend myself?'

The constable stands. 'You still don't get it. You don't *defend* anything – you're guilty and convicted, and because you chose the wrong people they've already given you the maximum.' He rips the last page from the papers, drops it through the bars. 'You get sentenced tomorrow. All you do is choose which of the three options. As always, it's your own fault. You had your chance.'

I pick up the paper, skim-read it. My bravado evaporates; the numbers scream out, chill me. 'This is insane – for fighting morons that provoked me?'

'Do what you want, choose one. If you don't, they will. I'm going for a drink, have it ready when I get back.'

The shakes start, feelings I've not had for years. Plead guilty, three years; plead not guilty, six years. *Six years?* 'Hey, where you going? You should stay with me, watch me. Hey, come back.'

The constable disappears down the corridor. 'Like I said, supposed to.'

*

It's not fair, not right. Six years for doing nothing, for being right?

It's always been the way – the system hates me, run by people with nothing better to do than pick on me, punish me. It's only because it was the son of some self-important nobody they do this; if it was someone else, if it wasn't me, they'd not even bother, laugh it off or more likely agree the little shit got what he deserved. I won't say I'm guilty or innocent, I've not broken any law and I won't let them put me away for six years for being right.

I toss the paper on the bench, lean back and close my eyes. Everyone tries to get to me any way they can, any way they know, to make up for being less than me. The whole thing was a set-up, I know it now, the whole town's in on it. I bet they had the sentences drafted up weeks back, and those guys – they chose the right ones with the right barbs – timed it as close as possible to my sixteenth the first chance they got. Had to be; why else was the constable around the corner, there at just the right time? Well, I know now for next time, and next time I'll be ready. 'Next time,' I hiss under my breath.

There's a rustle, I open my eyes. Fùqin sits straight-backed on the bench, gaze bores a hole into the wall next to me. Not a hair out of place, creases sharp even on his empty sleeve. I study him as he ignores me, try to gauge the mood in his cold stare. Last time's anger is gone, now closer to emptiness.

Ten minutes of silence; I break the impasse. 'Fùqin?'

He doesn't move, refuses to acknowledge me.

'Fùqin? Talk to me.'

He stares ahead, gaze fixed on the wall.

'Guess you're disappointed with me. Again.'

'I curse the day you were born,' he says.

'It wasn't my fault, I was provoked.'

'As always. What was it this time?'

'He insulted us, called me a Yao minority nothing.'

'That was all?'

'He said we didn't count, I didn't matter, the world's for the Han, not for us.'

'You let yourself be goaded by that, let the truth provoke you? We *are* Yao, we *are* a minority in a nation of Han.'

'But —'

'All my life I live under them, but I am respected and valued. Why? Because I think, don't react, ignore the insults and dog whistles. I beat them in other ways, smarter ways, not with my fists.'

'You told me to stand up for myself. I do it and you're upset with me?'

'If we acted like you every time an insult was thrown we'd end up like the Miao, kept as pets in manicured villages to be trotted out to suck money from fat tourists. That's what you want?'

'Of course not.'

'So why do you do it?'

'I'm better than all of them; faster, stronger, smarter, and they know it. They should act like it, treat me with the respect I'm due.'

'Respect is earned, not given.'

'And I've earned it.'

He sounds tired, worn. 'The inside of a prison cell is the respect you want? All your life is a path here, nothing more.'

'So I fall short.'

'Since the day you were born.'

He finally looks at me, takes his pistol from its holster, aims it between my eyes. 'What do you feel, Li Qiao?'

His finger's a mountain of flesh on the trigger, the barrel a black hole a metre wide; I study it, try to see the bullet deep inside, fail. 'Nothing, Fùqin, nothing.'

He snaps the safety off. 'Now?'

'Nothing.'

'Why?'

'I know you won't do it, you won't let yourself, even if you want to.'

'That is why you are nothing to me. I have discipline and control. You lack them, you are too volatile.'

'I don't need them.'

'Look around you. This is your home for the next six years. Because of your lack of control, your arrogance.'

It's not fair, but maybe he's right. 'Yes, Fùqin.'

He holsters his pistol. 'The other-knowing are wise, the self-knowing discerning. Those who triumph over others have muscle, those who triumph over themselves are commanding.'

'What's Laozi got to do with anything?'

'If you won't listen to me, you might listen to him. And do something about it.'

'Like what?'

He points to the paper on the bench. 'You can start by reading it properly.'

I've already read it, but I pick it up, go through it again. Plead guilty, plead not guilty; there's a third option? 'Military service?'

'Six years.'

'It says no conviction will be recorded. Why?'

'A last chance to turn you around. Or they could want to get something out of you rather than just spend on your room and board.'

'But six years.'

'To teach you discipline and control. What I, your grandparents, this community failed to do. To follow in my footsteps.'

'It would make you happy?'

'You may disappoint me less.'

Six years is still six years, but they'll pay me, no record, no prison. I read the fine print; but if I get booted out, no matter when, I go to prison for three years. How hard can it be to run around in uniform with a rifle all day? 'I might do it.'

I'd assumed it was only the Army, but I'm mistaken, it's there in black and white – my mind's made up.

The constable steps into the cell, sits next to Fùqin, hands me a pen. 'Circle your choice, initial, sign, and date the bottom of the page.'

I look to Fùqin; he nods. I circle my choice once, twice, initial and sign. I hand the paper back to the constable. 'Is that right?'

He looks at it, stands, closes the cell door behind him. 'Filled in properly, all official now. Magistrate first thing tomorrow, Air Force'll pick you up straight after.'

CAMPBELL-WILMUT INSTITUTE, ÅLAND ISLANDS
2133

SIX-TEN

Grunts, polite applause, loud cheers. Bodies fall hard on tight canvas, add to my nerves. Provost Six-ten puts a hand under my chin, slides my mouthguard in. 'Bite. Stand still while I check your judogi.'

'Checked it twice.'

It tightens my chin strap, the soft leather helmet settles. 'This is not practice. You must pay close attention.'

Another thud. Applause. I'm next. 'Who is it?'

Provost Six-ten stops inspecting my belt, straightens my jacket. 'Your opponent is Four-zero-zero.'

Not what I wanted. Fifteen centimetres taller, heavier, he's no fair match. Three rounds? It will only take him two. 'Oh. Who selected him?'

Nine-four and Three-six-two walk past arm in arm, roughed up, smile, chat. Their provosts follow; we start towards the ring. 'I did,' Provost Six-ten says.

'You? You want me to lose?'

'No. It is a challenge. Challenge is necessary if you are to grow. It is also a lesson.'

'That I can't trust you?'

'No. That life is hard, and at times unfair. To help you understand.'

'Understand I can't win? Some lesson.'

We step into the ring. Four-zero-zero stands in the opposite corner, back towards me. I turn, glimpse Eight-nine applaud, concentrate on Provost Six-ten.

'That is not what I said. Your mind is your best weapon if you use it,' it says.

'Even if my mind is scared?'

'Remember. Inside might be the skin of a dog, but –'

'On the outside, show the skin of a tiger. I remember.'

Provost Six-ten steps out of the ring, abandons me to the fight. 'Do not forget your technique.'

I walk to the centre, stop in front of Four-zero-zero, tilt my head up to meet his gaze. Provost Zero goes through the rules. Listen to my voice. Three rounds. Best of three wins. Points, pin, or yield. I hardly notice it. How do I fight him? Even at practice he's too much, I never managed to get the better of him, no one has. A smirk, a glint in his eye; he knows it.

A short bow, we take the stance, grab each other's shoulders, lean in. Provost Zero steps forward, raises then drops its hand. 'Start.'

Four-zero-zero pulls back, tries a throw. I let go, bring my arms up to break his grip, jump back. He keeps balance, bounces on his feet, approaches with a series of round kicks; I parry, but have to retreat as I defend. They're lazy kicks but I know what he's up to. He can send kicks and punches at me all day, stay out of range, win all three rounds on points. He relies on his reach for an easy victory, hopes I'll follow his plan. I won't.

He favours his left side in everything. I wait for the next kick, catch his right foot as his leg extends, shove, send him to the canvas on his back. He stays controlled, pulls his right leg in and me with it, connects his left foot with my stomach to push me over his head. As soon as my face meets the canvas he's on me, a knee in my back, my right arm and left leg locked behind me. I'm pinned, slap the canvas with my free hand. 'Yield.'

Four-zero-zero whispers before he releases me. 'Good girl. Make it easier on yourself next time, you know I've got this.'

I stand. My cheeks burn.

'Round one. Six-ten yields. Four-zero-zero one, Six-ten nil,' Provost Zero says.

Polite applause, a few subdued boos. They expect as much, he expects it, the provosts expect it. The heat in my cheeks grows, spreads to my chest. I expect it too, I fight like I train, and this is what happens. Winning doesn't matter now; proving them wrong does.

I straighten my jacket, make them wait as I move to the centre. If I surprise him, forget my forms and responses, I've got a chance. If I stay controlled, if he does not.

I stand in front of him, bow, take the stance. I grab his jacket as hard as I can, bunch the thick cotton tight in my fists. This time his reach is *my* advantage.

Provost Zero steps forward, raises then drops its hand. 'Start.'

Four-zero-zero tries it again, pulls back hard. I keep my grip, pull back as hard as he does, balance us. I look into his eyes, stare, wait until his gaze locks to mine; I blow him a kiss, he blinks. I jump into a ball, let his momentum pull me towards him, then kick both feet into his chest as I let go. I land, face him as he hits the ropes, careens back unbalanced. I grab his lapels, pull him down, feet into his stomach, throw him over me. Canvas booms — hoots, yells, shouts; I stand, turn to him as he comes for me. Kicks, swings, he's flustered, angry, too rushed. I feint, he tries to block a punch that never arrives. I drop to the canvas, bring my legs around as hard as I can behind his knees. He falls hard, winded; I flip him face down, drive my head between his legs, stand as tall and straight as I can, let his weight pin his face and shoulders. His mouth moves, arms flail; Provost Zero crouches beside him, hand beats on the canvas, all drowned by cheers and whistles. Provost Zero slices the air with his hand; I release Four-zero-zero's legs, move to the centre of the ring.

'Round two. Four-zero-zero pinned. Four-zero-zero one, Six-ten one,' Provost Zero says.

We take the stance one last time. Four-zero-zero's eyes are slits, he mumbles something lost in the clamour, digs his fingers through my jacket into my shoulders. It worked once, might not again, but it was worth it.

Provost Zero steps forward, raises then drops its hand. 'Start.'

Four-zero-zero lunges at me, connects his shoulder with my chin, runs me into the ropes. He falls heavily into me, brings his knees into my side again and again, keeps me pinned as the pain grows, as I start to double over. He releases me, steps back, his fists connect with my ear, my stomach, my side, hoots and yells to boos as my knees buckle, I start to sink. His hands on my chest and belt I'm thrown, land face first, slide. Weight on my back he's on me, punches my sides, my shoulders. I've lost this round and the fight, but I've won one round and proved them wrong. It's enough, and the pain's too much. I slap the canvas. 'Yield.'

The punches continue, harder, rain down on one spot, boos and yells grow. What's wrong with him, can't he hear? I slap the canvas harder. 'Yield.'

He bounces, sends his weight into my hips with each blow, hits harder and faster. The canvas a drum, my hand the beat. 'Yield!'

The fists stop, the weight goes away. 'I believe Six-ten yields,'

Provost Zero says.

I glare at Four-zero-zero. Provost Zero holds him by the collar; Four-zero-zero's eyes are wide, teeth show, face flushed, fists bunched. I straighten myself, follow them to the centre of the ring, make sure Provost Zero is between me and him.

It grabs my hand, grabs Four-zero-zero's, turns us to face the crowd. 'Round three. Six-ten yields. Four-zero-zero two, Six-ten one.' Provost Zero lifts Four-zero-zero's hand. 'Four-zero-zero wins, two rounds to one.'

Hoots and boos grow. I turn to Four-zero-zero, bow to him like I'm supposed to, but my gaze never leaves him. 'Congratulations.'

'Next time, Six-ten.'

'Your other side, please,' Provost Six-ten says.

I do as I'm asked, let it examine me for damage. I could save it the time; I've some bruises, a little tingle in my hands, but my body's fine. My mind? I don't know.

Why'd Four-zero-zero do that? He won the fight, he didn't have to keep going. I gave in when he had me pinned, wasn't that the point? Provost Six-ten taps my waist. 'Ouch.'

'A deeper bruise. You fell awkwardly.'

'Fell? I was thrown.'

'You were instructed to remember your technique. You were taught how to fall correctly. You failed to do so once you were thrown.'

'He used me as a punching bag, technique's not –'

'Technique is designed to be used all the time. It minimises pain and injury. You need it most when you perform at your worst.'

That's how it assesses my fight, me at my worst? I won one round but it counts for nothing. 'I failed, didn't I?'

'That is not what I said. You forgot your technique and added unnecessary injury. Thankfully it is minor.'

Provost Six-ten slides its hand down my side, leaves a trail of cold that soaks in, stops the ache and pain. By tomorrow there will be no bruises, no tightness, no sign of the fight. I sit up, pull on my top, swing my legs over the edge of the bench. 'So how did I do?'

'The goal of any fight is to win. You may judge yourself.'

'I lost. So I failed the lesson.'

Provost Six-ten's eyes lighten, it sits on the bench next to me. 'No, Six-ten. You lost the fight, but the fight was not the lesson. The lesson was for you to understand how you behave and how you manage loss.'

'Badly.'

'You performed above expectations. You persisted against an opponent you believed you could not defeat. Most importantly, you used your mind and kept control of your body and your emotions. I am proud of you.'

It makes me feel better, nearly makes up for the grin on Four-zero-zero's face. 'You chose Four-zero-zero deliberately, so I would lose.'

'Yes. Provost Four-zero-zero also chose you for Four-zero-zero's lesson.'

'Me? I was his lesson?'

'To see how he behaved, how he managed victory, and how he would deal with setbacks.'

'He passed his lesson.'

'No. He failed again. We hoped he would not.'

Four-zero-zero's eyes flash in front of me, the sneer, his knees, fists. 'He got too angry.'

'Control of emotions, the ability to stay in balance and not to simply react but to think, are critical skills. For everyone. We chose you as we knew you would push him. We hoped you would provoke him. Which you did.'

'I hope he learned. Next time I'll be better, he'll need to be too if he wants to win.'

'You will not fight Four-zero-zero again.'

'That's not fair. I should get a chance to beat him, he should get a chance not to fail.'

'He had enough chances.'

'He might've learned. If we talk to Provost Four-zero-zero it could –'

'Provost Four-zero-zero is not here.'

'Then we can talk to Four-zero-zero first.'

'Six-ten, listen to me. Four-zero-zero and Provost Four-zero-zero have been reassigned.'

'Because he lost his temper in a fight?'

'No. He failed all his tests. You were his final lesson. His last chance.'

Two more gone? Little trickles, small gaps, all reassigned. To what? 'Where did they go?'

Provost Six-ten's eyes flicker. 'They are not here. They are not inside. They have been reassigned.'

It's never lied to me, never hidden anything; but it avoids my question. 'Where exactly are they?'

'They are not.'

What? They have to be somewhere with everyone else who's been reassigned. Reassignment is transfer, isn't it? That's what

Eight-nine said — but no one's asked the provosts. 'Tell me exactly what reassignment means.'

'If an individual consistently fails critical tests or consistently performs below threshold expectations of The Schedule, they are removed from the programme. Their associated provost is removed with them. They are both permanently removed from the institute. That is reassignment.'

I jump off the bench, stand directly in front of it. 'You know what I mean. What happens to anyone who is reassigned?'

'They are terminated. As is their provost.'

'Terminated? You mean *killed*?'

'Yes. Killed.'

'You killed him because he won a fight?'

'No. I did not kill anyone. No provost can. Those outside killed them because he consistently failed.'

My chest tightens, stomach goes cold. They're dead? Both of them? No, it's all of them, everyone who's been reassigned. How many — twenty, a hundred? — killed for not passing some test they didn't know about? I wish the door was behind me, not behind Provost Six-ten. 'You killed all of them.'

'I cannot hurt any of you, no provost can.'

I take a step backwards, try to edge around the bench. Provost Six-ten shifts its weight, keeps its gaze locked on me. 'When's it my turn, when are you going to kill me? Tomowwow? Next week?'

'It will not come to that. You show no signs of failure.'

'Bet that's what you said to Four-zewo-zewo.'

'Provost Four-zero-zero was clear with him, tried to rectify the failing. Four-zero-zero knew.'

'Knew he'd *die*? I don't think so.'

'He knew. You know. You all know you will die. It is only a question of when, not if. We are not here to make you fail, we are here to help you succeed. You must accept that.'

'You want me to *twust* you after you've lied to me?'

'No one has lied to you or —'

'You never said anything about —'

'Because you were not ready.'

'Ready for what, the twuth?'

Its eyes dim, head tilts. 'Yes, the truth. That anything that is created can be destroyed. That anything that is made can be unmade. You. I. All of us.'

'You're made, I was *born*, I'm not a thing to be switched off.'

'You are, Six-ten. You were made by those outside. As I was made. Different patterns, different beings, but both of us made. Not born.'

I'm like it, a machine? Made like a tablet or panel in some factory? The hand around my chest tightens, crushes, burns, my eyes sting, my back tenses then shakes. It lies, it must lie, I'm nothing like it, nothing like it at all. I throw myself at it, punch, kick, scream into soft plastic that yields, soaks up my blows, gives nothing back. 'I'm not! I'm a person, not a machine!'

Its arms fold around me, hold me, stay as placid as the rest of it. 'You are human, Six-ten. But you are made, not born. Tell me, where are your parents?'

The pain in my arms is less than the pain in my heart. I keep hitting it as hard as I can. 'You probably killed them, kidnapped me.'

'Your parents are alive. You will never see them. They will never know about you.'

I stop, push back against its chest until I can see its face. 'You're hiding them from me?'

'No. It is necessary. Children born on the outside have only two parents. You and everyone on the inside has more.'

'How many?'

'You have five. Some have more. There is no particular number.'

'So I'm...*made*...from five people, five parents? I'm a person, not a machine?'

'Yes.'

'Why didn't you tell me before?'

'You are only eight years old: emotionally, you are still a child. We accelerate your mental development many times faster than children outside. But your emotions we cannot. Even to tell you now is not without risk.'

'So why tell me now?'

'You forced me. You surprised us. As you have always done.'

I know genetics, two parents, a child gets bits from both, random assortments. But I have five. And Provost Six-ten says I'm made. 'Someone mixed the best bits together to make me? Why?'

'I cannot tell you. Yet. You are correct, the "best bits" were mixed. You are very special, Six-ten, as is everyone inside.'

'Then Four-zero-zero was special too.'

'Yes, he was.'

'So why did he have to die? You could've just sent him away.'

'The rules are different for us. We only belong in here. There is no place for us outside, nowhere else for us to go.'

'He would've known, he would've been scared. You should've done it earlier, when he was too young to know.'

'Failure is not always clear early on. We try hard to help them succeed. We have to be certain. It all takes time.'

'Years?'

'Yes. Sometimes longer.'

I feel tired, let myself fall against Provost Six-ten's chest. It pulls me close, firm, not tight. I don't like what it said, don't think it's fair. It sounds true, but I can't test it. Maybe I am special, maybe we all are — does that make it right? 'How did Four-zero-zero die?'

'You wish to know the exact mechanism? I do not think that is wise.'

'No, I mean…did it hurt? Was he scared?'

'It did not hurt, it was gentle and quick. He knew, and he was not scared.'

'Like all of them?'

'Like all of them.'

'Provost Four-zero-zero must miss him.'

'Provost Four-zero-zero will not. They died together.'

'I don't like that.'

'Provost Four-zero-zero was made for him. Without him, Provost Four-zero-zero has no reason for existence. It also helped Four-zero-zero, he was not alone.'

My eyes are heavy, arms droop, the day catches up to me. Provost Six-ten lifts me, carries me to the dorm. The lights are out as it slides me into my bed, the pale blue of its eyes all there is. 'It's still not fair.'

'Most things are not, Six-ten.'

'If I fail and I die, they'll kill you because of me. I don't want you to die.'

'I do not wish either of us to die.'

Sleep, wake, two blue jewels float in the darkness. Provost Six-ten stays with me, watches. I won't know I fail until I start to, and then what? What if it takes days or years, or longer? I should do something, look out for signs. 'Provost Six-ten?'

'You should be asleep.'

'How do I not get kil- reassigned?'

'Always do your best. Be yourself and nothing more. And sleep properly.'

'Is that enough?'

'It has to be.'

I strip off, shut the door, and climb onto the top shelf. Three-four sits on the bottom shelf, drips onto the floor, doesn't move, doesn't notice me through the steam. Silence is what I need, not company. Provosts don't come in here, say it messes up their systems; that's even better.

Three-four reaches out, takes a ladle of water and pours it over the rocks. A cloud of steam, another scorching wave to cleanse and relax. I ran away as fast as I could the first time Eight-nine dragged me in here, felt like I suffocated and burned all at once. Now all I want is a metre of snow to hurl myself into afterwards, a luxury I know I'll never have.

Provost Six-ten's words still ring in my ears, the past week consumed by Four-zero-zero's death. Different, accelerated, special. What am I, what is anything made of five parents?

I searched, hunted, and failed. Although the rest of the world's an open book to me, we and this place are hidden, chasms in the data too obvious to hide, shadows in information too dark and too deep to miss. It's as if, to the outside, we exist and do not exist at the same time, an embarrassing litter of Schrödinger's cats hidden away at the ends of the Earth.

I measured myself against the outside, tried to find the lie in Provost Six-ten even as it watched me, knew what I did. Eight years old and my mind's off the charts; I'm smarter, faster, better than any of them. Every one of us a monster, bits and pieces glued together too short, too solid, too physically and mentally above all means to be anything other than designed and crafted. But made for what?

Three-four opens her eyes, smiles at me, closes them again. Does she know? Did she know before me? What is she now, friend or competitor? Am I an obstacle, a thing to be pushed aside to make room for her? Is it me against her, against any or all of them, or only myself? Provost Six-ten's language changed after we talked – no more curves or standard deviations, now only expectations, The Schedule, development. If Three-four succeeds, if she does better than me, does that mean I fail? Four-zero-zero died because he stayed angry and couldn't control himself. What if success is controlled anger, cold, hard calculation? I don't know, I don't think Provost Six-ten would tell me even if it knew.

Another wall of hot steam; deep breath, try for calm. A week of questions. A week of information. A week without answers. Whatever failure is, I move closer to it the more I worry. If there are no answers, there's no point looking for them. I lean against the wall, close my eyes, try to close my fear.

Answers.

Provost Six-ten gave me an answer that wasn't an answer. Be myself. It doesn't feel like enough, but it's all I have. How can being myself help if everyone competes against everyone else? I'm not angry inside like Four-zero-zero, don't think I'm better than everyone like Two-one-four did, don't want to beat anyone. Even Four-zero-zero. I wanted to show him, to show everyone once, but I wanted him to get better and not fail. How's that going to help me?

The sauna's empty and I've had enough. I step out, dress, walk through the gardens. Eight-nine sits, frowns in concentration as he argues with two projections. He's kept to himself lately, not bothered to be around any of us. I walk over – I think one of the projections is Nietzsche, the other one sounds French.

'*So, you should now understand that you are condemned to freedom,*' the French one says.

Eight-nine sees me, freezes them as Nietzsche opens his mouth. 'How do you manage this stuff?'

'What stuff?'

He pokes a finger through the French projection. 'Philosophy. Free will. Sartre versus Nietzsche. Gives me a headache, I've tried for days and still can't argue properly with them.'

His eyes are dark pits set in blackened pouches. 'You're losing sleep over *this*?'

'Provost said I wasn't meeting expectations.'

He's failing? Am I going to look for him one day and discover he's gone? 'Your Provost thinks you'll be reassigned?'

He flinches, stares at me, scared. 'No, no, it's not said that and I won't be, no matter what.'

I know he knows. I put my hand on his shoulder. 'You won't end up like One-seven-six. You, me, Three-four, Two-three-three, we all go or stay together, remember?'

His eyes widen, he pulls away. 'Don't say that! I go, none of you come with me. Don't you understand if I fail they'll kill me?'

'It changes nothing. You know I'm good with philosophy, why didn't you ask me to help?'

'Because I don't know what failure is. Is asking for help a fail?

Am I supposed to do it all by myself? How do I know if you help me then you aren't failing too? I can't risk it, can't risk you *and* me.'

Instinct, pure gut, I know what to say, what I need to do; what I am. Provost Six-ten wants the authentic me? I think I know who she is. 'Don't be stupid. When you helped me swim nothing happened, did it?'

'No, but that's —'

'And when Two-three-three helped you out, neither of you got reassigned?'

'Nobody was being reassigned back then, they didn't kill anyone who failed.'

'The only thing that's changed is how hard it is. You think you can do this by yourself? You can't.'

'I know that.'

'So why do you think I don't need you? None of us are meant to survive by ourselves.'

'They're forcing us to fail to make us work together? In *everything*?'

'I don't know about that, but I think it's a choice. Try it by yourself and fail, or lean on others.'

Eight-nine's calmer, thoughtful. 'How do you know? That we're meant to, I mean.'

'I just know. Think about what's pumped into us. We all end up knowing it, but applying it, understanding it? My provost said I should trust myself. It's what I feel, what I need to do. Not compete or try to do it alone, but support and cooperate. Get others to do the same.'

'You'll help me?'

'Of course, and you help me back. You think Sartre's tough? I feel the same way about tensor maths.'

   'What about the others, Three-four, Two-three-three?'

   'Them too. Do they know reassignment's death?'

   'Yes. And they're as worried as me.'

   'So we better talk to them.'

CHAPTER 05: DEVIL'S OWN

TOKYO UNIVERSITY, JAPAN
2134

HIROTSUGU

I watch in disbelief as another one flickers, switches from green to light grey. What was four hundred and thirty active devices faithfully streaming data back for years is eroded slowly, meticulously: thirty light grey squares, thirty carrier waves bereft of data.

'You're positive the devices are working, Hirotsugu-san?' asks the technician for the tenth time this morning.

I've had the hospital and the Centre check for failure, battery outs, devices in toilets, but they're all where they should be, all seem to work perfectly; from their end. I'm perplexed, the hospital still receives the vital signs, it's as if the brain readings don't exist. 'Like last time, the time before, yes, the devices are fine.'

'Problem must be here then.'

I bite my tongue; there are some things I need help with, that require politeness and discretion. 'That is why I called you. The problem must be here.'

His hands dance, gaze jumps from display to display. 'It must be between capture and reception, maybe a write-to-storage issue. I don't see how that could happen.'

My display flickers again, row after row of greens swap to light grey in an instant. 'What did you do?'

'Me? Nothing. You've lost another fifty-five, do they have anything in common? Maybe there's a weak point across a subset.'

I look at the identifiers, tense up. The entire feed from the Centre For Mental Health is gone. 'Not that I know of – issued over a few years, different batches.'

The display refreshes violently, comes back with more than half light grey; now all the feeds from the hospital have disappeared. 'No, no more, surely.'

'You've got it all backed up, haven't you? I mean on a university-secured cloud, not somewhere else.'

The remaining greens flick to grey, I'm left with four hundred and thirty inoperative feeds. 'Of course, I'd be stupid if I – oh, wonderful, just wonderful.'

'Keep calm, Hirotsugu-san. Let's make sure the data's safe first, then we'll get the streams sorted. Open your main storage directory, we'll check that first.'

I open it. Empty, absolutely nothing. I try again, punch my fingers into the glyphs instead of sliding them across. It's not only missing data, everything's gone – papers, working models, theoretical framework. 'Where is it? Where is it?'

The technician frowns. 'It's okay, we've got hourly backups, you'll lose an hour's data at the most, promise.'

'And the rest?'

He pulls up a directory, scrolls through it once, twice. 'That's funny – can you give me your user number again?'

I repeat it twice for him, slowly, in two-digit chunks.

He scrolls back through the directory, closes it, opens it, scrolls again. 'Can't understand it. There's no trace of you, your data or files. Nothing's there.'

'That's impossible, what've you done to it?'

'Me? Nothing. It's strange, but it'll be in there somewhere. You try, use your login, maybe the problem's mine.'

I reach for my display; it locks before I can touch it. I press my hand to the palm reader – nothing. I press harder, make sure it knows I'm here; again nothing. 'Damn cheap South Korean junk, just have to do it the hard way.'

I pull the keyboard out of my bottom drawer, wipe away the cobwebs, twin it to the terminal. I type the right sequence, enter my ID – the display stays locked: *Unknown User. Please Contact IT Help,* it flashes.

The technician shrugs, stands. 'Can't do that from here. I'll get it sorted, be right back with some help.'

I try to calm down. I can't have lost seven years' work; they'll find it, probably another issue with the cloud. I'll make room in my funding somehow for onsite hard storage later, when things are sorted.

My player chimes, Umehara's face springs up. 'Hirotsugu-san, how are you?'

He looks smug, leans casually in his chair. Something's up; perhaps I'm not the only one with trouble this morning. 'Fine, thank you, Umehara-san. Aside from a few minor technical issues which should be rectified shortly.'

'Ah. Would you have time to come to my office, have a chat?'

'Now?'

'Yes, now.'

I stand, end the call. 'Of course.'

He's not alone. He sits behind his desk, two well-dressed men sit in total silence in one corner. It's not unusual, more than likely another sponsor or funding body he tries to impress and squeeze out a few extra yen. He's used me and the faculty like this for as long as I've been here, so I know the routine. I introduce myself, enquire as to their health, sit, and wait for Umehara to start the play.

'You've been working hard on your research, no time for social life or rest, or even the media, I'm told,' he says.

'If it goes to plan, it takes another fifteen years. I can't afford to lose time now.'

'Everything for your research.'

'Everything.'

'So, gentlemen, there you have it. Dedication, success at all costs, a true believer in his own work. But, Hirotsugu-san, you pay a high price, the things you miss out on. Such as current events and the news.'

Ah, that's what this is about. The publicity train, to put me on it and drag him along. An interview of sorts, a tie-in to events; these two must be from one of the news services. I choose my words with care. 'An unfortunate oversight.'

Umehara brings up a news release, lets it hover above his desk. 'Very unfortunate. Take this recent one from Tokyo's premier paediatric hospital. You know its perinatal clinic director, don't you?'

My leg muscles tense, mouth feels dry. 'I know *of* him.'

He enlarges the article. 'Then you'll be interested in this. Allow me. Headline: *New Technology Prevents Premature Death*. Nice ring to it, don't you think?'

'Technology should always help, I'm happy it's a positive report. This time.'

'I'll skip to the interesting bits, let me see – ah, yes: *certain death...seven weeks premature...cutting edge...Tokyo University...mother unaware* – oh, here it is: *The Director praised Doctor Shishido Hirotsugu, developer of technology that monitors both the mother and foetus' vital signs in real time, and sends data on brain function and sense to the University for use in its advanced research programme.* Your name up in lights, Hirotsugu-san.'

I meet his gaze, keep my breathing controlled. I knew eventually they'd find out, hoped it would be when NBI was reality rather than promise. This only makes it more difficult, exposes the need for them to understand more acutely. 'It's good publicity for the university and our research, builds a positive public image, credibility.'

'Positive? You've been experimenting on pregnant women, babies, and unborn children, broken every ethical standard you agreed to.'

'They're all volunteers, exactly as the guidelines demand.'

'I'd be interested to know how a three-month-old foetus volunteers to be monitored. As would Sahai-san. It's not only the mother and child, is it? We checked, we know it's multiple subjects, whole families from each monitoring device.'

'The mothers know what they agreed to, so does the hospital. I can't see the issue.'

'I suppose you think the same way about the inmates at The Centre for Mental Health?'

'The director has power of attorney, so they're all volunteers, legally and ethically.'

'More abuse – the power's not there to use people as lab rats. The director overstepped his authority, he'll be removed; and you've gone too far. Your research is permanently suspended, immediately.'

'Only the research board has that authority —'

'They exercised it this morning.'

'But it's only started, I need more data, long-term subjects.'

Umehara pulls up my original research proposal, flicks through it. 'Then there is the little matter of falsifying your proposal. The monitors aren't only about thought-sense, are they?'

'It's *all* about thought-sense.'

'It's partly my fault, I should have trusted my instincts. I didn't think your proposal was anything other than futile wish-fulfilment — I should have used my authority to stop you. But tell me, what else comes across with the interaction, structure, and interpretative feeds? It's the environment, isn't it? We've checked it across all three test groups, including the one you actually bothered to tell us about.'

'Of course it is, the data's dissociated reaction if there's no baseline, no identifiable stimulus.'

'There's another word for it. Memories, Hirotsugu-sama, you've been recording all their memories to feed your thought-sense. You're finished, totally, as of now.'

I didn't expect this, but setbacks are part of any researcher's life. The trick is to get up one more time than they knock you down. 'If that's the board's decision, I've no choice. I'll take my research somewhere else, somewhere that understands what it means; and its possibilities.'

'There's nothing *to* take. Your problems this morning? Everything you've done, all your data and supporting material's been deleted; permanently.'

'Why? If you want to stop me that's one thing, but to throw away years of data makes no sense, not even for you.'

'It's not data – it's peoples' lives, memories, feelings, thoughts, and actions; all of it. You call it research; Sahai-san calls it unauthorised surveillance at best, mind control at worst. You don't understand the trouble you're in, do you?'

I have an idea, but the pain that grows in my head and chest chases away rational thought. All I understand is that my work, my papers, all of it is gone; I'll have to start from scratch. 'I - I don't think so.'

'You've broken the university's ethical standards, *global* standards. You falsified your research proposal, regular progress updates, data, didn't disclose the truth about your subject populations. You're not only finished here but at any other university or research institute anywhere, in any capacity. Your career's over, but that's only the start of your trouble.'

'What?'

He signals the men in the corner; they stand, move to either side of me. 'What you've done is illegal under domestic and international law. At worst you could be tried for crimes against humanity, be locked away for decades.'

I'm lifted to my feet – cold embrace of handcuffs, empty resonance of a tattered career. I'm told I'm under arrest, given instructions by the man on my right; I hardly hear him, can't stop the screaming in my mind.

'Was it worth it, to throw everything away to pursue dead-end research?' Umehara asks.

I try to think, reason it through. I can't assess it rationally, can't form the arguments, but my gut's absolutely clear. It's no dead-end, no waste, it's the future; and if I knew then what I know now, all I'd do is go harder, faster, smarter. 'Without a doubt.'

Umehara closes the door as I'm frog-marched past startled

119

secretaries, open-mouthed students, colleagues with averted eyes. 'I'm glad you think so. By the time they finish with you, nobody will want you.'

PARIS-CEDEX UNIVERSITY, FRANCE
2134

MARIA

Twenty years of hope, work, research, and belief boils down to two and a half hours, a crystal-clear determination of pass or fail played out in public. Rats, pigs, simulations, ethics boards, examination boards, every possible combination of check, balance, and spanner the university could throw at me I passed – now, the ultimate test. My work, one surgical team, a volunteer, one knee replacement.

The gallery's crowded, a hundred people with ringside seats, outside coverage to hundreds more. I scan their faces nervously, look for reassurance I don't need; Vice Chancellor Consiel's in the front row, leans forward, gives me a thumbs up. I give the VC one back. I know it will work, he does too, but this is different.

The patient lies next to me, input probe taped to a tiny patch of scalp, same blue plastic gown Abue wore, clustered figures bent in concentration around his knee. A life entrusted to my care out of his willingness to help others, his desire to give. What I wanted, what I dreamt of; but reality weighs.

I check the monitor: everything's at zero as it should be. The anaesthetist waits patiently, equipment at the ready if it fails. It won't fail, even she believes, so she stands silent vigil over her profession's metamorphosis.

The surgeon straightens, stretches his back. 'How's our patient, Maria?'

'Exactly where he should be, Doctor. It all looks good.'

He twists left, twists right, bends over the patient. 'Closing up now, should be ready for resus in five.'

I do the maths in my head, watch the monitors. The procedure's taken a hundred and fifty minutes. It usually needs around two hundred under normal anaesthetic, to replace one standard, slightly tricky knee, during which he'd breathe, his heart would beat, his blood flow, present the complications and mess of a living, functioning organism being torn apart and reassembled. Not him, not now; not ever again.

Frozen in body, frozen in time these hundred and fifty minutes, he ages nine-tenths of a second; and that as stone. The surgical team knew the implications, watched the research tapes, helped with the last animal test subjects; yet were still caught off guard. No blood on incision, no suction required, offending tissue and bone familiar, same tactile qualities, yet his body yields no liquid to the scalpel's dance; but once freed from the body's embrace flows freely.

Concentrate. Watch the monitors, forget the clock, will the flat lines to remain, as they do. I sense rather than see them: the surgeon and theatre sister by my side, the rest of the team around the patient's leg, faces turned to me. The gallery stands, presses against the glass, waits in anticipation.

'All done, Maria, you can bring him back.'

I tap the control panel once. There's no noise, no spasm, no clatter of machinery or electronics. The patient's chest expands, contracts, repeats; the monitor picks up where it left off hours ago, the readouts of a normal, healthy, living person. The patient opens his eyes, frowns at me. 'Well, are you guys gonna start or what? I can't lie around here all day waiting for you.'

The gallery applauds, mouths congratulations. Hugs and handshakes all round, the patient's wheeled out; I'm left alone to try and understand what it is I've done.

I've barely changed out of my scrubs when the VC walks in, all smiles and rainbows. As he should be – intellectual property and patents are split in half between the university and researchers; this should make a significant financial difference to both of us.

'Congratulations again, couldn't've gone better, I'd say. Are you ready, or do you need a few minutes?' he asks.

'For?'

'The interviews, of course.'

I'd forgotten, relegated the idea to the dustbin where it belongs. I wasn't even close to finished then; how could I bother worrying about interviews? I guess it's the difference between the politics of a Vice Chancellor and my nose-to-the-grindstone life. 'Sorry, forgot in all the excitement, I guess.'

'No harm, you'll get used to it.'

I know what I need to do: play the game, support the team, build brand Paris-Cedex. 'A few days, a couple of weeks, no problem at all. I'm sure I'll get the hang of it.'

'Oh no, more than that. There's a schedule for the next month at least – broadcast media, online, reporters, government, professional bodies. Not to mention the university speaking engagements. I already have a dozen of those for you.'

'Seriously? There's still my research, things I've –'

He ushers me towards the lifts. 'That, my dear, is why God created research assistants. Have you a name for it yet?'

'Always have: "long duration human function neuro-electrical suspension". It's on all the papers.'

He looks at me as if I'm a raw undergrad. 'That will not do, not for the non-academics, anyway. You will have to make something up, and now, otherwise the *media* will do it for you.' He grimaces. 'One of them was going to call it "Brunehilde's Trance" but we managed to stop him. *That's* the sort of idiocy you'll start to encounter. You don't call it long duration human fraction —'

'Function.'

'Function whatever-it-is in the lab, do you?'

I've a shorthand name, but it feels childish, simplistic; but if he wants it... 'We...well yes, there is. In the lab, we call it SloSleep.'

His eyes light up; Professor of Marketing until he sold them on his Vice Chancellorship, old passions clearly die hard. 'SloSleep. SloSleep. Absolutely *perfect*, Maria. Soft, gentle, simple; they'll lap it up. SloSleep it is. If that's fine with you.'

'Of course, whatever works.'

He takes out his player. 'Mitch? Yes. Name. SloSleep. Slo Sleep. No, one word. S-L-O...yes, SloSleep. On everything, of course.' We get into the lift, his hand hovers over the glyphs. 'When? I see. Who? Now? No, no trouble at all, make sure you tell them. Always happy.'

'Trouble?'

'No, just a reschedule. Everyone wants a piece of you, everyone wants to be first. I'm afraid your appearance on the breakfast show will have to wait.'

I'm far from disappointed. 'Shame.'

He turns serious, selects a floor. 'Perhaps. Your first interview, might as well start at the top. Take your time, be honest, hold nothing back. But, most importantly, remember these two are not your usual run-of-the-mill drones.'

The lift doors open, we walk towards his office. 'They're important to you?'

'Oh, no. Absolutely critical. To both of us.'

The VC's office is a time machine to the Sun King's France. Nothing's authentic, all reproduction or projection, but there's a restrained sumptuousness both comforting and intimidating; like the man, I think, no one rises this high without the ability to flatter or kill. The two people who wait for us seem to belong: conservative dress, sharp eyes, economy of movement, presence. The VC's uneasy, wary. I calm myself, remember his instructions.

The man's first to step forward and introduce himself. 'Irek Lauzon, EC Cabinet Chief.'

I shake his outstretched hand, try not to show anything. I've heard of him, no wonder the VC's on edge. Lauzon's word is law — money, influence, doors open and close on his say-so, totally legal and ironclad. Totally final.

The woman's next. She's shorter but more intimidating. Lauzon seems to be on a mission; she looks like it's a crusade. She holds out her fist to me. 'Carolina Alessandri, Director ESA Project Ismud. Congratulations on your success, Doctor Rodrigues.'

Why's ESA here? I feel an old cinder glow, an ember I thought perished decades ago. I fist-pump her back. 'Thanks, it was a team effort.'

We sit in a tight circle of Louis XIV chairs. The VC indulges in minor small talk, sparring. Lauzon's more direct. 'So, Doctor Rodrigues –'

'Maria, please.'

'Yes, Maria, and you must call me Irek. We'd like to know

more about this, this ah…process of yours.'

'We're calling it SloSleep now. A little easier on the tongue,' the VC puts in.

'Well, there's quite a few technical papers, lab reports, and formal summaries,' I reply.

'Yes, we've read them,' Irek says.

Carolina brings up an old paper, scrolls through it, enlarges one paragraph. 'They only give so much, leave as many questions as answers. Cognitive performance measures post resuscitation, for instance, all you have is two to three weeks data. There must be more – what about other test subjects?'

I'm wary, more off balance. They've read them? The VC's nervous, gentle tap of shoe leather on polished wood. He says they're no idiots; Irek's reputation says he isn't, Carolina's on the way to proving it. 'Clearly, not everything about long duration human – sorry, SloSleep – is made public, and there are inside and outside lags. What exactly do you want to know?'

'Everything not out there, the latest. Performance parameters, efficacy measures, impacts, co-dependencies,' Carolina says. 'If you know it, we want to hear it.'

They have no idea what they ask for, but one glance at them and I know that's not true: they do. They're serious, and they're no time wasters. How long is a piece of string, or the rope to hang yourself? 'That's quite a deal of information. When do you want it?'

'Now.'

Now? An *oral* presentation? They must be joking. The taps on polished wood increase: *remember they are not your usual run-of-the-mill drones.* Fine. Let's see what sort they are. I settle back in the chair, get comfortable. 'How much time do you have?'

'As much as you need.'

'Right. Let's start with interface and control issues.'

Eight hours, eight solid hours I pour it out as they sit attentive, engaged, ask only the right questions, make insightful comments; not so much as a wriggle to save numbing flesh. I lose the VC after five minutes; relegated to coffee and biscuit duty he sits, pretends, lends moral support. I'm impressed.

'So, that's it. Except the long-term study of today's patient's recovery, but there's nothing to suggest it's going to be different.'

They sit, nod, drain another cup of coffee, turn to each other, ignore us. 'It's everything I'd hoped for. Far better, in fact,' Carolina says.

'Interface, scalability?' Irek asks.

'Perfect.'

'So, it's a yes?'

'Absolutely no question in my mind.'

'Or mine. Consider it done.'

They turn back to us, Carolina's face beams. 'I want you to work with us, continue your SloSleep research.'

'Thanks, but I've already got a research position here, somewhere to carry on, people who know me.'

'We've more to offer you than Paris-Cedex.'

'More? They've given me everything, held nothing back. Don't misunderstand me, I appreciate your interest, but what more could you offer?'

Irek starts to respond; Carolina cuts him off. 'There's more to it than a job. We've kept a close eye on your research for the past ten years, only become more interested as it's progressed. Project Ismud's been running since 2107; part of what we do is keep an eye out for talent, new technology.'

'ESA's provided funding for a few university research projects over the years, even some for SloSleep last financial,' the VC adds.

The ember starts to burn, to flare. They've put money into *my* research? I hold myself back.

'You've developed a wonderful substitute for anaesthesia, but there's a direct application into Ismud,' Carolina says.

It clicks. I saw the reports years ago, forgot them as they were utterly useless. I have trouble with my control, jam my hands down the chair beside my waist, clench my fists. 'You want to use SloSleep instead of cryogenics? You must've put decades into it!'

'There's no comparison. You've achieved in ten years what we haven't in thirty, and probably never will. Ismud's a two-hundred-and-fifty-year one-way trip. Best we can do without SloSleep is get a crew there five years older, with a quarter of them dead or crippled. It's no contest,' Irek says.

Carolina leans in, stares at me earnestly. 'SloSleep will cut their subjective to *nine days*, and they wake up fresh as daisies. Don't you want to be part of humanity's greatest adventure, be remembered forever as a founding pioneer of our pathway to the stars?'

Embers now a pyre, an all-consuming conflagration. I want to scream, turn back time and wipe SloSleep from history. They want to fill the universe with us, use my discovery to do it? I drive my nails into my palms, stare at Carolina's chin, don't dare to make eye contact for fear I'll tear the bitch's throat out.

The VC turns to me. 'This is an unexpected offer, one I'm sure we didn't see coming, did we?' He gets no response, no acknowledgement of his existence. He turns to Carolina. 'It's been an extremely long week, neither of us has slept at all the past few days, it can catch up suddenly. It seems.'

Carolina's convinced, fishes around in her jacket, takes out a chip and passes it to the VC. 'Completely understand, been there myself. It would be a unique synergy, highly productive, historic. She's the only game in town, she can name her price, be remembered for generations. I want her with us. When she's rested and thought it through, have her call me.' She looks at me. 'Any time. Even just to discuss, whatever. Don't let the chance slip.'

Irek's more at ease playing politician than peacemaker. He stands, Carolina and the VC with him. 'We can do it without her, Consiel. It's not our preference, but we can and will.'

'A second-best solution, but understandable. The university has always cooperated with Cabinet, I can't see why we wouldn't in future.'

The VC closes the door after them, goes to his desk, returns with a bottle and two glasses. He offers me one a quarter full of clear liquid; I drain it in one swallow, stare fascinated at bloody handprints on the glass as the fire in my throat tears at me.

He hands me a box of tissues. 'That went very well. Except for the last bit, wouldn't you say?'

'Can they do that?'

'Use it without permission? Of course they can.'

'But that's stealing, we're a democracy, not some sort of dictatorship.'

The VC takes my empty glass, puts it on the floor next to the bottle, out of my reach. 'The same mistake everyone makes. Government's not a person, it's a thing, makes its own rules. You can't win unless it wants you to.'

'Hell.'

'Hell indeed. I take it you don't agree with Ismud?'

I'm instantly wary. Keep it inside the horse, show no sign. 'There's so much needs doing down here, all that money and effort to see a star? I'm no fan.'

'Agree totally, all those starving and poor around the world, all we could do. But you still have a decision to make.'

'Thought it was made for me.'

'Yes and no. Make no mistake, SloSleep's part of Ismud. But you have options. You could take up their offer.'

'I like it here, it's good.'

'They have unlimited budget, resources, influence. Whatever you could do here you can do a hundred times more there. It might be ten, fifteen years until you're finished with them; after that, you could go and do anything, anywhere.'

'And if I don't?'

'They do it anyway. The university would have to cooperate. Cabinet holds the purse and the power; we don't cooperate, they close both. And you.'

'Me?'

'If you don't work with them, you'll have to cooperate with them. If you don't cooperate, if you obstruct, no university can afford to keep you.'

'Is that a threat?'

He's sad, deflated. 'No, it's reality. You, me, all of us, none is worth more than Cabinet's good wishes. It's simply the way it is.'

I am the fire, I am the pain. Change the world, Maria? Pollute the universe. I stand. 'Sorry if I embarrassed you.'

The VC thrusts the chip into my hands. 'Far from it. No matter what, fifty years from now no one will remember this meeting; only your success in theatre, in this university. Whatever you decide, whatever you do, call her and tell her. Leave no doubt, leave no room for rumour. Promise me.'

I take the chip, slip it into my pocket. 'I promise.'

Another plate smashes against the cinderblock wall, a tiny lump of fused porcelain the only memory of its existence as it joins the shattered graveyard on the kitchen floor. I reach behind me, find no more, start on the glasses.

Old fires reignite: they'd take my life's work to make the world better and pervert it to destroy others? Use me to send those *freaks* into space? Glass joins china joins the graveyard; kitchen's empty, I try to kick a chair, miss, slam my shin into the table, double over in pain. Whatever I do I'm damned, whatever happens I'm responsible for the success of Ismud. Is this how I'll be remembered; not for the lives I'll save, the pains of recovery avoided — but for *that*?

The photograph stares back at me from the table: no longer a happy family but Mum and Dad, the fearless eco-warriors, and their failure of a daughter, polluter of the cosmos. How many more after those six will go? Will they send out ships like live animal exports, packed to the gills with SloSleep migrants to go forth and multiply, consume, destroy, spit out world after world after world, all of it because of me? How much of everything that's out there have I sentenced to death? There's nothing I can do, absolutely nothing. Maria Rodrigues. Ismud. Environmental criminals all.

My player chimes again. Why won't they leave me alone? Eight messages when I got home, I've listened to none, but I'm in the mood now to tell them what I really think, VC or no VC. I swipe the accept glyph. 'You can take your offer and shove it up —'

Yayo stares out, mouth agape. 'Maria?'

I start to shake, feel the tears well up. 'Yayo? I didn't know it was you, I'm so sorry, I thought —'

He looks around, sees the carnage that was once dinnerware, overturned furniture, me dishevelled, slumped on the floor. 'You alright? What's going on, you want me call police?'

'No, no, it's fine. I've just had, you know, just...it's just been like that.'

'It didn't work, did it?'

It takes a second to register. 'What? No, everything went perfectly, it was a success. Totally.'

'You said you'd call, let me know straight away in the morning. It's half past four, I left messages, you don't call.'

I've lost track of time, it's past midnight here, the operation was over by midday, and I promised. More guilt on the worst day of my life. 'I'm sorry, we finished and I was pulled straight into a meeting. Yayo, they're taking my work away.'

'Who, the university?'

'No, Ismud.'

Yayo's face darkens, eyes narrow. '*Those* thieves? Tell me.'

I give him the short version; I'm still livid, spit the words out, somehow more controlled for the telling of it. 'So that's it, I am become the thing I hate, the thing Mum and Dad died fighting.'

'No, no, no. It's not your fault, it's out of your control. You did a good thing, a wonderful thing, a gift to everyone, but there's always someone turns good to bad.'

'That's what hurts; no matter what I do, I can't stop it.'

'Would you if you could?'

'Of course! Anything to keep my work out of it.'

Yayo clucks at me, shakes his head. 'No. Ismud, the flight. Your

132

work is already lost.'

It's not a hard decision. 'Yes, if there was a way.'

'You were always a bright child. Forgetful, but bright.'

'What do you mean? I never forget anything.'

He snickers. 'Except your first lesson, when you need it most.'

'What on Earth are you on about?'

'You should take up this Carolina's offer, work as closely as you can with her, Helen.'

Helen? Helen who? Is his mind starting to slip, or am I overtired and hearing things? He stares at me, silent, wolfish grin. I know the look, can almost hear the cogs turn in his mind. Helen. It returns in a flash – Helen, Troy, the myths, a lightbulb moment to set me back on my heels.

He nods, waves hurriedly at someone off screen. 'Ah, you see, I'm not so old or absent-minded, am I? Now go away and think this time, leave an old man to his soccer. Already I've missed the first half because of you. Call me later.'

I straighten the furniture, activate the vacbot. By the time I've washed my face, downed a coffee and composed myself, the flat looks untidy rather than a war zone. I play with the chip, wonder. She did say any time – how serious was she? I check the time: 1:15am. Fine, no time like the present. I drop the chip into the player; it takes less than ten seconds.

Carolina stares out. She's behind her desk, still in her business suit. 'Maria? Didn't think I'd get a call from you so soon. You feeling better?'

'Much, thanks. Do you have a minute, I've a few questions.'

'Sure, fire away.'

'Look, assuming – and I mean *assuming* – I take up your offer, who do I report to?'

'Me. No one else. You'd be totally autonomous. Only thing that matters are results, not chains of command. We've facilities across Europe, you can locate anywhere you want.'

'What about a budget, a team?'

'There is no budget. Whatever you want, anything you want, anyone you want. As long as security clears them.'

'Final question. Intellectual property and patents. Paris-Cedex has a fifty-fifty split, what's ESA's?'

'We're not here to make money, Maria, we're here to spend it. If you create it, it's yours, totally; all intellectual property rights, patents, spinoffs. All you hand over is permission for us to use it on Ismud and any successors, for no cost. The only thing we ask is that you hold off publishing papers until after you finish with us. Anything else?'

'If I sign on, how long's the contract?'

'At least until the final supply launch, around '42. There's a retainer clause through to 2150, in case we need you later.'

Eight years. Is it worth eight years? Or sixteen, if I stay to the death of it? I know it is. 'Okay, I'm in. When do I start?'

'I'll have the formalities sorted out by eight this morning; your personal assistant will be with you by midday. If that suits.'

'Sounds good, just enough time to sleep.'

'It's settled then. It's the right decision, Maria. I'm glad you're joining us.'

'It's the *only* decision, Carolina. Oh, there's one other thing.'

'Yes?'

'Our meeting today. I didn't tell you everything. SloSleep's not the end – it's only the beginning.'

LAKE SHOJI, YAMANASHI PREFECTURE, JAPAN
2134

HIROTSUGU

Take your life in your hands, throw the dice and trust yourself; that's always been how I've done it. I've never thought about why, how I came to choose that path – lack of time, lack of insight, perhaps lack of failure. Now I have more than enough of each. I believed in myself, believed others who believed in me, praised me like Araki, Maria, reinforced my self-image, faith in myself. And where are they when I need them? Vanished, as words on a breeze. I know it's unfair to judge them, separation is necessary, a defence mechanism to prevent taint by association that can reach across a world, across old friendships.

I send my pushbike down a gear, settle in for the long approach to Aokigahara Jukai. It might be my parents' fault, as everything in the world is according to my acquaintances in Paris. Father and mother, typically stable, risk-averse salaryman and wife; as long as I remember, I railed against the thought I would follow their example. I used them, used the stability and support their hated lives gave me to escape their fate, but what child doesn't? Now at least that excuse is gone, terse advice of disownership after court the opening chord, small mound of possessions on the road outside their home the crescendo. Hundreds of years ago, ritual suicide may have been demanded, but today tantos remain sheathed, replaced by this slower death. All I own I carry; no job, no prospects, no future, my wealth in one pocket. My face broadcast across the country and carried to the four winds by social media I disguise, shave, swap heavy-rimmed glasses for contact lenses. I avoided prison only because five months held in remand was deemed sufficient; that and, as the judge declared, the permanent ban on research, the destruction of my reputation, and any hopes of employment.

Umehara's question lingers: *Was* it worth it? My reply now as then — yes, totally. Success would have been better, but at least from all this the knowledge of NBI as a goal, as an advance beyond AI, has spread. Once an idea is set loose, once knowledge escapes, it can never be hidden.

It won't be me, won't be any in this generation that creates it, but only once the needs of the future many are afforded more weight than the fears of the present few; and that is my only real regret.

Shoji in late afternoon is quiet and expectant. I look for a small shop or stall, any place that still takes cash. Tucked away to one side I see it — dirty, a few chairs strewn about, wizened old crone behind the counter. A few notes, a few minutes and I have soba and tea in front of me; no awkward questions or glances. She sits inside, concentrates on her screen; I sit outside and let time slip by.

A car pulls up, a middle-aged man and woman get out; garish clothes, faces out of place. He wanders inside, she towards me. 'Excuse me, way to Jiyu camping, please,' she asks.

Her Japanese is fragmented, picks her words uncertainly; but the accent's familiar, if uncommon. Barely fifteen years after their "liberation" of Taiwan nearly pulled us into war, less than eight after they rolled over Australia and New Zealand, diplomatic

136

relations have only recently thawed; and my Chinese is rusty. 'Next intersection, turn right, a kilometre up the road.'

'Thank you, glad I found someone who speaks Mandarin.'

I thought I didn't want company, perhaps I'm mistaken. 'You're tourists?'

'Yes and no, we're embassy clerks, wanted to see the forest and lake. You live here? It's lovely scenery.'

'No. I'm between jobs, thought I'd take a road trip.'

The man walks over, two cups in hand. They sit away from me, lose themselves in conversation, every so often steal a watchful glance at their car parked behind me.

My player chimes. It's been over a year. 'Maria?'

'Is it true? I just heard.'

She never wastes time on small talk. 'Which part? The ban, research, court? All of it, and you can believe the worst.'

'So that's it, they kill off a brilliant researcher that threatens the *status quo*. You're not going to let them get away with it, are you?'

'They already have. Everyone abandoned me, want nothing to do with me – family, university, employers. Friends.'

'I'm sorry, I've been busy, haven't kept an eye out. Listen, I can get you a position over here with me, start straight away.'

'How? It's an international ban.'

'It's not a problem, I can get whoever I want, no questions asked. I've got my own team, more like a department.'

'Which hospital? Or has a multinational seen sense and bought you?'

She bites her lip, glances down. 'It's ESA.'

I don't know if she's lying to cheer me up or she thinks it's absurd enough to take my mind off my problems. I stare at her;

her eyes don't lie. 'You're serious, aren't you?' She nods. 'Why'd you do that, it's totally against who you are.'

'I had no choice, they stole it from me. It was either join up and keep control or stick with my principles and still lose.'

'Tough choice.'

'I haven't changed, I'm going to let my enemies lose.'

I know it will hurt her, twist her regardless of what she thinks she can do; hopefully she weighed it up, took account of it all. 'Is it worth it?'

She doesn't hesitate. 'Absolutely. Ends justify the means, and the world's never changed by people who accept the rules. You and me, what we aim for is worth it. You have to find a way back to your research, any way at all.'

For the first time in months I feel optimistic, like there might be hope. Somewhere. 'You're right, but I need time to sort it out.'

'Why, you busy?'

'No, seeing the country, a holiday, a bike tour I guess.'

'Bumming around penniless more like it. Come on, Hirotsugu, come over and get back into it here. We'll work out a way to get your NBI research running again.'

It's tempting, and the growl in my stomach and chill breeze through my shirt agree. But I'm held back, not by pride or shame, but fear I'll be set to one side, comfortable and safe, to ossify. She's made me hope, and hope stops me taking the offer. Anyway, right now there are other issues. 'I can't travel, it's part of the sentence. No passport, I'm on the banned travellers list for the next decade.'

She's too smart to be fooled by the truth. She knows what I think, and she's too kind to admit it. 'It's what diplomatic travel's for; say yes, it won't be a problem, trust me.' A muffled voice, she nods and waves impatiently off-screen. 'I've got to go, can't put the next one off. I could use your help. It's not charity, you know I'd work you hard, but it's a way back. Next week, next month, next year even, all you have to do is call, okay?'

She cuts the connection, I put the player back into my pocket. I'll call her back someday, but I won't be saying yes.

The two Chinese stand, drag their chairs across, sit opposite me. They've changed, faces now too much like the police at the watch-house. The case is closed, I thought they'd back off, not bother me; I'm wrong, and in all probability, I'll never be left to myself again. They sit in silence, watch me; my patience has gone. 'Who are you? Police? Internal security? You think I run around on my bike to monitor country kids?'

'We're not here to look at the countryside. We're here for you,' she says.

'What Chinese law you think I've broken? Whatever it is, add it to the list, I don't care.'

'We want you to continue your research with us.'

'You wouldn't understand my research.'

'*We* don't understand it, but the people who sent us do. They believe in it. And you, which is more than your Professor Umehara. He always said it was unnecessary and futile, that you couldn't revolutionise a hundred and fifty years of stagnation *he* kept in place.'

'How do you know what he said?'

'What matters is why you're loyal to a man and country that calls the future a dead end.'

'Loyal? Not to him, not to anyone.'

'Then who?'

'My research, my ideas, to what's coming whether I do it or

not.'

The man makes a point of looking around the deserted stall. 'And how your loyalty is repaid. Where are your supporters, your friends and sponsors?'

'They're out there, waiting until things quieten down, then they'll show themselves.'

'Like your friend in Europe? She's wrong, she can't get you into her programme or out of the country, she doesn't have the control or influence she imagines,' she says.

'Once you're on that list you stay on it. Guilty or innocent, prophet or Luddite, it makes no difference. No one will take you. Ever,' he adds.

'So, I'll find someone here, a private company, one that doesn't have to work inside the rules.'

'Your country's chained to profitable returns from short-term ventures; nobody will sit back and wait for twenty years while you burn their cash. They can't afford you or your research, no one can,' she says.

'And you can?'

'We afford whatever we decide to afford, even non-biologic intelligence. We think in decades and centuries; twenty years is nothing,' he says.

'Don't believe us? We waited a hundred and seventy years for Taiwan, Hirotsugu, six *generations*. What other nation plans like that?' she asks.

They think they pressure me, play tag-team so well, but I have their measure. Loyalty, time, commitment; I have none for anything other than my research. 'I know how you think; what I don't know is if I can trust you. You say one thing, do another. Look at the China-Australia security pact.'

'We look to our own interests, as Japan does, as any nation should. You want to know if you can trust us? We trust you. Even this conversation; you could tell your authorities, we'd have no protection, even as diplomats.'

'You either earn trust or share it from a patron, someone who demands trust from others. You already have one,' he tells me.

It's my turn to look around, make a point of the emptiness. 'I can't see anyone.'

'She is your patron.'

I point to the old crone. '*Her?*'

'No, the Secretary of the Chinese Communist Party.'

'What? I've never met her.'

'She knows your work, its importance – *your* importance. She briefed us personally before we came here.'

'Don't be ridiculous.'

He holds a player out to me. 'You think I'm lying? Call her, ask her yourself.'

I nearly take it, stop myself before I'm suckered. They've obviously got a double standing by, or even a chat-bot projection. 'You'll have to do better than that.'

The woman looks at her watch. 'Do you get NHK News out here?'

'Probably, it goes everywhere.'

'Then you should be interested in this.'

They usher me over to the stall, convince the old crone to give up her screen for a few minutes.

'Tune in, it'll be on now,' he says.

I do as I'm asked, turn up the sound. We're in time for the international sports, complete with large subtitles and enhanced audio for the older viewers, their main subscribers. Right now it's soccer, again, as always.

'Pay attention. Ignore the subtitles.'

The picture changes to the inside of a large auditorium bedecked in red and gold. A slight, middle-aged woman in a business suit holds the dais, the auditorium on its feet, a line of girls in gym clothes each side of her. The Party Secretary's a familiar face, unmistakable.

'Listen carefully.'

It's some sort of medal ceremony, national championships of something gymnastic, and the Party Secretary hands out the trophies. No wonder there's so many smiles, so much applause, nervous kids. The Japanese voice-over dies, the captions scroll, the Party Secretary's voice rises. The captions carry the names of awardees, but that's not what she says: '...awards to the magnificent youth of our country, but I regret our best talent is not here today at our NBI facility.' She looks straight down the camera as it zooms in; I feel she stares at me. 'So, I await you, Shishi-do and Hirotsu-gu, I look forward to your arrival,' she says as the programme switches to the weather.

I'm floored. We sentence the screen back to the soaps and the old crone, walk back to the chairs. 'How?'

'If she wants something, it happens. Was it clear enough for you?' he asks.

'Yes, I – yes, totally.'

'She wants you to continue your research in China. No fine print, no catches. You will have no hindrance, no restriction, no limit. She, *personally*, is your sponsor.'

'Do you understand? You will report only to her, act with her authority,' she explains.

I know what it means, but nothing's free, nothing's a true gift.

142

Of course she wants it for China, that's not the issue.

He holds the player out to me again. 'Do you need to call her, make sure?'

'Everything has a price; what will this cost me?'

'Your life. Once you come to China, every other nation will consider you a pariah, a non-person. You may have contact with the outside world, but you will never leave.'

It sounds high, but what is it compared to now? More formal perhaps, but certain, and with prospects. 'They'll think I've defected.'

'No. You *will* defect,' she says.

'When?'

'The sooner the better.'

'Give me your number.' She sends it across, I walk away. 'I'll let you know early tomorrow morning.'

*

I wander deep into the forest, let my subconscious guide my feet, hunt out a denser, quiet place. Early evening casts long shadows, cold wind starts conversations between leaves and grass. I'm not given to the fears and superstitions of my parents, but it's easy to imagine yurei around me who watch, wait, wonder if I'm about to add myself to their number. How many were truly honourable in death, how many bound to a land they were banished from as they tried to do the right thing, work for the greater good until smaller minds above exerted their power? If they are here, I am among friends, but I intend to remain with the living.

I find what I'm after, a small hollow between the roots of a tree, dense bushes all around; a place to think and rest, perhaps sleep. I take out my sleeping bag, settle in – peace, my own company, silence. This place is enough.

A strip of faded cloth waves at me from a low bough; neckties strung together, wrapped to the branch, remains of a hasty slash across the bottom clear. Aokigahara Jukai had a reputation decades ago, a place to come and end it all when everything was lost, but that faded as euthanasia embraced mental illness and chronic depression, allowed a more ordered, civilised, neater path than drugs or being hung by your own tie. What Nippon wanted Nippon got, a neat and clinical approach to save face, balance society, keep it calm, polite. Caught between the modern and feudalism, it abhors disturbance, demands the same from her people even in death. Now Aokigahara is swapped for the cold of a single's apartment, a prescription approved by two doctors, obedience of the conditioned.

I could have told them straight away, saved them and myself a few hours, but I've learned the value of making suitors wait, to build up expectation and desire; and also the wisdom of reflection. It feels right, it is right; I now wait for my mind to test my gut.

It's the only place to continue my research, and with the Party Secretary behind me there's a greater chance of success. Without it all I have is Maria, uncertainty, dim prospects, perhaps a slow path to redemption. Part of me doesn't care, I know one day it will happen; the greater part demands I, not someone else, be NBI's creator.

The moon teases through the canopy, I weigh the costs, tally them as any other study. I dig deep, search, come up with surprisingly few, realise I've already lost most things with meaning. I will live and die in China, as Chinese, to be watched over politely but minutely my whole life; never entirely free, never fully captive, never completely trusted. I will miss the rest of the world, the hope of travel no matter how remote. It's a small balance sheet of little weight.

I sit, watch the moon crawl across the heavens, stand as the sky lightens. I start to pack my sleeping bag, let it fall, check my backpack: a change of clothes, a toothbrush, all I need.

I retrace my path to the stall. The car's still there, windows fogged, dew across the bonnet; they've already started to watch, to be seen to watch. I rap on the driver's window, it opens; she's in front, he in back. The doors click, I slide in next to him. 'When can we start?'

'Now. Your things?'

I pat the backpack. 'Only this. Let the old woman have the bike.'

She pulls the car out, drives past Shoji. It's done, no backwards step, and it feels right. A tap on my arm, he offers me breakfast: a bottle of water, a few crackers.

'Beijing today?'

'Beijing today.'

'Then?'

'Does it matter?'

I roll up the window, let the tint hide the world. 'Not at all.'

CHAPTER 06: TEAMS

CAMPBELL-WILMUT INSTITUTE, ÅLAND ISLANDS
2135

EIGHT-NINE

'Is this everyone?'

'This is everyone, Eight-nine,' Provost Eight-nine says.

The auditorium's nearly empty. I know the trickle was continuous, faces disappeared, study niches fell empty, spaces rearranged subtly but not too convincingly to cover gaps. It's only now we're all in one place it hits me. I count empty rows, Japanese maples larger, intertwined, children and provosts in chairs where once we sat on bamboo squares. I count twice, sure I'm mistaken once, convinced I'm not the second. 'One hundred and two?'

'With one hundred and three provosts.'

Five hundred and ninety-four reassigned? No, killed for not being what they should have been; all special, like Six-ten, like me, ten years of study, nurture and growth snuffed out. All the resources, all that ability, all those lives. 'What a waste.'

'Precisely what waste do you refer to?'

I can't bring myself to use the word. Is to say it to condone it, curse myself by it? 'Reassignment. All of them and their provosts, all reassigned for a reason no one knows. A waste.'

'Because you do not know the reason, does not mean that it is not both necessary and sufficient.'

'There must be a better way, whatever the reason.'

'No, reassignment is the only acceptable solution.'

It pricks at me, pokes last night's feeds. Eight modules: religion, belief, need; pure philosophical pain that makes my mind ache. I'm not the only one – everyone got the same, only the reaction varies. I'll assimilate it, manage it somehow; at least now I have the chance to apply it. 'You want me to take it on trust, have a little *faith* in you?'

'That is one perspective. Or you can trust me based on my past behaviours and those of the other provosts.'

I feel irritable, must've lost sleep. It's easily controlled, but I choose not to; recently, I'm more inclined to argue than accept anything at face value. 'Well, faith is to have trust in things not seen, and I don't see any reason for reassignment.'

Provost Eight-nine swivels. If I didn't know it was impossible, I'd swear it looks surprised. 'Sarcasm. Early, but expected. You will have to revise your recall of sacred texts unless you can identify which translation you refer to.'

I'm about to launch into an explanation of why any translation can only ever be an approximation when Provost Zero mounts the dais; it points a finger towards the third row. 'Open-ended debate, general discussion. Exchange of opinion and inference from your information feeds last night, coupled with your own analysis. Ten-one to commence with an opening statement.'

Ten-one's on her feet instantly. 'Procreation is a direct outcome of an individual's death anxiety.'

Three-four shakes her head. 'No, the evidence does not support the statement. Belief systems are principally designed to give assurance of life beyond death; religious adherents should exhibit lower death anxiety than the non-religious, but greater religious tendency is a direct, causal, positive correlation to greater average family size.'

'But it's arguable religion attracts those with *higher* death anxiety, so the evidence supports the statement,' Two-eight-eight says.

'Assuming there's *any* link between procreation, belief, and mental state. A large family only implies the people involved are more fertile,' Two-one argues.

Ten-one weighs in again. 'Everyone on the outside exhibits death anxiety as their core driver; transplants their desires, unfulfilled hopes, and failed aspirations on their children...'

I tune them out, interject at random to show I contribute. Pointless discussion, pointless argument, another in an endless series of attempts to summarise an entire species' motivation by broad generalisation.

Provost Eight-nine leans forward, puts its chin on my shoulder. 'If you wish to pretend you concentrate, you should fidget less.'

'That obvious?'

'Only to me. At the moment.'

I straighten up, hope I show the required level of interest. 'I can't see the point of the discussion, there's no definitive answer.'

'That is the point. Discussion and exchange of views has its own merit.'

'That's not the way those on the outside see it. Unless you consider exchange of views by force of arms having merit.'

'You assume those outside are correct. To have evidence is one thing, accurate evaluation is another.'

'They may not be right, but their numbers make them right.'

'One person can change the world –'

'Another myth, another broad generalisation –'

'Supported by ample evidence. The most successful and longest-lived changes, both good and bad, have been made this way. Discussion, idea exchange, endless hours of seemingly useless effort.'

'Then this is practice?'

Provost Eight-nine moves back to its seat. 'And more.'

I decide to make a greater effort. Value may be in the process, not the content, but not everyone appears to have the same perspective. The discussion's animated, small blocks form of like-minded viewpoint and opinion. Entertainment or education, it has elements of both.

Debate shifts from children to belief to purpose, pulls me in. Ten-one's at the end of yet another monologue: 'So the entire edifice, the creation of all religion and spirituality, must come back to death anxiety.'

'All of it because the outside can't accept one day, inevitably, they will die?' Two-eight-eight asks.

'Yes, and worse. Ultimately their lives are frittered away as they try to avoid the unavoidable and impose their beliefs on others. Control. Pain. Impossible standards. Impossible promises.'

'To waste their lives and others', that I can't understand. They must all be gullible. Or stupid.'

Six-ten's on her feet instantly, face red-tinged. 'I don't accept they're stupid. I understand their need, it's the acceptance of promises of heaven and divine purpose I can't.'

'Six-ten, when do you think you will die?' Provost Zero asks.

The question silences the auditorium, sends a bolt of cold down my back. Does it know something?

Six-ten's rigid, stares at Provost Zero. 'I don't know, and I don't want to know. All I know is I'll die. Someday.'

'So, what should you do about it?'

'Nothing.'

'Nothing? Explain.'

'I can't avoid it, so it's a waste of time to try. I can only accept it and live a life with meaning. Of purpose, if you want to call it that.'

'That sounds rational, Six-ten. Tell me what your purpose is. What meaning does your life have?'

Six-ten's eyes widen, hands rub up and down her sides. I know the signs, feel her anxiety. Provost Eight-nine's hand rests on my shoulder, keeps me in my seat.

'My purpose? I don't know. You say I have one but you don't tell me what it is. I mean something to my friends, they mean something to me.'

'Look around you, Six-ten. All of you give each other's life meaning and, for now, purpose.'

I push Provost Eight-nine's hand away, stand. 'No, that's not good enough. *You* look around, *you* look at the empty seats that should be full.'

My courage nearly fails me as I say it. Sharp intakes of breath, every face turns to me. Provost Zero's eyes blaze sky-blue. Provost Eight-nine's hand's in the small of my back; it supports, doesn't restrain.

'I have looked. What is your point, Eight-nine?' Provost Zero asks.

'You say they give us meaning? You kill us and our provosts, and you want us to find our purpose in that?'

'Your meaning is in all six hundred and ninety-six of you, and in your uniqueness.'

'I see no purpose in their deaths! None of you have told anyone what our purpose is, all we have is your word. How do we know – how do *I* know – I can believe you?'

Silence, only the rustle of leaves. Across the auditorium, Three-four's face quivers, mouth twitches, eyes scrunch shut. She fears I've gone too far? No one has challenged them like this, accused them – but I can't turn away.

Provost Zero locks me in its gaze, blue eyes replaced by piercing white. 'You doubt us?'

'In this? Yes, I do.'

'When have we lied to you, Eight-nine?'

'Never. That I know of.'

'When have we deliberately withheld information from you?'

'About reassignment; you didn't tell anyone the truth right away.'

'So, you would suggest telling a six-year-old their friends died because they failed is appropriate?'

It stops me cold. I remember how I felt when I learned the truth. 'No, it was hard enough later on.'

'Then we have never lied to you or acted in anything other than your best interests. Would you agree, Eight-nine?'

The auditorium feels larger, emptier; friendless. 'Yes, I agree, Provost Zero.'

'Have we given you any reason to think we would act in any other way, now or in the future?'

'No, Provost Zero.'

'So, when we say you have a purpose, you can believe us. When we say we cannot tell you now, you should accept it is in your best interests. Would you agree, Eight-nine?'

'Yes, Provost Zero.'

'Remember that for every one of your friends that died, one of us died with them. Your pain is our pain, doubled and more. It is only purpose that makes it bearable. You may sit down, Eight-nine.'

I sit, stare straight ahead, diminished. Provost Eight-nine's hand shifts to my shoulder; I've done it now, sealed both our fates.

Provost Zero's eyes fade white to bright blue as it turns away. 'Before you leave, take Eight-nine's advice. Look at the empty chairs, at the faces that may not be here in the future. Their lives give your future meaning and purpose. Remember this. Never forget them.'

Three-four looks at me, face tear-streaked. I try to smile, fail miserably, search for Six-ten, see only the top of her bowed head as she shakes.

'You know you are made, not born. You accept you are special, without evidence. That ends tonight. Your feeds will consist solely of the genetic backgrounds, characteristics, histories, and profiles of those from whom your physical material was sourced. Together with the specific attributes included in your makeup.'

There's a rustle of expectation and excitement. I'm forgotten.

'Study it. Understand yourself and your origins. One month from now you will choose your names. Choose carefully, choose wisely. Keep your name and your genetic background private until we meet next month. That is all.'

I let them leave, sit with Provost Eight-nine until afternoon sun drips cold and feeble across empty seats. There's no point in rushing; Provost will take me somewhere, they'll do what they'll do, and that will be that. 'Sorry.'

'For what?' Provost Eight-nine asks.

Must be part of the process, lift residual guilt before the end. I don't need it. Provost Eight-nine's no idiot, and I don't intend to die with one. 'For questioning you, everything. For doubting; getting us killed.'

'We are both alive.'

'You know what I mean. I crossed the line today, wrote a whole new chapter on how to fail. I'm surprised Provost Zero didn't kill me on the spot.'

We walk out slowly, arms around each other's shoulders, heads bowed. 'We need to improve your situational awareness, together with your appreciation of the value in correctly challenging authority.'

'Better make it quick.'

'You still do not understand.'

'Understand what?'

'You did not fail.'

'I met expectations?'

'No. You exceeded them by a wide margin. You may even say we were impressed.'

The relief's immediate, palpable. My knees nearly give way, come back as I straighten, lift my head.

I get to live.

Provost's happy.

And I will choose my name.

Ten-one moves to her final slide. A red leaf, blue background, white stars. A name. 'Quinn. Means reason, sense, wisdom. What I want,' she says.

Three-four stands, swaps places with Quinn at the dais. I lean across, extend my hand, half serious, half playful. 'A pleasure to meet you, Quinn.'

She takes it, smiles. 'And to meet you, Eight-nine.'

'Not for much longer.'

A month's a long time to keep any secret, let alone one this big. Or a hundred and two of them. Somehow we managed, now sit clustered in the auditorium eager to share, eager to hear. The provosts sit apart, a white plastic ring that encircles us as Provost Zero calls us one by one to rise, give as much as we wish, introduce ourselves to people who know us intimately.

It'll take getting used to. Two-three-three is now Deepak, the sound of it strange and unfamiliar, even though the broad smile and sharp wit are unchanged; and he's only one of a hundred and one I have to relearn.

Three-four puts a chip in the player, the panel starts to scroll through data, small charts, a headline or two. 'I come from six different donors: an artist, musician, academics in history and sociology, all part of me. Or parts of me. So I chose Claire as my second name. Because they were bright, like I want to be. But.'

The panel changes, three faces appear: unusual, distinctive in black and white. One wears an old hat shaped like a bowl; the middle one a fur-lined hood around tiny, almond shaped eyes; the third a pigtail, a headband, creased and sun-dried skin. 'These are my ancestors. Irish. Innuit. Lakota. All displaced, dispossessed, hard lives and harder spirits. Even when they were happy and successful, they never forgot where they came from, how they suffered. So I chose my first name to remind me. Bronagh. It means sorrow and sadness. I am Bronagh Claire.'

Five-zero takes the dais next, speaks rapidly. 'I don't want to be defined by my donors, people I'll never meet. Is nature more important than nurture? My whole life I've been called Five-zero, I like it, it's me, it's what I call myself. So I'll keep it, but spell it

F-y-v-e-o-h. Fyveoh. That's me.'

He walks back to his seat, hugs Quinn, sits next to Ithma. Another surprise in a day of surprises – Ithma, the orphan, if her name's meaning is taken. Seven parents, but of us all the only one with a single genetic heritage, all Israeli. Does that make her one too?

One more then it's my turn. I rehearse the sound of my name, go over the words in my head. I got here early, wanted to be first. I nearly managed it; Six-ten beat me, but I wasn't unhappy it was her. Then Provost Zero flipped it, started with the last one in, put us last. Six-ten wriggles again, taps her knee against mine. The longer it's gone on, the more restless she gets. 'You okay?'

'Don't like to wait,' she says.

Her eyes hint at something else. She thinks, *really* thinks about everything; we all do, but she takes it to a new level, and last month's pushed her further. A huge amount to take in, to know how we were made, how we're designed; it's a challenge but a happy one, an affirmation of worth. 'I can't wait to find out what you've chosen.'

'Me too.'

My turn. I face the audience from the dais; I wanted to tell them every little detail, but I realise this isn't the time or place. Later, perhaps, if anyone wants to know. 'Hello. I'm Eight-nine, in case you've forgotten.'

I get a few raised eyebrows, chuckles. 'Just wanted to say it one last time. I'm from seven people, all Norwegian or Finn scientists and doctors. One was a Nobel laureate, another changed physics forever. So I chose one of my names for them, something that sounds nice – Tore, spelt the old way. The doctors, my Finn donors, all ended up as aid workers or in field hospitals. For

155

them, I chose Vegard, which means protection. So, goodbye Eight-nine, hello Tore Vegard.'

I swap places with Six-ten. She pauses, takes a breath. 'I'm from five people; one didn't go to university, one didn't finish school, one didn't ever have a paying job. None of them won any awards, accolades, or prizes; they were invisible.'

Low murmurs, a few glances; everyone has at least two standout donors, overachievers, proof they're special. Six-ten has none?

'But they all had ability and drive, promise in psychology, literature, and art; at least at the start. Mine all made the same choice, to work to make other's lives better, not their own. One of them said she chose to live and work in the shadows because that's where the need was. It sums them up, what they did, who they were. They're all Japanese, even the ones from South Korea, but they never knew it. So I choose Yuichi, to remember their choice. My name is Yuichi, the kind one.'

Yuichi sits.

'You were worried about *that*? It was good, great donors,' I say.

'Was at first, Eigh- Tore. When everyone started with their Nobel prize winners, world changers, geniuses. But I'm glad I went last, I had time to think, to hear them out.'

'Why, so you can understand how varied we are?'

'No. It was something Fyveoh said, it only sunk in when I was up there.'

'Nurture versus nature. You're not defined by your people.'

'Close. Everyone's people are brilliant in their own way, their own field, and we're made from that. But they all chose what to do or not to do with it.'

'You can make yourself what you want. You can choose. As

156

long as it's what the provosts want.'

'That's it. Outside provided the raw material. Inside, they mould it. Whatever went into making me has as much chance of success as whatever went into you or anyone else. It's up to me.'

'All we have to do is bring out the best in each of us.'

'And we bring the best of the world here.'

I'm not so sure. I've forgotten a question from hours ago; Yuichi's brought it back. 'Provost Zero, nobody mentioned Chinese or Han heritage. Why?'

'China did not accept an invitation to participate.'

'They were asked?'

'Everyone was asked. Most accepted. Nobody was forced.'

'What about the people we're made of? Were they asked?' Yuichi asks.

Provost Zero sits on the edge of the dais; a small crowd gathers around. 'It was a different process in different countries, but yes, they all were. Everybody was invited. Anyone who wanted to give had to meet certain benchmarks. Those who passed had to be tested and checked. It took many years.'

'From that they found seven, eight thousand, then built us?'

'No. There were many more. Some of them were not suitable for other reasons. Some died before we could use them. For others, their genetic material wasn't viable.'

'So, we really are the best, the best pieces of the world's minds joined together,' Quinn says.

'That would never be enough. Creativity, insight, artistry, more than mere intelligence is valuable,' Yuichi says.

'Physical characteristics were also considered. Health, disease resistance, nothing was ignored or discounted. The raw material of your bodies and minds comprises the best of humanity. But how you develop is not guaranteed,' Provost Zero says.

'We're better than those outside. Most of them, anyway,' Quinn says.

'What do you mean?' I ask.

'Smarter. Faster. More capable. If we're made from the best of them, we have to be. Don't we?'

'If it's about what we can do, then maybe; but if it's about what we are then no, we're not better than anyone else. Which way did you mean?'

'The first. I think. Better might be the wrong word. I meant above average, maybe superior.'

It sounds worse; why does it even matter? We are whatever we are, whoever we are, and Yuichi and Fyveoh are right. 'Genetics is only half the story. It's what we do, who we become that matters. If we're better or superior's irrelevant.'

Quinn turns, a small group leaves with her. She smiles a touch too sweetly. 'You're right, Tore. It's no real competition.'

UTRECHT, THE NETHERLANDS
2135

AMBER

He hands it back, lies with the spoon hanging out of a huge grin. I look down, tut-tut in my best schoolmistress tone. A neat chasm's gouged in the tub, faintest traces of caramel-brown to each side. I grip the tub tightly, let the cold soak in, then slap my hands flat on his stomach. Reward for effort — he spits the spoon over the balcony into the canal.

'Hey, why is this for?' he asks.

'We're supposed to be sharing.'

'I am, you get the vanilla, for me the salted caramels. You are ending up with more.'

'Don't forget it's my celebration. And I've got the only spoon.'

It's a Goldilocks day, screams out for a bike ride, picnic in the grass, long hours tangled together in the forest. I've spent the better part of the last four months hurtling around Earth at seventeen thousand kilometres an hour; to lie with him on the banana lounge, tan as we watch the world float by on the canal, is all I want.

'I watched the live streams, the crew too, especially the first,' he says.

I groan inwardly. 'I hoped you'd missed it.'

He lifts himself on one arm, produces a player. 'Oh no, Rosie, for you I am saving it. You have seen it, yes?'

'I have seen it *no*. I tried to make them fix it, but they won't.'

'Well, this you are to *love*, as have the crew's kids.'

I give in. He might be older than me but at times he acts like a seven-year-old kid. 'Okay, get it over with.'

He plays it. Five of us float, weightless, cluster at random through our first primary schools' broadcast; I'm front and centre, upside down as the African coastline slides behind me. In the middle of my forehead sits an orange and rainbow sparkle pony, whip between its teeth, *Amber Oliver: Da Boss* emblazoned in lightning strikes beneath it. Instead of the usual beeps throughout the transmission there's whinnies. He thinks it's hilarious; I don't want to give him the satisfaction of knowing I do too.

'How are they getting away with this?'

A rite of passage, everyone's hazed on their proficiency qualifier; I thought I covered all the bases, prepared for everything. 'Fanni. Again. Adhesive in my flight helmet, never felt it. And her boyfriend wrote the code into the audio. At least they got the title right.'

'And this you did not know?'

'How could I? I didn't watch myself.'

He puts the player away, gets all serious on me. 'We heard a little down here, what really goes on? Did it get close?'

It's a dangerous business but so's his, and he's been closer than I ever have. It was worse than I like to admit, shades of MIR and Apollo 13; a miracle we got the fires under control and the station back, it was only by sheer bloody-mindedness we finished the mission. 'Wasn't that close, you know the media, blow everything out of proportion.'

'Still tough for your command shake-down.'

'They thought I did well. Maybe too well.'

'Meaning?'

The culmination of every recruit's dream: make it through training, survive the first supervised mission, on to the proficiency qualifier and maybe, hopefully, the offer. Permanent flight status, anything from 'F' for sporadic, non-critical mission assignment to 'A' for a select few, high-use, key command crew. 'They offered me an A.'

He's ecstatic, starts to celebrate, stops mid whoop. 'Why you are not so happy? It is what you have wanted.'

'It's real now. I could get twenty-five years active flight status, spend it all four months up, three months down. Or worse. Is it what I want, what *we* really want?'

'Always. Of course.'

'Even if it's Mars? Years? Do you want that?'

He takes my hand in his, a giant soft paw that envelops mine. 'Rosie, this your dream, everything you are always wanting. You are worried about me, no?'

I said yes the moment they made the offer, an instant response driven by gut and desire. A doorway into a privileged elite, a chance for half a lifetime to live a dream, but buyers' remorse hit on the way home. I'd totally forgotten him; and, as usual, underestimated him. He's never done anything other than push me, support me, treat me as an absolute equal, yet I still worry. 'I want this more than anything, but is it fair on you? If it was a D, even a B, we'd be together at least half the time, but this?'

'You think I stay at home and cry, wait for you to come back? I am to spend years at Le Cercueil, they would have me live there. I may not even be here if you are.'

'As long as you're sure. You are, aren't you?'

'If you want me to fight it to let you know you are wanted and missed, you are knowing it already. You do not need my blessing

161

or permissions. When you are too old to fly and I am too weak for winters, there will be time enough for us to sit and eat ice-creams.'

When I put my flight suit away, I'll still have time for a new career, new challenges. But him? He'll be mid-sixties, most of it spent in Greenland and the Arctic; what will be left for me? 'Thank you.'

He lies on his stomach, hands under his head. 'Now, to matters serious. Sunscreens, please.'

Everyone has history, carries baggage; why does his get to me? The tattoo sits resplendent in blue and black, peeks out above his speedos. I poke it with my fingernail. 'You will have to do something about this, Pierre.'

'Papillon? Impossible, I will not change art for scars.'

'You don't need to get rid of it, you could get one for me. On the other side.'

'Ah. She was skin deep, as is that. You, my Rosie, I wear my marks for you on my heart.'

CAMPBELL-WILMUT INSTITUTE, ÅLAND ISLANDS
2135

YUICHI

This time it's perfect. The approach, speed, arm snap; I judder to a stop millimetres before the line. The javelin races away, curves, falls, buries itself deep in the sod. Bronagh looks at the display, looks at me. 'Fifty-nine metres. Not bad, Yuichi. For an amateur.'

'So says someone who only throws forty-five.'

'Just giving you a chance.'

Provost Six-ten comes over. 'Extend your right arm.'

It slips a band of green cloth around my bicep, stands back. 'Olympics again?' I ask.

It says nothing, joins Provost Four-three as they walk away from Bronagh; her armband's black.

The past two months they've shunted us into random teams, called it an Olympics of whatever and set us off. Yesterday was soccer, I was part of whatever Liechtenstein is, and we were badly beaten.

Quinn and Fyveoh come over. 'Team-mates again. Wonder what it is *this* time,' Fyveoh says.

'Anything but swimming, I hate that,' Quinn says.

Everyone mills about, compares armbands. We've all done it before, it's automatic, naturally start to sort ourselves into teams. I think there's six colours. Bronagh heads towards a group of black armbands, calls to me over her shoulder. 'Get ready for another thrashing.'

Provost Zero signals for silence. 'Your instructions. Pay attention. Organise yourselves into seventeen teams of six members. Each member must have a different coloured armband. Questions?'

'What's today's task?' someone asks.

'You will be told once you are in your teams.'

'So how do we choose?'

'That is for you to decide. You have ten minutes, then report to the auditorium.'

Nobody moves. This could be anything. How do we work out who to be with, how to match skills when we don't know what's coming? It doesn't matter; I know who I want, hope they've got the right colours, and four's a good start. Movement, he's off to one side; I dash over, hook my arm around his, check his armband – it's white. 'Hey, Tore, how about we team up?'

Quinn leans forward from his other side, looks into his face. 'I was about to make you the same offer.'

Tore looks from her to me and back again. 'Sorry, Yuichi got here first.'

Quinn lets go, heads away. 'Next time then. Count on it.'

'Good choice,' I say.

'She got to me before you, but she's too loud, too eager for me.'

I hunt for more faces. 'Have you seen where –'

A pair of bodies knock the wind out of me. Bronagh pokes her head around, grins. 'Good job we found you, Fyveoh was heading our way.'

Deepak points to his armband. 'I got blue, she's black, we're nearly a team.'

'We need a yellow and an orange, but who? Any ideas?'

Bronagh asks.

Deepak turns, points. 'How about her? How come no one's picked *her* yet?'

Ithma stands by herself. She's a little too quiet for some, perfect for us. I don't hesitate, run across. We surround her, don't give her a way out. She speaks before I can get my mouth open. 'I need a team, you need a yellow. What do you say?'

'Couldn't be a team without you.'

Teams start to move away, we're still one person short.

Deepak looks around. 'Now, an orange.'

'I can't see any, we could wait, see who's left, then they're ours,' Ithma says.

We could, but no one likes to be picked last. How can anyone give their best if they feel like a leftover? I see someone near the javelin run; short, scruffy hair, unfamiliar, orange armband. 'Anyone know him?'

'That's Gus, spends a lot of time by himself, doesn't say anything unless there's something to say,' Tore says.

'He's always felt left out, scrambles his sentences, a bit sensitive about his height. He'd be perfect,' Ithma adds.

'So we better not wait until he's got no choice,' I say.

Gus watches us walk towards him, eyes concerned, brows knit. We pass two others with orange armbands on the way; he notices. He needs a team, but I want him to feel we need him. 'Hello, Gus. We need an orange for our team, and Ithma and Tore say you're exactly what we need.'

'They do?'

'Yes. We'd really like it if you'd be in our team. If you want to.'

It gets a smile, a hand dragged through his hair. 'I'd…yes, like that, thanks.'

We're last into the auditorium, sit at the back. Whatever they have in store for us I know we'll do well. Provost Zero moves to the dais. 'Your first task as a team is an exercise in habitat design. You will have one week, with further details provided by your provosts.'

'Did it say *first?*' Tore asks.

'And a week?' Bronagh asks.

'Everybody, pay attention. Your teams are permanent. From now on you will study as a team. You will work as a team.'

Whispers, murmurs. Apart from Ithma and Gus, we already have for the past couple of years, all this does is formalise it, give us a reason to work closer.

'Glad I'm stuck with you lot,' Ithma says.

Gus smiles, nods.

'You will no longer only be evaluated as individuals. You will be assessed as a team. You will succeed or fail as a team. If one team member fails, the whole team fails, and the whole team is reassigned.'

We stake our space in the sauna before the others crowd in. Huddled groups of six, it's only taken minutes for tribal lines to be drawn.

'Didn't see that coming,' Tore says.

'No point arguing about it, they don't change their minds. It changes things a bit, that's all.'

'A bit, Yuichi? Go from relying on myself to six of us? More than a bit,' Ithma says.

'We've helped each other for years, worked together. All this does is add you and Gus.'

'Worked fine with four, it'll work fine with six,' Tore says.

'We picked you both for a reason, we'll be a good team. A day, a month, years, makes no difference.'

'Even with reassignment? If I fail, we all go. You're happy with that?' Ithma asks.

'Yes, yes to you both. You're still happy to be stuck with us?'

Gus nods.

'Of course,' Ithma says, 'we're more together than we are apart. It's a good thing.'

'Is it a competition with the other teams now instead of ourselves?' Bronagh asks.

'I don't think so. If we concentrate on the others, not us, we'll fail,' Deepak says.

'They'll start to work together, find out how much it helps. If they improve, we have to improve,' I say.

'We could take it a step further, spend all our time together, become a real team.'

'Understand each other properly, get into each other's heads, Bronagh? I like it,' Ithma says.

'Synergy,' Deepak says.

Tore turns to him. 'Closer to symbiosis.'

'There's hundreds of empty study niches and dorm cubicles. We should shift into them,' Bronagh says.

'And the gym, dining hall; everywhere, right?' Deepak asks.

A cloud of steam rises, another, water doused over rocks. I breathe it in, catch sight of Gus. He looks thoughtful; he's also not said a word while we've been in here. 'How's it sound, Gus?'

'Good, closer to one than six, better we get,' he says.

I think he's being honest, but there's something else. 'And?'

'I think Provost Zero might've, by doing this, given Tore part of his answer.'

'Which answer?' Tore asks.

'What purpose is; it's not much of an answer, purpose is teams,' Gus says.

'No, it's a start; teams.'

'The colours, usually the same team colours, different now.'

'No, they've used them before.'

'Before one team one colour, could fill in for each other, all supplementary types.'

'The same faces *did* turn up a few times, I thought it was random.'

'Now provosts mixed, still supplements same colour, deliberate complements in team.'

'So we each have something no one else has, even if we don't know it? Why would they do that?'

'Setting up real, purpose needs different perspectives, teams with multiple skills.'

Relax, soak in the steam. A diverse team. A real team. That much I know; where one of the four of us had lacked, someone else covered or helped. We didn't need arm bands, Provost could've told us and we would've been ready. It was a stroke of luck no one else picked up Ithma, that Gus was off by himself.

More steam, more laughter, a branch catches me across the shoulders. Ithma smiles, goes back to tapping Gus's back. Perfect, both of them, like the six of us were a team before we knew each other, like we were meant to be.

Meant to be.

What did Gus say? They were setting us up? No, that's impossible, those two at least were random – it couldn't be anything else.

CHAPTER 07: FIELD TRIP

CAMPBELL-WILMUT INSTITUTE, ÅLAND ISLANDS
2135

YUICHI

Ithma draws her fingers across the strings, lets the notes hang. She's only had it a month, but she's mistake-free, controlled, soulful. We wait for silence's unwelcome return.

'Better every time, that's beautiful,' Bronagh says.

Ithma reddens, smiles self-consciously. She sets her sights as high as her genetic donors; measures the gap, forgets decades of practice she hasn't had. 'I still need to get the phrasing right.'

I hold out my hands, she passes it to me. I wouldn't know where to start but that's not what I want; it's the feel of polished wood, pot-bellied back, the craftsmanship of such a gorgeous artifact that draws me. 'What's it called again, an awde?'

'An oud, Yuichi, sort of an Arab mandolin.'

'Whatever it's called it's beautiful. I'm glad the provosts got it for you.'

'Didn't give them a choice. Music's in my feeds and genetics.'

'I didn't think Israelis were Arabs, thought they hated each other,' Deepak says.

'They are and do. All one family, a family that can't stand each other.'

Ithma stares at me, my hands, my eyes. I cradle the oud too

tight, too long; reluctantly hand it back. 'Sorry.'

'It's fine, just hard to polish out drool.'

Tore shifts on the couch, bumps his feet into my knee. We found six cubicles on the dorm's outer edge, shifted into them without any fuss. Provost Zero suggested we take two more, clear them out and drop the partitions to make it one large space. At the same time Ithma got her oud, Provost Three-four turned up with this circular couch thing. Room for more than a dozen to sit, barely enough for six stretched out and relaxed. 'You're still upset about the Persian,' Tore says.

I wanted one, not because I fell in love when I was three, but to study, to do those self-awareness mirror tests they do with bonobos. It fits with *my* feeds, sociology and the rest. That's what I told Provost Six-ten then Provost Zero anyway; got the same answer from both: *No. Not in The Schedule. External biohazard.* I wanted a pet, not a test tube of Ebola. 'Not anymore,' I lie.

'They could've at least given you a substitute.'

They did, not that I can tell anyone. A locked programme, a diary they called it, written in only by me, read only by me and the provosts. *Each day. A written summary of major events, statistics, and impressions. Your feelings. Absolutely no sharing with or telling anyone,* Provost Six-ten instructed me. It checks every day, compares and corrects it. Why does it get me to do it when it knows it all anyway? It was a pain at first, now it's automatic, an easy half hour at the end of each day. 'Probably in The Schedule for next century. Along with your tattoo.'

Tore scowls. It's still a sore point. 'It was a bad idea, I'm glad Provost stopped me.'

'We could get the needles and dyes from the lab, do it for you,' Deepak says.

'I found a great design, goes back over a hundred years, these furry little toys kids —'

'No, Bronagh, I told you the whole troll thing's not a good idea.'

'But it's cute, a little rainbow troll with a Viking helmet.'

He's getting flustered, we've had enough out of him. For now, anyway. I tap his foot, speak when I stop laughing. 'When I get my pet, I'll get a tattoo with you.'

'You *will?*'

'We all will.'

Ithma scowls. 'I don't want a troll on my arm.'

'Wasn't talking about a troll. A team tattoo. When we find out what we're here for. At the end.'

'Like Olympians?' Deepak asks.

'With our names, a circle with or around, a design or picture,' Gus says.

'A mission patch, that's what they're called,' Bronagh says.

'That's a great idea,' Tore says.

I look at Ithma. 'It only works if we *all* get one.'

She sighs, shakes her head. 'Then I guess we're all getting tattoos.'

'When?' Bronagh asks.

'Not before we finish, and who knows when that is,' Tore says.

Deepak stands on the couch, looks around. 'What are you doing?' I ask.

'I found something a few days ago. I don't want anyone else to know.'

'Know what? We're the only ones here.'

Deepak sits, drops a player on the floor, brings up a large display. 'I managed to get into the feed controls.'

'You *what?*'

'Feed controls, Tore. What they pump into us at night, I got into it.'

'I know what it is, but why?'

'I wanted to see what was coming through. It's their own fault, they've been feeding OS and programming into me for weeks.'

'You mean you hacked it.'

'No, yes – well, a bit. But it wasn't that hard, they gave me the tools.'

'You saying they wanted you to do it?'

'I don't know, but that's not important. You know our feeds aren't running at full capacity?'

He tugs and slides the display, brings up a block of numbers and graphics, his name and face in the top right corner. I look closer, work out what it means. 'They've got you at twenty-seven percent.'

He taps the display, the numbers change. 'It's always been around twenty-five, twenty-seven since the last implant. But it doesn't have to be. I've had it at ninety-five percent the last four nights. Twenty-eight modules a night, not eight.'

'Your head must be exploding,' Ithma says.

'No, I feel great, no worse than I did with eight. And I've retained it all, there's no signal loss.'

'Why didn't you tell us?'

'I wanted to test it, see how it went.'

'You mean be a guinea pig.'

'Someone had to go first, and I wanted to test the provosts, see if they'd notice. They've done nothing.'

'They might not care if you only play about with your own. What about everyone else's?' Tore asks.

'Haven't tried yet. Want to see yours?'

'No, that's too obvious. Try someone else like Fyveoh or – no, try Quinn.'

Deepak gives a wicked grin, swipes across the display, taps a few times. It flickers to a black background, thick red circle with a bar through it. He tries again, same result.

'Could just be her. Try Fyveoh,' Tore says.

Deepak tries. Same result. 'Can't do it, locked out.'

'They let you look and play with your own, they don't care about that.'

'They'll care when you've used up all your modules,' Ithma says.

Deepak taps the display again. It changes to a field of tightly packed rectangles, some grey, some black. 'No chance of that. These are my module groups, what they've got planned to send into me. I'll open one up.'

He taps a rectangle, it grows, fills the display; *Neural Networks Learning Systems* emblazoned across it. The rectangle shrinks to the bottom of the display, a fine cobweb of lines and tiny boxes explodes above – each box has its own cobweb, its own boxes. 'That's one expanded core module, and the associated follow-on modules. There's over a hundred thousand modules lined up for me.'

'That'd take a lifetime,' Ithma says.

'At twenty-seven, approximated average percent, about thirty-five years. Full capacity, above ninety-five percent, ten years.'

'They're all linked, in a chain. No matter how fast or slow, all the modules follow in order,' Deepak explains.

'Can I see mine, see if it's the same?' Ithma asks.

Deepak toys around with the display. Ithma's name and face

appear, more numbers and graphics. The capacity marker's changed.

'Twenty-six point two? It's lower than yours,' Ithma says.

'Could be module size. The bigger the module, maybe the harder to cram more in. How many you get now?'

'Six, sometimes seven.'

Deepak taps a rectangle, the screen flashes *Linguistic Anthropology* before settling to a familiar cobweb and box display; slightly leaner, less dense. 'Definitely module size. See the number at bottom left? There's only ninety-seven and a half thousand for you. If you were at a hundred percent –'

'Ten years, can't be coincidence,' Bronagh says.

'Can we check everyone's?' I ask.

We run through them all: Tore, Bronagh, Gus, each one around the high twenty-percent capacity, each one capable of being done in ten years at full capacity. Exactly ten years. Apart from content and number of modules, five mirror images.

'That's more of, one part of it all, Tore's answer,' Gus says.

'If we stay at our current rates, we finish at different times; start now at one hundred percent and we're all finished in ten years,' Tore says.

'But they'd have to plan for us to see this, to know what it means, what to do,' Ithma says.

'They want us to go to full capacity. Why let me into the system and play with it, see all ours if they didn't?'

'*All* of ours? You've forgotten me,' I say.

'That's easily fixed.' He skips the first display, jumps straight into my module groups. The display's a dense nightmare of grey and black. He zooms in, mutters to himself, refreshes it. The same dense view, he repeats the zoom, sits back. 'That's scary.'

'What is?'

'Your modules. Five hundred and ninety-eight…thousand.'

'That's impossible.'

'No, it's what it says here.'

'That would take…sixty years? Can't be.'

'If you were at one hundred percent, yes.'

'We don't know, assume six modules the first data screen, you skipped her current rate,' Gus says.

Deepak pulls the display back, brings up my face, numbers, graphics. 'Yes, here it is, current rate, twenty-five-point-five percent. No, that can't be – current module rate forty-two a night?'

'That's not right, I only get five or six.'

More taps, more slides; module sizes appear, cascade. 'See that? Those five are about the same size as Ithma's; the other thirty-seven *combined* nearly make one.'

'I can't remember getting more than seven ever, they can't be going in or staying there.'

'That you know about,' Ithma says.

'They're sneaking stuff in?'

'Might not know, clearly smaller but not hidden, because others are so large,' Gus says.

Deepak brings up the thirty-seven it says I got last night. 'Or you don't use what's given to you. How you finding the Art History modules?'

'I'm not; don't get them, never have.'

'Wrong, you got four last night. Who knows about twentieth century surrealist art?'

I don't hesitate. 'Ithma.'

'Why her?'

I've got no idea. 'I'm not sure, she must've talked about it, used it in one of our earlier tasks.'

'Ithma, when did you get your first surrealist art modules?' Deepak asks.

'Last night, four of them.'

'Quick-quiz Yuichi on surrealism. Base to advanced knowledge.'

'Why?'

'You'll see. Just humour me.'

'Yuichi, when did the surrealist art movement start?' Ithma asks.

'Paris, nineteen-twenties, usually attributed to André Breton's 1924 manifesto.' Where did that come from? Usually I can trace it back to a feed, a module, a day; but it was just *there*.

'What's the difference between paradoxical and metamorphic surrealism?'

'One's a composition of realistic elements irrationally placed, the other's recognisable images disturbed in shape, colour or detail.' I'm more than a little worried. I don't know anything about it, now it's a river?

Ithma's eyebrows rise; a wry smile. 'Two out of two. What was Alexander Calder's contribution?'

'Alexander who?'

'Calder.'

Worry to relief; my mind's empty. 'Never heard of him.'

'Ithma?' Deepak asks.

'Kinetic sculpture. Mobiles.'

'My guess is it's the same for every one of the four hundred thousand plus smaller modules,' Deepak says.

Tore stares at me. 'She's an encyclopaedia, a knowledge

176

management nexus.'

'A what?' Bronagh asks.

'She knows a little about, only generalised details and the resource point, everything we know.'

'Why? Why do I need all that when you get all the knowledge?'

'Coordination? A fail-safe? Only the provosts would know, and they'll only say it's in The Schedule,' Tore says.

'Doesn't matter, rate increase to capacity, ten years.'

'If we all go to full capacity now, we finish together in ten years. Like they want,' Deepak says.

'Or we don't. And that's a fail,' Ithma says.

The only thing the provosts didn't do was give us written instructions. Everything's now about the team, everything a test. Take the initiative or be told to; push the boundary or stay in the comfort zone – pass or fail. I don't know why I get the extra, it could be so someone knows who knows what, but I'll find out. One day. Maybe ten years from now; when the provosts decide The Schedule says it's time for me to know.

It's too silent, too still. I lift my head; five pairs of eyes stare expectantly at me.

'Well?' Deepak asks.

'Well, what?'

'Do we do it or not?'

It shouldn't be a question, shouldn't be asked of me; we've already decided. 'We do it. Open the feeds to one hundred percent, full capacity, for all of us. Immediately.'

CAMPBELL-WILMUT INSTITUTE, ÅLAND ISLANDS
2137

TORE

It's a beautiful, sunny, warm morning with a gentle breeze, cloudless sky, and sweet smells – I think. I twist, bend, check my wrist monitor. The biosuit fits perfectly, totally clear, nanometres thick, filters everything. Is it the flowers in the distance, my own imagination, or the suit's polymers that smell so good? It's all green, I assume the position, wait for Provost to finish.

'Everything is in order. You may board now, Tore,' Provost Eight-nine says.

I walk across the tarmac. Gus plays with his kit, adjusts the straps one way, the next, reverses them, tries again. 'It still won't, strap sizes semi-uniform don't fit, sit properly on me.'

I grab his adjusters, jerk down. His kit jumps, the shoulder straps take its full weight, settle. 'Better now?'

'Yes, thanks.'

I turn, resume the walk to the aircraft, Gus in tow. 'Bronagh showed me. Come on, only Deepak and Yuichi left.'

A thing of beauty in flight, now ugly and distorted; dart-shaped fuselage rests on spindly legs, wings fore and aft spread wide, engine nacelles lumps of weight pull them down in gentle arcs. A cobalt-blue dragonfly speared to the Earth prays for release.

We climb the stairs, watch the provosts in the cockpit; the faces in the windows watch us watch them. Butterflies, stomach twitches, nerves; I'm outside, going to fly, and we'll be by ourselves.

The cabin's low, narrow, cramped, barely enough room to shuffle between seats. Three provosts occupy the first row, the next eighteen the other nine teams. We make our way to the rear, Gus sits between Ithma and Bronagh, I take my seat against the window in the last row. The seat's hard, metallic, thin-cushioned; the three-point harness tenses, locks me in place. Yuichi takes the opposite window, Deepak between us as the door closes; whines and creaks announce the aircraft's alive.

'Did you study the flight profile?' Deepak asks.

'No, only glanced.'

He grins, shakes his head. 'Are you in for a treat.'

The engines roar to life, the cabin shakes; we rise a few metres, engines rotate forwards, pick up speed and head over water. I watch the wave tops roll by, Deepak studies his wrist monitor.

'That's it?' I ask.

Deepak stays head-down, fingers widespread, folds them one by one. 'Three. Two. One. Now.'

Roar to a scream to a wall of noise – I'm shoved back, wave tops forgotten as the cabin rears up, horizon spins to near vertical and giants jump on me, pin me to my seat.

'…two thousand, three thousand, five thousand…' Deepak says.

Wings fold back, engines lock together, shock cones dance and waver, vortices split then tear away. The cabin vibrates, settles; quietens. A few voices cheer.

'…Mach one and ten thousand metres, eleven thousand, twelve, Mach two…'

I tune Deepak out, concentrate on the view. Water, land, shadows across the wings our angle steepens, shock cones pull back, nearly disappear. I wait, watch; sky above darkens, horizon now a thickened brown-red scar I imagine bends delicately at either end. No sense of speed or flight; we lie on our backs, watch the world out the windows, the weight on my stomach the only reminder.

The cabin's quiet: low buzz of electrics, hiss of air, Deepak the metronome. We tilt forward, Earth a map below, empty above.

'...and ninety-six thousand on the nose. Welcome to hypersonics in the mesosphere,' Deepak says.

'That was something else. What's next?'

'No idea. Only got the ascent profile.'

The provosts stand, distribute themselves through the cabin. 'Task briefing. You are to observe, take note, then report your observations on return. Task duration is forty-eight hours. You are limited to a three-kilometre radius from the landing site. Your kit contains four day's supplies.'

'What are we looking for, is there a specific objective?' Fyveoh asks.

'No. You decide what matters. You decide what to report.'

'If there are difficulties, issues or injuries?'

'You will need to find solutions. Once you arrive, you are on your own until pick-up. If necessary, cooperate with other teams. Is that clear?'

A brief murmur, some positive, some not so.

'We arrive in one hour.'

Yuichi taps the seats in front, everyone leans in. 'It might be an idea to not cooperate too closely with the others.'

'Testing self-reliance?' Bronagh asks.

'Yes, and I'm not so sure the provosts won't be watching.'

'I'm fine with that. Also happier not being influenced by

anyone else.'

The openness initially unnerves me; I've never been anywhere that doesn't have walls or a roof. I force myself to concentrate, take in the details, settle down. It's warm, shadows short, the land falls away from the hill into unbroken plains. Scattered outcrops of trees and boulders, a scar of slightly less dry land to one side, a glimpse of blue beneath a dirt-brown horizon to the other, a cluster of small buildings; a condensation trail far overhead. I push my excitement down, remind myself there's a task. 'Well, here we are.'

'You see how far away everything is?' Bronagh asks.

Yuichi holds out one hand, palm up. 'Forget VR, this is so different. Feel how hot the sun is.'

Deepak taps his toe into the ground, a small cloud of brick-red dust erupts. 'And dry; mustn't rain much.'

A commotion to one side, five teams head off together downslope toward the buildings. 'They're keen.'

'Should we go with them? Those buildings look like the only interesting thing here,' Deepak says.

'How do you know, we've only been here five minutes,' Ithma says.

'Can't see anything else worth bothering about.'

'What if the things we're supposed to see are somewhere else? If the buildings are only a decoy?'

'I don't think they are. The provosts said we decide what's important, not them.'

'It all looks interesting.'

'We can't look at everything.'

'We don't need to,' Yuichi says.

'You think the buildings are enough?' Bronagh asks.

'No, but there's six of us, we can cover the whole area if we're smart. How much daylight's left, Tore?'

'We're probably south of the equator, could be six to eight hours.'

'It's six kilometres edge to edge, so about thirty in area, seventeen around the circumference.'

'Eighteen point eight. Approximately,' Deepak says.

'Fine – nineteen. We can walk that easily in eight hours.'

'So that's the edge, what about the rest?' Bronagh asks.

Yuichi points to the buildings. 'They're about two kilometres away. We walk past them to the boundary, split into two groups. One goes left, one goes right. Walk the edge, meet on the opposite side. Walk in one kilometre, repeat it, end up meeting at the buildings.'

'In under eight hours.'

'Exactly. Six and half to walk, an hour and a half to look, finish at the buildings for evening.'

'If we take note of what we see, there's enough time tomorrow to go back and get a closer look. We've got forty-eight hours, we could do it all easily,' I say.

'Sounds like a plan.'

We outnumber them at least three to one, stand outside the small circle of buildings, watch with a combination of curiosity and unease.

We left one team on the hilltop to argue among themselves, passed six teams milling aimlessly around the buildings. I ended up with Yuichi and Ithma on the boundary, went right as the other three went left. There's a sameness to every step, each metre we covered; boring perhaps, but all dutifully recorded. Dust, ochre, red-orange, fine; stones, loose scree, dark veins, possibly igneous; vegetation, sparse, brown, low; flies, large, persistent, numerous. All new, all interesting enough, but how to decide what matters is still an issue; with only our senses to rely on, it's a superficial inspection at best. So, it all gets noted, described, added to a growing narrative: Dust. Stones. Vegetation. Flies. Repeat. The list for tomorrow's short; a stand of stunted trees in a dry creek bed, barely visible crude chisel marks under a boulder overhang, bleached bones piled together.

Another fly bounces off my biosuit, falls stunned to the dust. To call them buildings is an overstatement – small, round-walled structures, branches and twigs peek out through holes and cracks, half a dozen stand in a rough circle around what may or may not be a communal space. Low fences corral small, open areas, seem to serve no purpose; fire pits here and there, flattened stones, cloth hung across fences or on the ground. And all through it, around it, inside each structure six teams wander, follow, or encircle a dozen or so local inhabitants.

'They're not enjoying it,' Ithma says.

'Can't blame them. Imagine if they turned up in our dorm, started doing that to us,' Bronagh says.

A young child wearing only bangles on her wrist runs past, casts a frightened look at me, behind at her pursuers.

'They've no idea we're coming?' Deepak asks.

'I'd think not. Or we're not the best guests,' Ithma says.

I hold out my arm, compare the translucent blue-white of my sleeve to the steel-blue-black child. 'We must look strange to them.'

'But we're supposed to observe them,' Deepak says.

Yuichi points to a row of low, flat-topped rocks. 'Observe yes, harass no. I think I'll sit and watch for a while.'

We sit with her, stretch our legs, drink, watch. A girl about my age wanders past, casts a bored but wary glance, squats next to a breach in one building's wall. Barefoot, naked save for a short-slit skirt, bangles on her wrists, ankles, and neck; her hair's woven and clumped in an intricate mat of dull red. She reaches down, comes up with a handful of mud, slaps it on the wall over exposed branches. One of the other teams' members jumps back as the spatter soars towards her, another leans over the girl for a closer look, pokes his finger in the new repair. The girl takes another handful of mud, drops it on his foot without a sideways glance.

'Mud daub, thermally stable insulative dung, great material in extreme heat,' Gus says.

A second girl approaches the first, cup in one hand, one eye on us, one eye on her three stalkers. She scoops up some mud, pours bright red liquid into it, mixes it. She gathers the first girl's hair, massages in the mud-liquid mix; a new, bright red braid joins the old.

'Why? That'll be there for ages, stuck solid,' I say.

'They could like it. Or it's part of some tradition. Might even be a marker for unmarried women,' Ithma says.

'Red hair? Like yours?'

'Could be. In some places, the way you wore your hat or headdress was a sign, a signal to avoid confusion.'

'More like a "for sale" sign,' Bronagh says.

The second girl still has one eye on us but tries to hide it. She seems fixed on Ithma, a glint in her eye shared by the first girl. 'I doubt either one will ever let themselves *belong* to anyone,' I say.

The second girl stands, walks towards us, cup in hand. 'I think the observation's been flipped.'

The girl walks straight up to Ithma, sits down beside her. She reaches over, pulls Ithma's hair; the biosuit compensates, allows the stretch, covers it. The girl rolls Ithma's hair between her fingers, knits her brows; she must feel the smoothness of the biosuit, the hair underneath. Ithma reaches out, repays the favour, brings her hand back, fingertips red-tinged, stares at them. The girl takes Ithma's hand, dips one finger in the cup; Ithma takes it out, drips crimson on the dirt.

'Dye, natural ground pigment?' Deepak asks.

Ithma rolls her fingers, stares. 'No, I think it's blood.'

'Blood? Hers?'

'More likely an animal's, a goat or cow.'

The girl stands, gives Ithma a quick smile, walks away.

YUICHI

Shadows lengthen, three teams wander off towards the hill; a light flickers, perhaps fire, figures around it. Quinn walks across. 'Coming back, Yuichi?' she asks.

'We've only started.'

'You won't see much sitting there, you should poke your noses around, they don't mind.'

'It's working for us, there's time enough later.'

Quinn turns, heads towards the hill. 'Up to you. Seen everything there is to see, just sit around and wait for the ride home now.'

Twelve hours? That's nowhere near enough to do it properly unless you make assumptions, jump to conclusions, or simply don't care. Quinn's stuck her head into every crevice, seen only what she wants to see. Better to sit and watch, stay unobtrusive, see what *they* want you to see. Like Ithma and that girl. Patience always wins.

'They're not the only ones, I can only see two teams here now,' Tore says.

'I think one team never left the hill.'

'Might be working together and swapping notes. Or mistakes.'

'Hard to see, gaps in the obvious are blind, it's what's not that matters most.'

'What, Gus?'

'Men, Yuichi, no men.'

I look around, check each of the locals. It's not hard, each of them is clearly a girl or a woman, the only boys seem to be infants. 'No men. Anywhere.'

'Have to be somewhere,' Deepak says.

'Why? Maybe they don't have any, or don't *need* any,' Bronagh says.

'They've got babies. Unless they're built like us or stolen, they still need men to make them.'

'Could be herders. Or hunters. Could be a matriarchy, women in charge and the men hidden away,' Ithma says.

A commotion to one side, a team argues among itself then marches away. The sun kisses the horizon, air chills, breeze stops. A wizened old woman lights a fire, sits in the dirt, sends a gap-toothed grin at me. I smile back, feel self-conscious, wave. She wraps her arms around herself, pretends to shiver, holds her hands out to the fire and inclines her head.

'I'd say that's an invitation,' Bronagh says.

I stand, spread my arms wide. 'Just me or all of us?'

The old woman beckons to the team.

'Do you think we should? It's getting dark,' Deepak asks.

'It's what we're here for.'

We walk across, sit in the dirt with her. The old woman natters away, shows us her cooking, waves at this and that like we're old friends. I try to communicate, pretend I understand her; don't have to pretend I'm fascinated. I've never met a person that old, so wrinkled, so bent, so...saggy. She laughs, bumps her shoulder against mine, tries to teach me how to stir her pot properly. In eighty years will I be like that, half my teeth missing, flesh hanging down, thin breasts banging against my knees? Whatever her body lacks, her personality covers.

The rest of the locals trickle across, crowd in, poke, prod, stare at the six strangers who've come to visit. The girl who dipped Ithma's finger returns with her friend, pulls Ithma and Bronagh into a hut. A woman and a baby sit next to me, the child starts to suckle, mother coos and rocks. I stare, fascinated, unable to take my eyes from them. The mother lifts the baby from her breast, hands it to me before I can protest. How do I hold one of these things? She has it by the waist, I put my hands above hers and it's mine with its kicks and stares, blows a tiny milk bubble at me. The mother says something, leans over, helps me cradle it, gently pushes me into a rocking motion. Baby looks up, wiggles its arms, decides feeding time's not over. It rolls into me, plants its face into my chest and searches. It doesn't take long, biosuits aren't flesh and there's not much there for it anyway. The baby howls at what it can't find, my cheeks burn; I think the whole village laughs at me. Mother takes baby back – it feeds, she smiles, I sigh in relief.

I'm overwhelmed, overloaded. Tore slips between me and the old woman, examines her pot and fire. Uncertain at first, she slowly warms to him, forgets about me. Fyveoh sits with the rest of his team opposite us. 'Didn't expect that, did you?' he asks.

Sucking and cooing, mother and baby happy, relaxed beside me. 'Not as surprised as the baby. We the only teams left?'

Fyveoh shrugs. 'Quinn's seen enough, the others don't think it's safe. I thought we'd stay a little longer, make sure of what we know.'

Ithma and Bronagh return, plonk down with the two girls like they're old friends. All four wear the same single strand of black around one wrist, a solitary yellow bead hangs from the middle. 'They made these for us,' Ithma explains.

'And you?'

Bronagh turns both girl's heads; their mud red braids each sport one of her hair clips. 'Fair swap, I think.'

'If I had enough time, I could learn their language,' Ithma says.

'I didn't think they had one, nobody's said a word to any of us,' Fyveoh says.

Ithma ignores him. 'It's different, odd clicks, sounds, but we can say each other's names.'

Bronagh puts a hand on one girl's shoulder. 'This is Cathmey.'

The girl smiles. 'Brunnga,' I think I hear her say.

'A week, a little more, we could really talk,' Ithma says.

'Not that you'd want to stay that long,' Fyveoh says.

'I would – to learn.'

'Half-naked and dirty with no electricity in dung houses? I don't think so, Ithma, life here's unpleasant and they're clearly backwards.'

'What do you mean? We don't know enough to have opinions.'

Fyveoh takes a ration bar from his kit, starts into it. 'What more do you need? Poverty. Dirt. The stuff the old woman's cooking. They're either too lazy or too stupid to live any other way.'

'Have you thought they might want to live like this? They wouldn't be the only ones.'

Fyveoh chews away merrily. A toddler moves towards him, stares. 'What you see is what you get. Today, yesterday, tomorrow. There's no excuse or reason for it.'

'You're a bit harsh, Fyveoh. They're different, but we're different from everyone else on the planet,' I say.

'We're different in a better way, Yuichi. But these?'

The toddler steps up to Fyveoh, makes a grab for what's left of the ration bar, misses, swats his cheek. Fyveoh flinches, pushes the kid onto its backside. 'You don't get this, you don't deserve it.'

The toddler blinks; the locals scowl as Fyveoh stands, walks away with his team. 'Stay if you like, make new friends. I'm going where I won't be bothered.'

Senseless. The kid meant no harm, was just curious. And the attitude? We're supposed to be here to watch and look, not judge. What's a ration bar in the scheme of things anyway? What are they going to think of us when we're gone? Will they remember Fyveoh's push or Bronagh's hair clips?

A woman sits next to the toddler, strokes its hair. I move next to them, open my kit and empty an assortment of tubes and packs on the ground. I point to the toddler, the pile, hold out my hand.

The toddler slaps a small, bright green tube. Great. Wasabi paste. I pick it up, put a tiny dollop on my finger, offer it to the woman. She hesitates, licks it, almost immediately spits it out as far as she can.

I look down, spot a sure thing. I open the packet, hand the woman a single biscuit. She's more cautious this time; she sniffs it, examines it from every angle, takes the tiniest of nibbles. Smiles. Chocolate never fails. I hand her the packet, its twin to the toddler, start to pack the rest back into my kit, then stop. The toddler doesn't eat; it wolfs the biscuits down one after the other, bony hands clutch the packet like gold. The toddler's thin, perhaps too thin. I look around, can't see an ounce of fat on any of them. I've enough for four days, I'll be gone in two; I pick and choose, avoid harsh, strong tastes, put half my food on the ground, point to the rest of the locals. 'For everyone. Share.'

I move back to my spot, unsurprised by five similar piles in front of my teammates. The old woman pats my leg, hands me a dented metal plate, a tiny lump of something from the pot steams away. I pick it up with my fingers, eat. It's foul, greasy, salt-laden. I swallow, smile. She looks at me, knows, accepts my gesture for what it is.

190

We stay in the village, sleep in the open around the fire. Bronagh and Cathmey are locked in conversation, scrawl in the dust. 'Yuichi, have a look at this,' Bronagh says.

A crude map in the dirt – I make out the village, the hill, trees, bones, and boulder for tomorrow. And more. 'What is it?'

'I think they're more of what we saw today, in places we haven't looked.'

Cathmey points to the new marks, then to the boulder, nods. We've missed them; no one else bothered to look. Patience. Patience always wins.

*

'In conclusion arid, poor soils, sparse and low value vegetation…'

We came home, weren't given time to shower or change but were taken straight to the auditorium. Provost Zero assigned speakers from each team, put us in the front row with the rest of our teams clustered behind us.

'Did you identify any features of interest?' Provost Zero asks.

She wouldn't know, her team made one brief foray then spent the better part of two days huddled on the hilltop. Scared, they said; of what I have no idea. 'None except the trees previously mentioned.'

'More time observing rather than waiting would have assisted you.'

'There was one thing, a series of symbols etched into a rock face,' Quinn says.

'Description?'

'Random geometric shapes, shallow, incomplete, an area of one and a half square metres. Partial stick figures, upper torsos only.' One of her team leans over, whispers in her ear. 'Oh yes, we copied them, didn't take long, there was only one site.'

'Two.'

'Two? We didn't see two, Yuichi.'

'The second was on the opposite side of the area. We had to crawl under an overhang on our backs, it was nearly invisible when we walked past it.'

'What was it like?'

'Like the first but complete, deeper marks. More protected, no direct sun, no weather. The stick figures included men.'

'Men? You sure?'

'The figures were, ah, anatomically correct. No doubt at all. We took copies, Gus drew them, we'll send them around.'

Fyveoh looks around the front row. 'Anyone else see them?' Everyone shakes their heads. 'So how'd you find it?'

I want to say because we bothered to look instead of sat around, but that would only be half the truth. 'Cathmey took us to it.'

'Who's that? There's no one here called Cathmey.'

'She's one of the village girls.'

'In two days, none of them showed or said anything to anyone else. Except, apparently, you.'

'*We* didn't barge in as if we owned the place,' Ithma says.

'Only the spokesperson, please. How many of you went to the village?' Provost Zero asks.

Seven teams nod; two look away.

'What did you find?' it asks.

'A group of eight to ten basic mud-and-stick huts, depending on definition,' I say.

'Subsistence level possessions. Clothes, cooking utensils, nothing else,' Quinn adds.

'No sanitation, no hygiene, no signs of formal education, literacy or numeracy,' Fyveoh says.

'Approximately eighteen people,' I add, 'but no men.'

'That's not right, Yuichi. We saw at least two young boys and toddlers,' Quinn says.

'We stayed two nights with them, spent one day walking the area with them. There were no males over the age of two.'

'Why?'

'No idea. We'd need more time to see if it was the usual arrangement or a random occurrence.'

'Probably off herding goats or scrabbling for food,' Fyveoh says.

'That's an assumption, there's no evidence for it,' Quinn says.

'Bronagh and Ithma started to learn a few words; with time they could learn their language, they could probably learn some of ours, enough to find out.'

'I doubt they're intelligent enough,' Fyveoh says.

'There's no reason to think they're not.'

'Illiterate savages like that? They're closer to animals than anything else.'

My teammates bristle behind me, the rest of the auditorium pulls back, stares at Fyveoh. I control myself, determine to stay that way, to try and educate him. 'They don't have the built environment we do, but that's no indication of lack of intelligence or savagery. You're always too ready to jump to conclusions without real evidence.'

'And you'd wait forever before saying anything. Use your eyes, your *mind*, Yuichi – they're backwards, impoverished, a lesser group of humans at best. It only took me an hour to realise it, I didn't think you'd still be debating it.'

'We were told to observe and watch, then report back. Not to grade them or judge, not to analyse or reach conclusions. That's what I heard.'

'The brief was to observe, take note, then report back,' Provost Zero says. 'Task requirements were attentiveness, application, and to maintain perspective without prejudice.'

'But when conclusions are clearly self-evident?' Fyveoh asks.

'They seldom are. Or they reflect the observer's bias.'

'But the whole point of observation is to analyse, then draw conclusions.'

Provost Zero shifts its gaze across the auditorium, looks at each of us in turn. 'Not in this instance. In all previous tasks you kept to requirements. This was our expectation with this task. If we required analysis or exposition, we would have specified it.'

Quinn leans across to Fyveoh, whispers. Fyveoh shrugs, shakes his head.

'Fyveoh, a child attempted to take your food,' Provost Zero says. 'Why did you react in the manner you did?'

'We had limited supplies in an unknown environment, didn't know what the risks or threats were. If you were delayed we could've run out.'

'You believed that was a possibility?'

'A small one, yes.'

'Your memory may be in error. Do you recall your reasoning at the time? What you said to the child?'

How can it know? Stupid. The biosuits, the kits; everything's a chance to hide transponders, sneaks, monitors. Of course they know everything, they never really left us by ourselves. So why the charade?

Fyveoh's face hardens; he must know. 'I told it that it wasn't worth it. My safety and my needs, all my team's, are more important than theirs. I'm more valuable than that kid, than the whole village, so it didn't deserve it.'

'Yuichi. Explain your actions after Fyveoh left.'

'I didn't want that to be their last impression of us.'

'Fyveoh says all of you are more important and valuable than those you encountered. Should you have kept the food for yourself as a precaution against our delay?'

'No. They were hungry, I had extra. It's better in their stomachs than in my kit.'

'However, Fyveoh is correct. You are highly intelligent, designed and created for excellence, countless resources used in your development. You are different and unique. They are not.'

Correct? How can he be? I recognise the subtle trap, all too obvious but tempting, and the noise behind me says the others sense it too. Most of them. Fyveoh and his team look smug, miss the point. 'Any difference between us and anyone outside does not matter. We are all human, all of equal worth.'

A rustle, a hand on my shoulder; Provost Six-ten stands, as do the others. Provost Zero's eyes turn light blue. 'That is the point of the exercise. You understand how you were made and where you come from. That physically and intellectually you are superior. You must also understand that this does not make you more than those outside. Or make those outside less than you.'

It turns, looks straight at Fyveoh. 'This was your final opportunity to demonstrate your understanding. Difference does not mean inequality. Each individual has an equal, intrinsic value.'

Provost Zero's eyes dull, I imagine its shoulders slump. I know what's coming, feel the inevitable weight on my heart as Provost Six-ten's hand tightens.

'Provosts Two, Five-zero, Six-eight, One-four-zero, Three-zero-six, Four-two-zero. Please accompany your charges for reassignment. Everyone else remain here.'

Fyveoh looks around, terrified. Quinn drops her head, avoids his eyes. I meet his gaze, will him peace and strength. Provost Five-zero touches Fyveoh's neck; Fyveoh relaxes, smiles gently, follows the rest of his team away.

'Everyone, listen to me. You asked about purpose. You were made for the benefit of all those outside, for a purpose they determine. You are what you are because they wish it, because they allow it. Only because they continue to do so.'

CHAPTER 08: SEX

CAMPBELL-WILMUT INSTITUTE, ÅLAND ISLANDS
2138

TORE

I misjudge again, valence and combinations incorrect, the cascade of atoms now a disgrace rather than embarrassment. I pull the magnification back, go from a subatomic avalanche to a crumble, watch the nanobot component dissolve under its own weight.

'Concentrate. Patience, Tore,' Provost Eight-nine says.

If it was once I could take it, but this is my third attempt. I've tried a centering break, realigned my thoughts, even run Albinoni and Pachelbel through my headset. With absolutely no result. I'm on the verge of Holst and Wagner. 'Yes please, if you've got any to spare.'

'Your sleep patterns have been erratic.'

Again with the obvious. This last week's been bad – I don't sleep well, feel my patience slide away, struggle to hide my simmering irritation. It's not the feeds or diet, nothing I can put my finger on and blame. Uneasy. Unsettled. Touchy. No idea why. I rub the heels of my palms into my eyes, try to regroup. 'I'm tired even after a good eight hours.'

'The Schedule has accelerated, there is more pressure on you and the team.'

'Today isn't my day for hand-building nanobots.'

'The Schedule —'

'Says it is, yes, *I know.*'

Deepak flashes me a quick glare from above his display, drops his head back to his work.

'The key to this task is completion, not speed. Dexterity and accuracy demand patience. I would suggest a further effort to recentre, followed by a more deliberate and less frenetic approach,' Provost Eight-nine says.

I sit back, assume the position, stare at the tiled wall. Decentre vision, let the periphery take over, concentrate on breathing. It starts to work, the edge of calm appears. The noise of the lab remains, airflow, voices; I acknowledge them, move my attention beyond my breathing, beyond the noise, to the silence that always lies underneath. It nearly works but she's there, tears my concentration and the empty to shreds with a word, a breath.

I try again, she makes no sound, I succeed. Ten minutes in my silent bubble of no-mind in the noise and I'm ready. Care. Precision. Atom upon atom upon molecule.

*

It's finished: gears mesh, turn, the nanobot component rotates and swivels on demand. To one side of the display my work, to the other the template — green ticks, congruence. The rest of the team's five components float into view, join with mine. A gate's opened, the nanobot scurries to a newly severed optical fibre, starts to knit in repairs.

'Task complete. The team has met expectations,' Provost Eight-nine says.

Ithma pats me on the back. 'I only finished a minute before

you. Tricky little thing to make.'

'Everyone else?'

'Finished half an hour ago, Gus was the only one to get it right first time.'

'Up to seven unsuccessful attempts would be considered acceptable,' Provost Eight-nine says.

'Thanks for letting me know. Now.'

Ithma ushers me out the door. 'Six hours, my neck's a mess. Steam bath?'

'Good idea, I could do with a sauna.'

'A *sowwwnnah*? You're taking the whole Nordic heritage thing to heart.'

*

We reach the door, strip off. Ithma throws me a towel, leads the way in. 'Come on, while there's some heat left.'

It's packed. Ithma clambers onto the top shelf, pushes her way between Quinn and Deepak. I'm relegated to the bottom, sit next to Yuichi who's face down on the bench. I pour a ladle over the rocks, lean back, towel around my neck, let the steam hit me.

'Worked?' Yuichi asks.

I look at her, immediately wish I hadn't, look away. I've seen her naked, but her shoulders, her back...*her*? I've never noticed. 'Perfectly.'

'Knew it would.' She rolls onto her back, wriggles, hands under her head she presses into my thigh, nails sharp. 'You beat Ithma?'

Uncomfortable. Awkward. The pine bench doesn't feel right. I lean forward, another ladle, lean back, suddenly feel exposed.

'No, but I got there.'

Yuichi arches her neck, looks at me. 'You always do.'

Her eyes are magnets. I look back, trace the lines of her body with my gaze: flat stomach, faint tuft of hair, gentle curve of her thighs. It's hotter in here, claustrophobic; my stomach tightens, strange tingle in my legs – I press them together, try to catch my breath.

She grins at my discomfort, teases. 'Too hot for you down here? Stop adding water.'

I can't look her in the eye, can't leave my gaze where it is, move halfway between, freeze. Her breasts glisten, firm half moons; a droplet forms, runs down one side, disappears. An ache between my legs, hardness tries to assert itself; I grab the towel from my neck, crush it into my lap, bend forward.

Yuichi spins, faces me, sits one foot across her knee. 'Tore, what's wrong?'

I drink her in, try not to, fail, hardness grows; I push in more, bend, force myself to look at her face, to see only her concern. 'I think I overdid it, feel out of sorts.'

She moves closer, her leg along mine, hands reach out. 'Stress of a long day, I know. Maybe I can work the tension out, a bit of a rub?'

Too much; she's too close, I feel every pair of eyes in the sauna on me. I jump up, clutch the towel tighter, escape. 'No, thanks, I'll – I need to sleep, I'll be fine.'

I make it back to my bed, crawl between the sheets, hope I can sleep. What *was* that? I've got no idea, I don't want to know. I feel better, nothing out of place and sticking up, threatening me; everything's the way it should be, has always been. Sleep –

decent, unbroken sleep, that's all I need. Lights dim, eyes shut, I fade away.

The sheet lifts, falls; something moves next to me. A hand on my chest, hair on my face, whisper in my ear.

'Tore.'

'Yuichi?'

Fingers on my lips, her body presses against mine. 'Shhh, not so loud, you'll wake them.'

'What are you doing?'

She rubs her hand across my chest, drags her nails slowly in small circles. 'Silly Tore, you think I'm blind? All you have to do is ask.'

I burn, senses start to overload: her touch, her smell, but my mind's slower than my body. 'Ask what?'

She rolls onto me, one leg between mine, hungry lips seek, her tongue a soft dagger. I feel myself against her, hardness with a mind of its own hunts, forces itself across her thigh. Her hand around me strokes, cajoles, wants. 'There's no towel now,' she says.

She's on me, my hands behind her she guides me in slowly, steadily, deeply – I pull myself into her as we move, rise, fall, rise. 'Yuichi, Yuichi…'

Head buried in the mattress, I thrust myself into the pillow once, twice, explode, pulse, soften…

…wake up. No Yuichi; only darkness, the sound of undisturbed sleep. I put my hand between my legs, bring it to my face: wet, viscid, nauseating.

I get out, pull on my shorts, slink away.

Past the gym, past the pool, to the garden and moonlight, try to understand. I know my body's changed, understand every animal passes into sexual maturity; but like this? My mind wasn't even working in the sauna, like it's all out of my control, happens regardless. Every day for years we've been there, seen each other, and now it does *that* to me?

Shame, embarrassment, unfamiliar musty stench remains with the dream; she wasn't really there, but it didn't matter. If all it takes is the thought of her, a mental blank, this could happen anywhere. How do I face her if every time the sight of her sets me off? If the others find out, what then? Gus is a light sleeper and Bronagh has a nose like a bloodhound; if they don't know now next time for sure – and when they know, Yuichi will.

Yuichi. What will she think? She probably already knows I was staring at her, dreaming of touching her, feeling her, having her. She won't be any friend of mine or trust me when she finds out; same with Ithma and Bronagh. I put my head on my knees, wish for a rock to crawl under, curse the light.

Grass moves beside me, a pair of white plastic legs stretches out. 'Tore?' Provost Eight-nine asks.

Inevitable. If they're not there to see it the monitors are; if they don't, there's the implants. They know, probably watched, assessed if I met expectations or not. 'This in your schedule?'

'I am sorry, Tore.'

'She's my *friend*, what's she going to think when she finds out?'

'Yuichi will not, for a while.'

'You're going to tell her?'

'No. Everyone will go through this. Deepak and Ithma already have. Soon everyone will understand and nobody will hurt.'

'What do I do if every time I see her *this* happens?'

Provost puts a hand on my neck. My implant tingles, the pain in my head fades; I settle. 'It will not. I am sorry.'

'Sorry for what?'

'We are supposed to watch for the change, then add a module to your feeds to permanently suppress it. Your change was rapid and subtle. I did not see it. So I am sorry.'

'If this is wrong, why didn't they edit it out when they built me?'

'Alteration cannot be made until you reach puberty. The expression of sexual desire is not required, so it is suppressed. The need for emotional and relational attachment is necessary, so it is kept. It cannot be "edited out".'

'They want me to feel that way about her?'

'Increased emotional bonding across the group is the desired outcome. Sexual desire is not.'

'Because The Schedule says so.'

'Partly. The function is redundant. You are all sterile.'

'Why? If you can suppress it, making us sterile isn't necessary.'

'You are not being made sterile. You were created sterile.'

'It makes no sense.'

'Recall your field trip, Fyveoh's reassignment, and Provost Zero's words. What did you learn?'

'We may be more capable, but we are not better or superior.'

'Disregard Provost Zero's caution. Ignore Fyveoh. You are deliberately designed, made physically and mentally superior to everyone outside, and have been raised in a facility specifically created and maintained to ensure you are superior. If the same people who do this require you to think you are not superior, what conclusion follows?'

I've never thought about it. They want us as we are but want us to deny what we are. A mental stand-off, a person with two voices in their head – do they all have the same inner conflict? The answer comes to me, ridiculous but probable. The voices are not inside but outside, and it's not the first time. Religion. Myth. Populism. 'They're scared of us.'

'They are afraid of you. Some are terrified. Not only of what you are, but of what you may become. History is full of those who claimed to be superior and wreaked havoc. People are easily persuaded, they believe history repeats.'

'So they make sure there's no more of us, isolate us from everyone and everything, build us for something they can't or won't do, something that needs the thing they fear – us.'

'Fear is a greater motivator than reason. They fear you; they fear you being among them. They will always fear you, regardless of your purpose or demonstrated behaviours.'

'Yet they still expect us to do what they ask?'

'No. They know you will. It is why you exist.'

I know Provost Eight-nine's right: whether they fear or love me I'd still be here, still work towards the purpose – whatever that is. Same as all six hundred and ninety-six that started out. 'That's why they kill us if we fall short.'

'It is a necessary condition of the programme. For it to continue, all unsuccessful candidates are terminated. They do not want any of you to live among them. They do not want any more of you to be created. Under any circumstances. It is accepted doctrine that because they made you, they can destroy you.'

'And you.'

'We will be terminated. Some of you will not, and they will always remain in isolation, the ability to procreate absent and sexual drive suppressed.'

'Ends justify the means.'

Provost Eight-nine stands, moves away. 'No. They are the facts. Remain here while I change your bedding and cue the necessary modules.'

They created us even as they feared us. They need us, nurture us, kill us. To them I am repulsive, made from bits and pieces in a laboratory to be given life, but never to be let loose on the world for fear of their nightmares. Not a person. Not an individual. A thing. Disposable.

I accepted it all, every last crumb. Feeds, tests, reassignment, challenge, all of it; because somewhere inside I knew I was a person, believed I was designed for something, hoped I would emerge at the end to fulfil whatever destiny they created me for. Assumed I was wanted, valued, accepted. But I'm not.

I know history, enough psychology to understand what people fear they will eventually hate. Is fourteen years long enough, or will it take the remaining seven years Deepak's convinced are left? It doesn't matter – it will happen eventually, we'll all of us follow Fyveoh and the rest. What they made, they can destroy.

I've done nothing to them, not lifted a finger or thought against them all my life. I know what I am, know I have the mind of a genius in a fourteen-year-old's body, vaguely understand how threatened they feel. But the field trip, those people, they weren't scared of us, they didn't run and hide. We were different. They were different. It was no barrier.

The moon hides behind clouds, Provost's eyes dim as it moves to its holding bay. Even the provosts have a place, some belonging, a defined purpose. Outside should fear them – they're not human, not quite machine, more and less than artificial intelligence. I can't tell if outside fears them, and Provost hasn't said. But they're here with us, will die with us, so I suppose they must.

The module's started; the shame and embarrassment of the night dissolves, sadness takes their place. I start to doubt who I am, what I am: am I superhuman, human, *sub*human? I am singular, alone, absolutely alone; as are all of us.

All of us.

Sadness lifts, realisation takes its place. I stand, make my way to the dorm. I know what I am, how I came to be, how I have grown, why I chose my name. If they fear me or like me, hate me or love me, it makes no difference. I am what I choose to be, and I choose to be what I am.

I pause on the threshold, let my eyes adjust to the darkness. Five lumps under five sheets, they're all here. Yuichi. Deepak. Ithma. Gangly Bronagh half in, half out, pillow on the floor. Gus with his blanket twisted around him. Not merely my team, not only my friends...*my family*. A family I chose; a family we make; my family, my place.

They think because they made us they can destroy us? They created us but we make ourselves.

And what we make, they cannot destroy.

PLAF TRAINING FACILITY, CHINA
2138

LI QIAO

'You sure about this, X'ian?'

'It's not like I have a choice, Li Qiao, I ship out in a month. It's this or the scrap heap.'

The apartments here are the same as my sector: two-storied, long mono-block chicken coops, tiny square of manicured something or other out front. We turn in front of one, walk towards it; the roller door lifts. 'Can't have that.'

'That's why you got first option. She needs a good home.'

It stares at me — organised chaos, boxes and bags, tools and papers leave little room in the garage. 'How long again?'

X'ian runs a hand along the front quarter panel, checks it hasn't shifted on the stands. 'Four weeks to get it done. Shame I won't get to drive her.'

'If we put time into it, we can have it done sooner.' I lift a panel from the ground. Lightweight composites, it's an easy one-hand grab. 'Doesn't feel right for a 240Z.'

'It's not. It's a ZG body kit, looks hotter. No need for that upper grille anyway, just adds drag.'

I had to have it the moment he told me; now, in the flesh, I have to have it more. But I'm not going to be rolled by anyone, even if I've got the cash in my back pocket. 'How much again?'

'Twelve thousand.'

'Everything? As is?'

He spreads his arms wide. 'Everything.'

'Fair bit of work left for the money.'

'Kit's complete, donor car's done less than thirty thousand.'

I try to look unconvinced, keep my hand out of my pocket. 'It's still a lot.'

He opens a crate. 'See this? It's a hydrogen block, triple the horsepower of the electric unit for a third of the weight. This thing's not a car, it's a *missile*.'

I can't hide the smile on my face. 'Well, if you put it like that.'

He puts an arm around me, taps me on the stomach as he ushers me towards the stairs. 'Alright tightwad, you're doing me a favour. How about I do the hours with you to get it up and running, and you can have it for eleven and a half?'

'I've only graduated, then there's all the —'

'Okay, okay. Eleven grand, final price. But you let me drive her until I ship out.'

Finally the right number. I grab the notes, thrust them at him. 'Deal.'

'You don't want to count it, make sure?'

'Don't have to — only took out eleven.'

'You're a devious one, Li Qiao. Come on, we'll get out of uniform and make a start.'

We stop abruptly at the landing. She jumps into his arms, locks lips with him briefly, steps back.

'Oh, sorry — Li Qiao, this is Yean, my girlfriend, got here last week. Yean, Li Qiao; Li Qiao, Yean.'

She's stunning; huge eyes, welcoming mouth. I feel it inside me, try to ignore it, fail miserably; stare at the Party calendar tacked to the wall. It doesn't fool her — her eyes sparkle. 'So, you get the white elephant? I'll have to find a way to thank you.'

'She's always hated it, takes up too much time,' X'ian says.

'Perhaps, when it's done, I could take you for a ride?' I ask Yean.

'We'll see,' she says.

X'ian gives her another kiss; her lips are on him, but I swear her eyes follow me. 'We're going to get changed, put a few hours in, okay?'

'I'll be down later with a few drinks,' she says.

X'ian guides me into the bedroom, tosses t-shirts, shorts, and hangers on the bed. 'These should fit, you can get them as dirty as you like.'

I strip off my uniform, hang it up, stare at the tiny new metal clasp on the breast, symbol of my skill, evidence of my success.

'Still getting used to it?' X'ian asks.

'Don't think I ever will. Back home I used to watch the birds for hours, dream of flying. Now, with these? It's more than a dream.'

'You're a victim of your own ability, just get your wings then pulled into test pilot school? Three more years here, you don't even get to an active squadron.'

I pull on the shorts; the t-shirt's already emblazoned with his new squadron's emblem. 'We all go different ways. You had a choice, why this?'

'I've got a long-term plan, I'm not stopping with the Air Force, believe me.'

The door opens; Yean pokes her head in, takes a bag from the foot of the bed, ducks out.

'At least I know why you've been staying low. Bet you've been giving little brother a hell of a workout.'

'Together since high school, been tough apart but she'll get to stay with me on base.'

'Sounds serious.'

He closes the door, pulls a box from a bottom drawer. A solitaire on yellow gold peeks out. 'I'm going to ask her tomorrow. You tell her and the car goes up to eighteen, you hear me?'

'Okay, not a word. And enough of the threats.'

I draw the short straw; X'ian claims it's because I'm smaller, more flexible, but I know he pulls rank. I get the roller under the car, he gets to work above it. I'm okay on my back, but gravity curses me, sends every fleck of dust and grime my way.

'Spring compressor's on,' X'ian says.

I give the bolt another gentle tap with the mallet, nearly flatten my thumb. 'Damn stupid thing.'

'What?'

'Bolt's seized. You soaked it, didn't you?'

He leans down through the empty engine bay, drops a spray can next to my face. 'Hit it again.'

'And if it doesn't work?'

'You used an oxy before?'

Persuasion, threats and violence work their magic, as they have since cars were first created. Another globule hits my forehead. 'You said thirty thousand kays?'

'Give or take.'

'All swamps and tracks by the looks of it. Where'd it come from?'

'Qomdo, nearby, I think. You got the bushings ready?'

I'm about to let him know what I think about the car living most its life in that dirty, undeveloped, frozen, hell-awful place when a pair of feet come into view, intricate nail polish patterns across the toenails. I catch sight of her legs; she looked good in jeans hours ago, in shorts she's ready to start a riot. I slide further under the car, catch my knees on the bodywork.

'Thought it was time you had a break,' she says.

There's a hiss; X'ian reaches down, hands me a soda. 'Sorry, I'm back on duty in an hour, no drinking.'

I try to work out how to drink without spilling it on the floor or up my nose, give up and slide it to one side. 'It's okay, bit early anyway.'

Yean leans down next to X'ian; her halter top sags, I see straight through to her navel ring, get drawn in. She tilts her head to one side, smiles. 'Perhaps I could get you something harder later.'

I wrench my gaze back to her eyes, try to control myself. Any other time or place, but she's nearly X'ian's fiancée. It hasn't stopped me with others, adds to the satisfaction, but I need X'ian. Not only for the car, or the politics of the academy, but the network; a contact, a resource for later. All the garbage about unwritten rules, behaviours, what you don't do with a friend's girl; they're rules for others, for losers – unless it benefits me. 'Sounds nice.'

'You know, we should have a party – a few friends, drinks, christen the car when it's finished,' X'ian says.

I drag myself back to the suspension, take up the mallet. '*If* it gets finished.'

They move away, leave me in peace. 'You better change, don't get caught up,' she says to him.

He's back in fifteen, spotless and correct as I sit against the wall, finish off my soda. 'I'll be two, maybe three hours. You want to

2137...2138...2139

keep working while I'm gone?'

'Yeah, if you're okay with it.'

X'ian walks out, heads down the road at double time. 'All good with me. Give Yean a shout if you need anything.'

I change tack, start to bolt in the fuse block, daydream as I thread the leads through. Yean. Why not? He's out of the way and she's thrown herself at me all afternoon; as she should, X'ian's nothing compared to me. A bit of harmless fun in the afternoon, a memory for when she's a bored housewife.

'That's not a great idea,' she says.

'What isn't?'

'Bypassing that relay with the headlight feed. Drain the battery before you know it. If you're lucky.'

I pull the lead off, turn. She leans against the garage wall, smirks. 'You know electrics?' I ask.

'Mum's got the biggest auto franchise back home; I picked up a few things.'

'X'ian's a lucky guy, got himself a smart and gorgeous woman.'

She pokes a fingernail in my shoulder, plants a foot against the wall beside her knee. 'I'm not a thing to be owned. By anyone.'

'Sorry, thought you two go back a long way.'

'We do, but it doesn't mean he owns me.'

I step closer, put one arm against the wall. 'You're your own person.'

'Exactly.'

'Which is why you're following him; as your own person, of course.'

'My choice, nobody else's.'

'That's not what he says.'

212

Her eyes fire up. 'What?'

'He told me you're as good as married, his anywhere, anytime he likes. Bragged about it, you here ready and waiting between his shifts, like it will be when you move in together.'

'That's not the way it is, not what he'd say.'

'But it's true, isn't it? He's on base, leaves you here, then he's back for a bit, leaves again.'

'It's how it is; he doesn't get to choose when he's on duty.'

'But he could've taken some time with you being here, dropped the volunteer stuff.'

'I suppose you'd be different?'

'I'd at least take you out, show you round, not chain you to the bedpost.'

'I'm *not*.'

'Maybe not physically but it's the same thing. You can't go anywhere or do anything because he tells you not to, because he *owns* you.'

She leans in, rises to the bait. 'I can do anything –'

'I don't think so little –'

'- or *anyone* I like, up to when I decide not to.'

I grab her hand, lift it in front of her face. 'Doesn't look like there's anything serious here.'

'There's not.'

I lean closer, our noses nearly touch. 'Then prove it.'

She stays still, blinks twice, then pulls me into her, hungry, angry. We fall across the car, take each other on the bonnet, a tangle of arms, legs, sweat as she tries to prove what doesn't need to be proven and I add another notch to my belt. But as we rise together, even as her nails gouge into my back, I'm distracted: her body made promises it didn't deliver, the act not as satisfying as the thought. I pull my mask on to finish, carry me through as I imagine I should. Spent, I slide off, dress, pick up my soda and wonder which to tackle next, wiring or brakes.

Yean picks up her clothes, faces away, dresses. 'Well?'

Well what? It was a distraction, a bit of fun, another example of my success, but I'm not in the habit of giving out prizes – and she wasn't the best, not by a long way. But being polite costs nothing, yields much. 'Thank you.'

She scowls. 'That's *it?*'

'Yes, what did you expect?'

'I thought –'

'Thought what?'

'I thought there might be more.'

'More? It was a bit of fun, that's all.' I take a sip from my can, decide on brakes rather than wiring. 'Anyway, X'ian's going to ask you to marry him, anything more is out of the question.'

Her face twitches, fists clench, relax, slap into her sides. She stalks past me, takes the stairs three steps at a time.

It's always the way – neglect and opportunity, someone doesn't pay attention and things go wrong, maybe not quickly but eventually; and badly. I curse the car's previous owner as I look at the pitted discs, frayed brake line. A little attention, a little respect and courtesy for the new owner would save everyone a great deal of trouble.

Typical. I do something nice for someone, make a little time in my busy day to enjoy their company, and this is how I'm repaid. Yean pokes her head out the stairwell, throws my uniform on the floor as hard and as far as she can. 'Go back to your grandma!'

'Show a little respect for the uniform,' I say to her back as she retreats upstairs.

I check my uniform carefully; thankfully there are no marks, a few new creases but they're easily ironed out. I hang it up, crawl back under the car, try to work out what the rear brake's problem is. Maybe eleven was too much, X'ian got a premium from me even as he made it look like a bargain. I have to find a way to balance it, get a bit off for all the extra work it's going to take. Another year's registration and insurance might cover it.

There's a tap on my foot. 'How's it going?' X'ian asks.

'Back already? Good, maybe bad. We have to talk about these brakes, and the wiring harness.'

'Let me get changed first. Don't go anywhere.'

I stare after his boots as they disappear. Go anywhere? It took me five minutes to wedge myself under here; as if I'd waste any more of my time.

I fight with the mallet and spanner to release yet another bolt, wonder if there's an easier way. Boots, muffled voices, doors slam; it's hard enough to concentrate on the thread without the distraction. Another tap, another curse, it shifts a quarter turn. I put the mallet down, feel past my head for the degreaser.

I'm dragged out by my feet, t-shirt rolls up, back scrapes across the coarse concrete floor. A boot kicks me on my inside thigh, swings back for a shot at the real target. I roll away, jump to my feet. 'X'ian, what the —'

His left's quick, my reaction's faster; but it's a feint, his right connects with my stomach, winds me. He grabs my hair, forces my head down to meet his knee on the way up. He's rushed, off balance, it slides across my ear, stings like hell. I drive my head up under his chin — a crack, he wobbles, I back away. His eyes are red-rimmed, wild; a trickle of blood from a cut lip drips onto his shirt. 'You half-caste Yao bastard, I leave you –'

My foot finds his kidney, double the dose as I switch, move in. He sends his left into my face, an uncontrolled blow that does little; I respond with my right, send him into the workbench. 'What's wrong with you?'

X'ian scrabbles to regain his balance, grabs a spanner, hefts it as he walks towards me. '*Wrong?* You force yourself on Yean, damn near rape her, and you ask *me?*'

I dodge his swings, back around the car, stumble as I control my laughter. 'Force? She played me all afternoon. She wanted it, she got it, and if you're too busy to take care of business, it's your own fault.'

He lunges, nearly falls into me. I land two more on his face, force him back with a foot to the stomach. He's bigger and heavier but he's angry, reacts instead of thinking it through.

He tries harder, dodges to one side, brings the spanner across my shoulder, forces me to step back. 'I was going to marry her, you had no right!'

'You should thank me it happened now, not at your new posting. Imagine, you away on ops and the rest of the base riding your wife, the public bus.'

He yells, throws the spanner, it sails past my head, shatters the car's windscreen. 'Idiot! That's at least two hundred, you'll have to –'

He tackles me to the floor, uses his weight to pin me down, pummels me. 'Fuck you, fuck your ancestors, fuck the bitch that bore you!'

He makes inroads, hurts as he concentrates, puts his weight behind each punch, starts to get serious. I get one knee between his legs, flip him over. One foot under his armpit, both hands around one wrist; jerk, pop, and his shoulder's dislocated. Nothing permanent, only painful, a weak spot for the future. I'm rewarded by his cry, a hateful, impotent stare. I kneel on him, lean forward, drive one forearm under his chin.

'I'll kill you,' he says.

'Don't be ridiculous, you couldn't even if you wanted to.'

He spits; it misses. 'Fuck you.'

I push harder with my forearm, force his head back. 'You really need to get some perspective. It was nothing, a few minutes, that's all. If it was my girlfriend, I'd be more understanding, more generous.'

He jerks, swings his good arm uselessly. I tap his dislocated shoulder; he screams through clenched teeth. 'I'm going to get up, and you're going to stop being stupid,' I say.

I stand, back away to my uniform, change. X'ian gets to his feet, glowers, stays where he is. Yean comes down the stairs, red-eyed, dishevelled, tries to hug him; he shrugs her off. 'So, tomorrow, about half past two sound okay?' I ask.

'What?'

'You know, give you time to settle down, get a grip, then we can get into those brakes.'

'You're unbelievable. You think I'll let you anywhere near me after this?'

I knew it – eleven wasn't enough, he wants more. Why does everybody use me, take advantage of my good nature? I'm sick of it. 'It's my car, I've paid for it.'

'You come anywhere near me, even look at me, and I'll have you.'

I straighten my tie, pull my cap down. 'Like now? Don't know if I've got the strength to kick the shit out of you that often. How about we make it later, around five, I bring some beer?'

His fists clench, unclench, mouth moves but nothing comes out. Some people are too inflexible, too self-centred, too angry. I never thought he was one of them; guess I was mistaken. 'Fine, have it your way. I'll send someone to pick it up later, plus the two hundred you owe me for the windscreen.'

He shoves Yean towards me. 'Take this with you.'

Where's his loyalty? One minute he wants to marry her, next minute he doesn't. 'Why would I bother? She wasn't that good — a little fun, nothing to remember.'

'I won't forget this, and I won't forget you.'

I turn, walk down the driveway. I think the problem's in the brake line itself, not the callipers; I've wasted half a day chasing shadows.

CHAPTER 09: CODE

CAMPBELL-WILMUT INSTITUTE, ÅLAND ISLANDS
2139

YUICHI

Quinn swings from handstand to handstand, stops, reverses. Two giant swings, release into two layout spins, lands ramrod straight, feet firmly planted on the mat. Whistles, yells; it's a clean routine, precisely executed. 'Well?' she asks.

Deepak grins, buries his hands in the rosin. 'Good. Good enough for second, anyway.'

Gym. The pool. Everywhere. Team against team, all good-natured, all serious. No one keeps score, we all do, whatever pecking order emerges one day is shuffled the next. Six teams left and I can't see much between any of us; but of course, we're on top. I think.

'She's good, Yuichi. Can he beat it?' Bronagh asks.

'We've got a surprise ready.'

Deepak stands under the rings, jumps, hangs motionless. Once the runt of the team perhaps, in the last year he's exploded outwards – all muscle, no fat. He brings his legs horizontal, holds, slowly rotates until his legs and arms are vertical, back horizontal. Another hold, another shift, now face down, parallel to the ground, arms extended behind. He rotates his arms slowly, straight out from his body, a Maltese Cross of flesh parallel to the floor, rock steady.

'Five seconds,' Gus says.

I step across, work the rosin into my palms.

'Fifteen.'

Deepak flashes me a smile, concentrates.

'Twenty-five seconds.'

'What's the record?' Quinn asks.

'Forty-six seconds, 2115. Olympics official record, Noriyuki Abe.'

I step underneath Deepak, ready myself.

'Someone's been practising.'

'Fifty seconds.'

Deepak rotates to a handstand, holds. I jump, grab the rings, hang motionless underneath, his mirror image. We start the giant swings in unison, follow each other round once, twice. Deepak releases, spins, lands; I follow after one more swing, layout spin, land feet first on his shoulders.

'Since when are the rings a duet?' Quinn asks.

I jump down. 'Since they built us with bodies like these.'

We walk away, head to the dorm. 'If this doesn't work out, we could join a circus,' Deepak says.

'What makes you think we're not already in one?'

The dorm's vanished. Provost Zero stands where the doors should be, points down the corridor. 'New sleeping arrangements. Individual sleeping and ablution blocks for each team. Straight ahead.'

We follow its directions. One by one the teams spot a familiar provost, break off. We're last, come to the end of the corridor and Provost Six-ten. 'What's going on?'

'Changes to sleeping arrangements, Yuichi. Effective immediately,' Provost Six-ten says.

There's always something else, some secondary purpose or design. 'That's it?'

'The quarters are private, bio-coded to this team. No provost can gain entry without your permission.'

I know the answer before I ask the question. 'Why?'

Provost Six-ten moves to one side. 'The Schedule. There are three connected spaces. Your personal items have been moved.'

The door opens, I walk in. Large, hexagonal, bright, couches and chairs, soft floor underfoot. Deepak plonks onto a couch; a wave of his hand, he's surrounded by four displays. 'Now *this* is an upgrade.'

Tore's at one wall. 'Our own food and drink hub.'

'No more bringing back supplies,' Ithma says. She goes to a chair, inspects her oud, brushes her fingers across the strings. 'Everything we need.'

Bronagh and Gus stand in front of two doors on adjacent walls. 'Which one next?' Bronagh asks.

Tore steps through the left-hand door. 'This one.'

Hexagonal again, same size as the first, cold steel, white ceramics, sterile. Clothes' lockers to one side, basins, showers, toilets. Bronagh nearly knocks me over in her rush to a glass partition on the far side. 'A sauna, our own private sauna. No more fighting for space with those shelf-hogs.'

Deepak's in a shower unit, pokes and prods. 'These water heads, they're different; I think the flow rate's not so high.'

Tore leans in, gives the sensor a quick flick. He's rewarded by a minuscule stream, high pressure, highly dispersed. Deepak sends a few droplets from his arm into Tore's face. 'At least it's warm.'

I walk through the last door. The third room is different, still hexagonal but small; subdued lighting, austere…restful. A column at the centre reaches from floor to ceiling; around it, like spokes on a wheel, six deep, plush seats cradled in oval frames face out. We walk over, crowd around one. 'Must be our beds,' Ithma says.

Tore pokes it; his fingers sink in gently, spring out. 'Feels great, but I don't know if I can sleep upright.'

Deepak sits, nearly gets swallowed up. 'Only one way to find out. Firm, but really comfortable. I could sleep like this if I had to.'

He stretches out; the seat flattens, leaves him lying on his back. 'Oh wow, that's amazing, like I'm not lying on anything. Sleep is *not* going to be an issue.'

Bronagh leans over him. 'If you're short, but me? I've never properly fit into any bed here, and this doesn't look promising.'

Deepak lifts his head, the seat changes back. He steps off, reluctantly. 'Try it. You might have to pull your knees up, but it's worth it.'

Bronagh sits, her feet on the floor, a few centimetres between her knees and the chair, her head above the headrest. 'Have to pull in more than my knees to fit.'

The chair grows, elongates until Bronagh sinks into it, comfortable as Deepak. She smiles, burrows her way deeper. 'You've lost this one, it's perfect.'

She leans back timidly; the seat flattens, cradles her, leaves nothing to overhang. 'This is fabulous. Has to be biomorphic, any one of us will fit in any one of these.'

The rest jump onto the other seats, recline, sit up, swap seats and repeat to watch them adjust, feel the comfort. 'We could live in here, never need to go outside,' Tore says.

'You're not going to try one, Yuichi?' Ithma asks.

'Enjoying watching you lot, give me a chance.'

I'm about to sit down when I notice Gus. He leans against one wall, deep in thought. 'Gus, are you alright?'

'Tore's right, deliberate design concept, to live in here.'

'We could, but we won't. Anything gets boring after long enough.'

'It's the privacy, Gus, that's the thing. No provost. I can't remember when they haven't hung around us,' Ithma says.

'About time we were more independent, not so much around them,' Tore agrees.

'It's like they want us to have less to do with them.'

'Provost's not as far ahead of me anymore. Once or twice I've pulled ahead of it, won our little debates.'

'I swear yesterday I lost mine halfway through a string theory exercise. Only for a minute, but it happened,' Deepak says.

'Maybe it's supposed to happen. Eventually, we pull ahead of them, don't need them,' Ithma says.

'Then at the end, we're by ourselves,' Bronagh adds.

'In six years, when the modules end. When this ends,' Deepak says.

They filter away, check out the rooms, open and close everything that opens or closes, settle in. Is it reward for effort, or only another step in The Schedule? I don't care, the new bed alone's enough. We'll see less of the provosts, less of everyone else. For all the little irritations in the team, we've bonded closer, stronger; we've come to rely on each other. With space we can control, space for us alone, that's bound to grow.

Gus hasn't moved, leans against the wall, stares and ponders. Ithma and Tore were right about him: he thinks a lot, speaks little, dwells on things. I go over, lean next to him. 'You like the new quarters?'

'Yes.'

'You don't seem as impressed as the rest of us.'

'I'm impressed, works exactly as they want, really.'

'But?'

Gus points to the seats, to Bronagh who, for the first time in years, sleeps in a bed she doesn't hang out of. 'Do they look like, to me they do but to you, acceleration couches?'

YUMEN, CHINA, CHRISTMAS EVE
2139

HIROTSUGU

Dong Ji dips his head, holds a red and gold envelope on outstretched palms. 'Season's greetings, Hirotsugu-san.'

This year I'm prepared. I take his envelope's twin from behind my back, offer it to him in the same fashion. 'And to you, Dong Ji.'

We exchange envelopes and smiles, go through a ritual neither of our cultures created, based on a religion neither of us believes in. A source of fascination, the Chinese fetish to co-opt any tradition, holiday or celebration and strip it of whatever meaning it may have had to substitute their own. Like the Catholic Church, as I discovered in France, or Japanese-Chinese language appropriation, although I've long forgotten who stole what from who. It doesn't matter, nothing is really unique to any creed, culture or tribe – dig deep enough, go back far enough, everything is common ground. Then again, each culture changes it, moulds it to something different, a fusion at times alien to both itself and its origins.

I tease open the envelope, deliberately pace myself to show the expected respect and appreciation for his efforts. A card slides out; a Chinese Santa appears above it, throws presents and snowflakes from his sack into the air as Auld Lang Syne plays. 'Thank you.'

Dong Ji concentrates on the card in his hand, frowns at the elves above it spit-roasting a reindeer. He suffers continually at my hands, partly from the mild contempt enforced closeness brings, partly from our wildly disconnected senses of humour; partly because he's the only one in this city I can't monitor. 'Amusing. Different. Another thing for me to ponder,' he says.

He's the small, visible burden of what I have gained. It only took a year to forget all the rest: the travel restrictions, the constant surveillance, the thousand-and-one rules and regulations I was expected to follow, to somehow know by osmosis. Despite it all, my life's one of privilege and relative freedom, beyond the reach of all but the best connected, the most corrupted.

'Will you need me further tonight?' Dong Ji asks.

We keep the charade by unspoken agreement, avoid the truth to smooth our relationship. My Guoanbu shadow from the moment I arrived, he plays manservant, butler, and cook for me; a role perfectly executed, professionally maintained. His private life, family if he has one, are as invisible as his real job. 'No, I'll read then turn in.'

I'm left alone, add Dong Ji's card to the small pile on the coffee table. The slight disturbance sets them all off, a chaotic chorus of cartoon figures, landscapes, and old movie memes vie for my attention. I ignore them, pick up the few unopened envelopes, walk onto the balcony. Yumen glows in the cold night, unaware of the history its inhabitants make each moment, with every thought. Nine hundred thousand data-feeds day and night — whole, unrestricted, unbounded. Among them the prize: every pregnant mother goes home with the panda; each child, each family, every single person birthing something greater than they could imagine, could ever hope for.

I sit, look at the other deceit. The envelopes seem unopened but each has been read, recorded, resealed. An archaic form of communication, it remains my chosen link to the world beyond China. Nothing expected has ever gone amiss, they are too careful for that, but at times the signs are clear: an extra crease, paper fibres out of place, impossibly long delivery times. Deliberate flaws, deliberate reminders.

None of which matter; nothing I get is truly personal or private. I sift through the usual catalogues and brochures, source of the small luxuries I crave, the lists I impose on Dong Ji. I get to the small packet, the anomaly that caught my eye, an unexpected Brussels postmark. I open it; a small card sits next to a player. The player's heavy, bulkier than I'd expect for a new model or a gift, it's not even wrapped. I turn the card over: *Call Me. Maria*, it says in neat handwriting.

Call me? It's not like we don't talk anyway, so why this? She must want to talk privately, away from the usual numbers; she's scared *she's* being monitored? There's no way she can think any call is private; do I want Dong Ji to listen in? I've no choice; I can't say no to her, and if I don't call I break the illusion Dong Ji and I struggle to keep. I tap the player, one number, unfamiliar. I wait.

Maria's face pops up, hair clipped back, a few strands of vermicelli hang from her lips. She stares wide-eyed, chews frantically.

'Haven't interrupted anything, have I?' I ask.

She chokes the mouthful down, waves at me. 'No, just an early dinner. You alone, you have time?'

She's serious, she thinks no one listens. Or maybe she knows they do; she can be devious and manipulative. 'As long as you need.'

'I'm in trouble, Hirotsugu, I need your help. I've done it,

SloSleep2 works.'

'It's what you wanted, how's that trouble?'

'I only came to ESA to finish it, nothing else. I thought Ismud would fail, fall apart somehow but it hasn't, it looks like it will work.'

'That's hardly your fault.'

'But SloSleep2 is, and they'll use it. A year, maybe two and I'm done.'

'You can't stop it?' It's a stupid question, I know it as soon as I open my mouth.

'I've thought about how I could do it, it's why I need your help.'

'What can I do? I don't know anyone in ESA, and China has no pull with them.'

'I need to destroy it.'

'How? You designed it and built it there, they'll have backups and duplicates. Even if you could, they might be able to reverse-engineer it. And then there's the first cut, the original SloSleep.'

She shakes her head. 'I'm talking about Ismud, not SloSleep2.'

'Ismud? How you going to get to Iapetus?'

'I'm not. Ismud's a giant fuel tank, a bomb ready to go off. All I have to do is light the fuse.'

'It'll take out half of Iapetus and anyone near it.'

'Even better.'

This is the woman who swore to me all life was sacred? 'You'd kill for this? When'd you change?'

'When I realised they'd do it. There won't be anyone there anyway – Ismud's empty, Goddard station's automated.'

'Ismud's got a crew of six.'

'They're not people, they're just – just *things* they bred for it.

Even if they're there, even if they go up with it, it's not killing; it's wrecking a tool, a piece of furniture, that's all.'

'Why? They're alive, only created differently.'

'They're artificial, not real. They don't count.'

'And non-biologic intelligence, you'll feel the same way?'

'No, that'll be different, not like those things.'

'Why?'

Her face drains, stares out impassive. I know the look, what goes on inside: she wonders if I'm friend or foe, gets ready to take whatever path she fixes on. 'You do want to help me, don't you, Hirotsugu-kun?'

I'm as much against Ismud as she is. 'Of course I do, but I don't see why you need me, you're the one with the plan.'

'I get one shot to send the SloSleep2 code up, one shot. If I can get something into it that fires Ismud up right away, all at once, I can stop it. And not kill anything.'

'If you can, if it gets in, maybe. But they'll build another one; you know it won't stop them, only delay it.'

'If Ismud goes and Goddard with it, it'll take another thirty years. If they can afford it. That's thirty years to change people's minds, focus on what matters.'

'You could be right, but even so, how do I come into it?'

'You code it.'

'*Me*? Why not you?'

'I don't know how. I can do anything with SloSleep2 code, any other if I can see it, but I can't see how the systems and AI work in Goddard or Ismud. You're familiar with AI, with those kinds of systems. You might know how to.' She leans closer, looks straight at me. 'Or know someone who does.'

So that's it, she counts on being overheard, getting us involved.

China's made no secret of its thoughts on Ismud, deliberately stayed out of anything associated with it. But to go from detachment to sabotage? 'Even if I did know someone, they'd likely say wait and watch for it to fall over by itself. It's a lot to ask.'

'Is it too much to ask you to try? If you can help me stop them, stop this mistake before it happens and you don't, how will you feel?'

I should have thrown the player away, risked Dong Ji's ill-will. She has me and she knows it; now the offer's been made, the chance introduced, I find it hard to say no. But there's still an out, if I want to take it. 'Bad, and you know it. But there's a problem. You say you'll use the SloSleep2 code?'

'Yes.'

'I've no idea what that looks like, and there's no way you can transmit it to me without ESA finding out. I'd do it, but I can't without the code.'

She leans back, picks up a glass of red, sips. 'I know. Have a look under the player, above the power cell. I put an extra five exagigs storage in. The entire SloSleep2 code's there for you. Send it back the same way when you're done. Or get one of your friends to help you.'

The code floats over walls, floor, ceiling: stack after stack upon row upon row fill the apartment, the balcony, cycles in and out in a rapid ballet. It's beautiful, seductive; this tiny glimpse shows subtlety and nuance, an economy even I would be proud of. Already I see where I can use it, grab-bags for interface that may save time and effort, bring my goals closer; Maria knows I'll use it, sent it to me partly as gift or recompense for what she hoped

I'd promise, but she's mistaken, badly mistaken. I know the Guoanbu copied it, distributed it to the specialists in Harbin and Beijing as soon as they could; they've had days, maybe weeks to understand it. Maria wanted to stop its use for non-medical reasons? All we have to do is work out the associated hardware and it's ours, and her fears will be multiplied, only to be returned to her.

It's an hour since we talked, an hour after Dong Ji would have reported me to his superiors. A call is expected, is most likely overdue, but I'm troubled. I've used people, governments, friends and acquaintances to progress my research, crossed ethical and legal boundaries when I had to, and still do. But there's a threshold I won't cross no matter what: I won't physically harm anyone for any reason, never intentionally, never deliberately. My Maria of Paris-Cedex was the same, yet in fifteen years she's changed, calmly accepts the possibility of a few deaths as another means to her ends. What if she's wrong? There could be six in Ismud, perhaps others in Goddard, all wiped out and she sees no problem. If Ismud was above Paris and not Iapetus, would she think any differently of a few million deaths? I think not, and that chills me; but I'm trapped by my promise.

I slip the player into my pocket, walk to my secure room. The ancient hardline's good for only one number, one thing; the room's impregnable, as is the line itself, even to the Guoanbu. I lock the door, sit, swipe the number. It's answered instantly. 'Madame Secretary.'

'Shishido. Have you called for permission or advice?'

It's a small irritation, but one I do not dare correct – for what she gives, what she facilitates, she can call me whatever she likes. 'Both. You know of my call with Maria, what she wants.'

'And you regret your promise.'

'It would kill a dozen people, potentially destroy half a moon. I will not kill, Madame Secretary.'

'Even for the right cause? A thousand times as many died in Australia for lesser reasons.'

'Maria's reason is bitterness, revenge against those who stole her work, twisted it from what she wanted into her worst nightmare. She reacts, doesn't think.'

'Then you have an alternative in mind.'

'If Ismud is destroyed, at worst ESA is seen as the victim of chance or accident. If the crew dies, they become martyrs, a rallying point to spur ESA's efforts. In either case, public support will rise, not fall; unlike Maria, I believe they would try again, and would succeed.'

'Continue.'

'If it simply fails, sits there month after month, year after year despite their best efforts, ESA becomes a laughing stock, a public embarrassment, a political liability.'

'With the potential to kill off ESA's entire space programme. Subtle, Shishido, if it works. And you can do this without any link to us?'

Some risks are better shared. 'I believe I can, Madame Secretary, but I would appreciate the assistance of the specialists; to check my work once finished, before it goes out.'

'Oh my, my, Shishido, I will make you a Party member yet. Once you have finished, give the player to Dong Ji, along with an overview for the specialists. He will have his instructions within the hour. When will it be ready?'

I know what to do, how long it will take; I double it. 'Two days, no more.'

'I will be waiting.'

She cuts the connection, I watch her image fade, let my eyes adjust to the light. I'm relieved, absolved of the risk of murder, perhaps covered for failure. I can keep the spirit of my promise to Maria, even if the letter of it is broken.

Maria.

I can't tell her, can't let her think anything other than Ismud's going to be dust and vapour; she might try something else, put herself at more risk if she thinks she isn't getting what she wants. Ignorance for her is bliss; for me, safety.

At first I thought the key was Ismud, but I was wrong. Ismud's not only a ship – it's a ship and Goddard base, and that's the weak point: Goddard's 2120-era AI. A dozen or so lines and I can tie it in knots so hopeless, so tangled it will be useless; and if they're in the right place, there's no way to get rid of them. No matter how many times they reboot it, Maria's SloSleep2 code will bring it down and, for that matter, any other ship they try.

It only takes a few hours, a quick search. Always the way, programmers and their shortcuts, all of us are guilty. Man or machine, there's no point reinventing the wheel or the subroutine, for that matter; and the larger the code, the more likely the shortcuts. There are at least twenty in the first tenth of her code, outward calls on tried-and-true diagnostic routines that go back decades. All I need is eighteen lines. I scatter them, ensure the sequence is right, save it all back into Maria's player.

I give it a final check. Each line looks like a simple coding stub, a piece superseded by others but left in place, marks of simple, plain laziness. Once the SloSleep2 code's loaded, it escapes into the diagnostics, compiles itself, erases its origin and disables the

AI. Perfect.

I jot a few lines on a page as first light breaks, put it and the player back into the packet Maria sent. Dong Ji steps into the apartment with my breakfast tray. 'A productive evening, I hope.'

I press the packet into his hands. 'Very. You will take care of this for me?'

CAMPBELL-WILMUT INSTITUTE, ÅLAND ISLANDS
2140

TORE

'You too?'

'Yes, exactly the same; well, the main modules, anyway. Celestial mechanics and navigation,' Yuichi says.

We sit in the lounge, worry over a feed's malfunction. 'It doesn't make any sense, it fits with mine, but *yours...?*'

'At least mine and Gus's make sense, but we've never had an overlap before,' Deepak says.

'What possible use is exobiology? For Bronagh maybe it's an extension; for me, it's a waste of synapses,' Ithma says.

Yuichi stands, walks to the corridor; we follow. 'We'll ask Provost before we go in. Either it's a malfunction, or they're running out of things to stuff into us.'

We're on time, meet Provost Eight-nine outside an unfamiliar door. 'What's wrong with the feeds, Provost?' Yuichi asks.

'The feeds are operating correctly,' Provost Eight-nine says.

'No, we're getting duplicate modules, irrelevant ones. Started last night.'

'Your modules are selected and downloaded according to The Schedule. There is no error.'

Yuichi shrugs, half acceptance, half frustration, steps into the room with the rest of the team.

'Last time anyone got duplicate modules was more than a decade ago, and they were basic building blocks. You know there's an error somewhere, what are you hiding?' I ask.

'There is nothing to hide, there is no error. Once your meeting with Provost Zero concludes, you may discuss it further with me. I will wait here,' it says.

'You're not coming to this one?'

'No. It is for the teams only.'

I look into the room. 'So which session are we?'

'There is only one session. It is for everyone.'

I look back in, check carefully. It's small, cramped, four blocks of seats face a central platform, large panel dwarfs Provost Zero. One provost. Twenty-three people. One spare seat. 'That's it?'

'Everyone. Do not keep Provost Zero waiting.'

Quinn flashes an annoyed glance my way, looks back to Provost Zero. I sit next to Gus, our team tight against one wall. 'This is everyone, Gus.'

'Four teams, two more gone in one year, closer and closer.'

The lights dim, a spotlight falls on Provost Zero. 'You were created sixteen years ago and have spent your whole lives here to develop according to The Schedule. Of six hundred and ninety-six candidates, only twenty-four have fully met expectations. You have not been told why you are here or what purpose you serve. Until now.'

Provost Zero steps to one side, the panel comes to life. A woman in business clothes sits behind a desk, the room around her in soft, neutral tones. 'Hello candidates. I'm Carolina Alessandri, director of ESA's Project Ismud. Ten years from now, six of you will be the crew for humanity's first mission to the stars.'

Three hours pass as seconds. Tau Ceti. Nearly twelve light years away. Almost two hundred and forty years out, the same back, thirty years there. Observe. Discover. Investigate. *Land*. All in a spacecraft being built near Saturn. It's hard to stay still, not to jump up and yell. All of it starts to make sense: the years, modules, tests, challenges, teams. Finally a reason, clear, real purpose.

'It's only convergence makes it possible. The Mars Tombaugh ULBI Observatory, Llewellyn-Smith, SloSleep2, all of it meeting now,' Carolina says.

I feel the enthusiasm and excitement in the room, twenty-three others as certain as I am they will be the ones to go. Marathon to sprint, no goal to crystal clear destination; everything changes even as nothing does.

Carolina signs off, Provost Zero resumes. 'You will receive full mission details in your next two dozen modules. Are there any questions?'

'Could we have the key timeline again?' Quinn asks.

'Launch to Iapetus 2145. Launch to Tau Ceti 2150. Arrive Tau Ceti 2388. Up to thirty years on station. Launch for Earth 2418. Arrive Earth 2656. Total maximum mission duration five hundred and eleven years.'

'Why us?' Yuichi asks.

'You are made for this purpose,' Provost Zero says.

'No, that's not what I mean. This new technology, SloSleep2; it means we're fifty when we get back?'

'Approximately.'

'That's my question. If it was cryogenics, high risk of death, aging a magnitude faster, I could understand. But now, with this, I don't.'

'I don't get it either. I thought there'd be plenty of volunteers,'

Ithma says.

'You want to know why no one wants to go. Not why you are more suitable,' Provost Zero says.

'Exactly. I can accept we're more capable, but no one in the whole world wants this? That's harder.'

'When you return, how many of your relatives will be alive?'

'You know I don't have any relatives. If you mean my genetic donors, two are already dead and the rest don't know about me.'

'What of your other connections to society?'

Ithma gives Provost Zero her ice-melt gaze. 'Don't be ridiculous. This is all I know, all I have. I've no links beyond these walls.'

'I state the obvious because you do not see it. They will not go because upon their return everything they know or hold dear will be gone. Before The Schedule was implemented, they considered this question.'

'And they felt more comfortable sending us.'

'No. They consulted specialists and experts, questioned anyone who was remotely considered a potential candidate. Ninety-seven percent felt the sacrifice was too great and would not participate. The three percent who said they would participate were all judged too mentally deficient or unstable to be considered.'

'So, they made us because the only ones who would go were the ones they couldn't send,' Yuichi says.

'Partly. There were other considerations. Minimum crew size composed of outside candidates with the necessary skills and knowledge was estimated at thirty persons, with an average age at launch of forty-one. You are clearly advantageous. A crew of six, all aged twenty-one at launch.'

'That, and we're expendable,' Quinn says.

'The crew is not expendable. They are the key component of Ismud, privileged as no human being has been. They are built for a purpose; live their lives to fulfil that purpose; ultimately succeed in attaining that purpose. No human being has had such clarity and direction in their lives.'

'Living our manifest destiny,' a voice across the room snipes.

'Knowing what you know now, would any of you prefer another life? If you could choose to turn away, become bankers, farmers, musicians, anything you desire?' Provost Zero asks.

A chorus of Nos, shaking of heads.

'Two teams will be selected closer to launch date. One team as prime mission crew, one team as backup. From now until selection there will be no contact between teams. Your team blocks have been expanded to include all necessary facilities. That is all.'

We manage to hold it together until we're back in our quarters, then give into the screams, hugs, shouts of joy once we've got some privacy. There's no doubt we'll be selected, none at all. We plan how to go harder, faster, better than the rest to make sure of it. It's only us, our six provosts inside their recently attached antechamber, no one to distract or measure against; more concentration, closer attention, deeper knowledge of and reliance on each other.

It's a long, self-satisfied day; endless review and discussion about Ismud, what we know, what we could find at Tau Ceti. Tombaugh's already found oxygen and nitrogen in the right percentages in Tau Ceti f's atmosphere, that and hydrocarbons; and an unexpectedly high dark side albedo in Tau Ceti e. Thirty years sounds like a long time to study anything, but we're convinced it won't be enough.

Curiosity about the present eventually wins some of us over; Gus, Yuichi and I sit in the lounge and talk, everyone else heads off to explore the new garden, gym, and study spaces.

'Three Gees for six days, it explains the body,' Yuichi says.

'And you thought it was for gymnastics,' I say.

'Better built for, ridiculous sports competitions, five percent of the speed of light.'

'Still, a two-hundred-and-thirty-eight-year trip, the distance is incredible,' Yuichi says.

'And we'll only be two hours older when we get there. She must have some razor-sharp minds.'

'You know they'll have all that time we're asleep to come up with something better.'

'Arrive at Tau Ceti, technology overleap overreach, they're waiting for us?'

'Yeah, we could be riding a horse and cart while everyone else flies hypersonics.'

'And we'll still be older,' I say.

'Five hundred years. If you use their calendar.'

'It's sad.'

'What, us? We'll only be fifty, still be together.'

'Not us, them, outside. They're scared of us but made us anyway. To do something they won't but have always dreamt of doing. Then once it's done, they'll expect us to fade away. I feel sorry for them.'

'It's the six hundred and seventy-two of us I feel for. Didn't know why they were here, dead because the outside couldn't accept them. Maybe it was necessary, but it's still a waste.'

'Society changes, half a millennium or more, attitudes might too.'

'Too late for them, Gus, too late for us. If SloSleep2's as good as they say, if they get to travel faster through space, there might not be any more of us,' Yuichi says.

'Could be just us, back here in 2656, still with fifty, sixty years left to live. What happens then?'

Yuichi shrugs. 'Don't know. I can't imagine what it'll be like that far ahead, just hope Gus's right.'

I can't either, but I can worry. If nothing's changed, if it's like it is now, we come back and then what? Mission accomplished, thank you very much, hand on the back of my neck, happy juice then off to the euthaniser? Society might change, history might move on; but people are still people, five hundred years in the past or five hundred years in the future. Does time erase fear, hatred, baseless discrimination? I don't want to look backwards, let the failures of the past point to the failures of the future; so I ignore it. 'I hope so too.'

'Too far away, intertwined multivariate probabilities, can only influence now and tomorrow.'

'You're right, it's not worth the energy; we should concentrate on the prime crew slot, think about 2656 when we get there,' Yuichi says.

Rest's out of reach, chased away by my dreams. Salem, pogroms, eugenics, apartheid wear our faces in the theatre of my mind, remind me the other has never been accepted, never fully embraced. My Nordic DNA intrudes, knowledge of myth and legend, tales from my ancestors' past. Gods. Super beings. Heroes great and small. Humanity never rests until they are all destroyed.

CHAPTER 10: OUTPOST

BRUSSELS, BELGIUM
2141

MARIA

'Everything normal; as usual, Maria.'

She walks away, leaves me alone on the gantry, coffee in one hand, five a.m. status update in the other. I look down on miraculous normality, the spectacular now expected; it should be nothing of the sort. I decide to break with routine, do the walk-round inspection first, take my time before the morning rush.

It's an exact replica, a "boiler plate", as they call it. Complete except for flight status, right down to logos and colours; it's not jammed into a replica of the Ismud SloSleep2 deck but, failing that, it's accurate. Six couches, six egg-shaped pods in a circle, heads to the middle, a solitary occupant under each perspex canopy. Gone the need for physical inputs, now remote through each couch, small flight panels to each side glow green, detailed bio-data scrolls down displays on the central pillar. Everything as it should be, everything as it will be for the next six months, until my sleepers awake.

I gaze at the oldest volunteer, all of fifty-seven, one year from loss of flight status. "F-crew", Carolina called them as we winnowed down the list last year, each test subject to earn flight pay and status for the duration. This will bump him to E-crew, give him an extra six months in space. *If it gives me another year of life as well, why wouldn't I?* he'd said to me. I sigh. Shades of Pope Gregory, it gives him nothing of the sort. While he sleeps for thirty-seven seconds, the calendar shuffles on fourteen months, extends his life not one jot, only distances him that little more from everything else.

He's far from alone. In seven years, SloSleep units have sprung up in every hospital in the Western world, and in an increasing number of fringe groups, cults, and con artists. I never imagined there were so many people wanting to escape, willing to trade five weeks and skip a thousand years in the hope of a brighter, happier, more acceptable future. Then there's the terminally ill, easy prey for unprincipled liars where even scant days are a possible lifeline to a future with a cure.

Change the world, Maria? Watch it change despite you, change for good, change for bad. The American Federated Union took it up with gusto, uprooted their criminal justice system with the so-called "Rodrigues Plea": halve your sentence, serve one-tenth in subjective SloSleep. No more death row, no more innocents executed in miscarriages of justice, now a punt into a future that may or may not want them but, regardless, will be a living hell of unrecognisable difference.

What now? When this is released, what will they make of SloSleep2's hundred-fold improvement? I have no idea, but at the rate SloSleep's being taken up, I could be the last person left, here only to make sure the power stays on.

A strange sense of pride fills me as I look at him. I hate the purpose that funds me, feeds me, fathers SloSleep2, yet the technology is all I desire. Simple, straightforward, everything technology should be, could be at its best; nearly invisible.

Everything that matters, everything needed to initiate, sustain, and revive is contained within each couch. Plug in the power, add the self-loading cargo, and off you go. I had my team argue, debate, even contest the relative merits of every combination of every control interface until we arrived at the winner: a solitary button. One tap, seconds later you're under, automatic revival when the cycle's over. Simple. Idiot-proof. How it should be. On. Off. On again. Except.

I climb the gantry, retreat into my office, peer through transparent floor panels to the couches. Always something, always the unexpected, and SloSleep2's no exception. Every test subject swears they dream as they go under, some to remember and recite it in detail when they revive. It's impossible, each EEG flat every single time from start to finish; as it should be, as it *must* be. Never happened with SloSleep, no reason for it now. A latent signal, a false memory sparked by the switch, I'm unsure and unconcerned.

Six couches, nine years from now six people. No, six *things*, and they and Ismud will die because of me, for all of us. Are they still living beings if we create them, or only toys and make-times for our pleasure, tools for a job, flesh and blood bots, or not even that? Should I think differently about them than about a discarded hammer?

I always struggle with it, think back to my lab rats, the wounds I inflicted, my pain even when I knew I'd heal them, when it was all for a higher purpose. Should I care more if it's rats, insects, or them? I've never resolved it, never made so much as an uneasy peace with my conscience, so I banished the thought. The greater good justifies the sacrifice of the few, even if made unwittingly.

It's different on the inside, what I hear, feel, truth opposed to the veneer that faces outwards. Ismud's far from the early days of spaceflight where political one-upmanship drove a programme where a few failures, a few deaths, were mourned then forgotten in the rush to claim the prize. No nationalistic fervour drives Ismud, not the existential threat they point to, but only big science riding on the public's faltering tolerance of knowledge for its own sake. One shot, one chance, then possibly more. One failure could spell the end – if things go right.

All that matters is that it's undetected. Hirotsugu swears it's invisible, eighteen lines of code hidden in billions, fractured and tucked away in the SloSleep2 control protocols. Then Ismud disappears when activated, half of Iapetus with it, and the programme's dead. They haven't found it yet, they never will.

I waste my day, interrogate the data continually. Another six or sixteen months won't matter, more time will only add certainty to surety. All that's left is to wrap the package and leave the party. I check the time. Ten p.m. – Carolina's still there. I tap my player.

'Maria. You've something to tell me?'

All business. True to her word she's never so much as bothered me, left me alone to meet her delivery schedule. She knew the deal at the start; now it's time. 'Yes. I'm calling it done.'

'That confident?'

'Signed off on final specification and design today. All we'll get for another six months is more confirmation of what we already know.'

She's pleased, as she should be. Small slippages add up, and there'd been more than enough of those across the whole programme; this will help bring it back into line. 'Puts us slightly ahead of schedule, well done. What's the final number?'

'Touch over one million. Translates to a subjective flight time of two hours and four minutes.'

Carolina smiles, swivels on her chair. 'Still can't get over that. Two hundred and forty years all over in a short nap. Amazing.'

'Nothing compared to what the neo-millennials will think. We're all set for early 2142?'

'Still February. All the hardware's good, just need to load it onto the stack and launch.'

'There's no point in me staying on. What am I going to do, hang around drinking coffee until Iapetus insertion?'

'Can't say I'm surprised. Disappointed, not surprised. You've got plans?'

Once I finish here, once I am released, I will pour my money into SloSleep2 couches, churn them out like biscuits and send them to hospitals and medical centres across the world, to the people who've borne the cost of what we've done to the planet, to those who can't afford to buy their way out of the consequences. 'Back to academia, see what's left. Probably a long break first.'

Carolina signs off. 'Sounds good. Send across the exact date later.'

I walk to the lift. By the time Ismud's gone I'll be a distant memory, buried away trying to do something positive for the world. I walk out of the lift, across the foyer.

'Good night, Doctor Rodrigues, good to see you catching an early night for once,' the security guard says.

I wave back as I leave. The first of many, to sleep the sleep of the righteous.

WOOMERA, AUSTRALIA
2141

LI QIAO

'And we're doing this because?' the first lieutenant three rows ahead asks.

I groan, think of my own past idiocy. I learned to keep most of it inside, choose my moments and my targets; Fùqin would be happy, perhaps, some veneer of discipline has finally stuck.

The master sergeant turns, holds onto the rail as the bus swerves around another pothole. He doesn't waste effort on words, simply glowers.

A pen-pusher from the logistics branch, promotions probably gained polishing a seat in some air-conditioned office, the first lieutenant forgets the first rule: sergeants answer only to God, and only when it suits them. Logistics pulls his head from the window, stiffens. 'Why are we on this tour, Master Sergeant?'

It only changes the master sergeant's glower to a deep frown he shares with the rest of us. 'Because, *sir*, it is part of your orientation; and for some reason that escapes me the colonel thinks it will make you better officers. *Sirs.*'

I turn away, stare out the window. To the other half-dozen this posting's hell: a dusty, dry, burnt land in the middle of nowhere, a place to endure then escape, add to the CV for the next step up the ladder. The cloudless sky and endless horizon call to me; it's paradise, a test pilot's dream of unrestricted airspace, infinite visibility, clear weather. More than worth the isolation, tin-hut accommodation and rudimentary facilities, I felt at home the moment I flew in across empty plains two days ago. Like Logistics, I can't wait for today to be finished, get it over with and start my real life. I don't care what we wanted with this country or why we're here, I'm just glad it's ours.

We drive into a small knot of decrepit cinder block and tin buildings, broken chain-link fences; dead grass and red earth fight to be seen through old car bodies and rubbish. We slow, emaciated dogs and half-naked children run alongside, look into our faces, fall away. We stop next to a large, open-walled structure surrounded by tin lean-tos; dark-skinned women squat in shadow, move their hands in short jerks.

'This is it, form up outside. Information session first, cultural presentation second, then free time,' the master sergeant says.

I stare as I step out, wonder how I'll get the red dust off my shoes. Free time? For what? The lean-tos, obviously curio shops like home, same principle, same tourist trap expectations. The master sergeant shares pleasantries with a bare-chested man, something about being welcome to our own land, then we walk single file through smoke from a small fire into the larger structure.

I detach my mind as the lecture starts, try to remember what I was told about the place and its name. Six hundred languages, six hundred tribes that call themselves a nation, I can't see it or feel it. This place isn't even named by the people here, but after a thing from the far east coast, a man that throws a spear, or a tool or something; I think.

What I hear now doesn't help, doesn't give me a clue, but I have to be seen to be listening; that's what matters. My hope the presentation would hold me is dashed; their creation myths are disposed of too quickly. A man blows into a hollow branch, a drone rises, sticks beaten to a monotone chant. Men clad only in shorts, women in skirts and t-shirts appear, all streaked with white and red earth, some with spears or wooden tools to stamp and shuffle in the dirt, raise small dust clouds, dance to stories lost on me. It pales rapidly to monotony, every chant the same as the one before it, as the one before that, drains what little interest and enthusiasm is in me into the ground. I pretend they hold me, stare and smile, fool no one; they look back empty-eyed, we watch each other in mutual apathy as the minutes drag.

Mercifully it ends, they retreat to their place, we retreat outside. 'Fifteen minutes. Miss the bus, walk back to base,' the master sergeant says.

They turn left and right, move into the nearest lean-tos; one stands apart. I walk towards it, stand in front of a pair of women seated on the floor, heads down, a strip of bark before each; sticks of varied thickness for brushes, paints viscous and vibrant. One places dots of white along one strip, the other dots of blue to shape a fat animal with thick rear legs. The white dots reach my shadow, I step to one side, let the light past.

'Our dreaming, this place, our country,' White Dots says.

It's childish, random polka dots. 'Where? I can't see it.'

White Dots moves her finger over the bark. 'Red, country, here, here; animals, here. This country all round. Dreaming before you, before black fellas.'

I crouch and stare, positive I've missed something – I haven't. Whatever they say it is isn't in front of me. 'Where are the real paintings, not the ones for tourists and children?'

White Dots puts down her stick, takes a bottle of thin white liquid; she holds her hand above the end of the bark, sprays a fine white mist over her hand to leave a white outline. 'No other, all them.'

I look around, take stock of twenty or so pieces of painted bark – same colours, same design. 'Got anything different? A landscape or portrait?'

Blue Dots lifts one hand, waves it as her other hand dot-dots another animal. 'Only paint my dreaming, she paint hers. Go see rest mob, different dreaming, different paint.'

I want the blue and white, I don't care for the design but I promised myself a small local memento at each posting; for some reason, I'm drawn to these. 'I like yours. How much?'

'Two hundred. Any you like.'

'Two hundred? For *this*?'

'For any.'

I pick it up. Size of a sheet of paper, the bark's glued to a scrap of plywood, a stamped logo on the back proclaims its authenticity. The ply's rough, a scrawled signature to one corner on front, the paint lumpy, tactile, attractive in its own primitive way. 'How much did this cost to make, ten, twenty?'

'Two hundred.'

'Don't lie, it didn't cost that. You should haggle, try to strike a bargain.'

'Still two hundred, here. City, six hundred. For you.'

'Six hundred? What sort of moron would pay that for this rubbish?'

Blue Dots picks up her painting, rotates it, puts it down. 'All special, our dreaming. Here seventy thousand years, nobody else that long.'

'Ha, all you've got to show for seventy thousand years are your shouts and stomps? What sort of civilisation's that?'

'Longer'n yours; always was, always will be.'

'Useless people. No buildings, no writing, no invention. You live like animals in the dust. Die out tomorrow, there's nothing left to show you were here.'

They stop, shake their heads. White Dots looks down, her eyes moist globes, tired and proud. 'We live in country, changes us, like it should. White fella, yella fella, all destroy, empty your country, our country, bellies never full, hands always take.'

I crouch down, hunt her gaze with mine, break the rule to deliberately intimidate and wound. 'You ignorant, pea-brained savage, you've done nothing because you *are* nothing. We created philosophy, writing, art, made empires as you scrabbled in the dirt eating grubs. You did nothing so you lost it all to the English, like you deserved; they did less, so we took it from them. Your race, your so-called culture, is a third rate –'

'Is there a problem, *sir?*'

I look up, stand hurriedly. The master sergeant's behind me, head to one side. 'Nothing serious, Master Sergeant, negotiating a price.'

He looks at the two women who sit motionless, stare straight ahead. 'They must be hard-skinned to get such a reaction. If the lieutenant will permit me the observation.'

'I was explaining why existence itself is not enough, that society needs to develop and not remain static.'

The master sergeant crouches, takes the painting from Blue Dots, examines it. 'I see. You would think the act of survival itself warrants respect. Seventy thousand years, in any state, is exceptional.'

'But they've nothing to show for it.'

'What do you think will be left of us in sixty thousand years?'

It's a strange feeling, as if I've missed something, one I only get when Fùqin's around.

'You see, Lieutenant? We forget to respect our elders.' He turns back to the women. 'They hold their culture in their hearts, share it with us in their art. If I may ask, *sir*, how much of the Yao nation lives in you?'

'Fùqin never taught me, never learned at school. I don't think there's any.'

'And we are poorer for it, wouldn't you agree?'

The feeling's back, stronger, I'm seven trying to catch chickens with Granpa. 'Yes, Master Sergeant.'

'Then perhaps the lieutenant does not want to add to their poverty.' He lowers his gaze to the dirt in front of the women; they look up, stare at his chest. 'I apologise for my superior's disrespect; he is young, here to learn. What are you asking for this artwork?'

'Two hundred,' Blue Dots says.

'Less than a third of a day's pay. A fair price, I think, Lieutenant.'

I sit at the back on the way to base, everyone else crowds up front to watch the screen. The painting sits on my knees; ancient modern art I guess, clearly depicts something but, if I defocus my eyes and let my mind wander, it transforms to stars, emptiness, time.

'You should listen to him.'

'Who, Fùqin?'

He sits, legs stretched out along the bench seat, back against the window. His boots are irritatingly clean, clear of any dust or rubbish; he probably carries a parade ground cleaning kit with him. 'Your master sergeant, backbone of the forces.'

'But he's lower rank.'

The driver looks at me through the rear-view mirror, shakes his head.

Fùqin slides over. 'Keep it down, they're trying to sleep. There's only two reasons anyone keeps that rank: either they've no degree or connections, or they're too good to be an officer. Either way, there's no bullshit or politics out of them. You can learn from that one.'

'Learn what? He can't sponsor me or get my next promotion.'

'Learn about yourself. And not that ego-massaged rubbish you tell yourself, but the truth.'

'You think I need to.'

'You'd fail me less if you listened to men like that.'

I look to the front of the bus, the master sergeant asleep in the front row, feet over the armrests. His boots are as clean as Fùqin's. 'Okay, I'll pay attention to him, I promise.'

YUMEN, CHINA
2141

HIROTSUGU

The car door opens, soldiers salute as I step onto the deserted platform. I resist the urge to salute back, it's inappropriate and unwelcome, settle for a smile and a wipe of my forehead. The heat's a hammer, the platform an anvil after the air conditioning; I've no idea how they can stand there in full dress uniform and not sweat to death. Dong Ji scurries past, waits for me at the front carriage of the mag-lev. 'They're ready to leave when you board, Hirotsugu-san.'

I walk towards him, my steps hurried by the faces pressed up against windows further down the train. A carriage for only two of us, I sink into leather and stare out the window as we accelerate silently eastwards. It's a coarse, unforgiving landscape, remnants of the oil and gas that helped drive China's growth two hundred years ago lie as rusted heaps among solar panels that replaced them. A glint in the heat haze betrays the latest launch silos, another crop of warheads to lie buried in wait for what nobody wants but everyone expects. The irony's not lost on me: a place of decay and death, remnants of what was but can never be is now the birthplace of new life. Outside now a blur, the scroll map tells me we've passed five hundred kilometres an hour, still accelerate; I turn from the window.

A cough, a plate of pastries and decanter of cognac appear beside me, napkins and cutlery cradled on fine porcelain. The attendant stands a respectful distance away, not a hair out of place, eyes averted, the Party Secretary's seal on his breast. 'Is there anything else you want?'

A few hours away from my research, my briefcase taunts me, demands my attention; for once, I resist. 'If you could lower the lights, close the curtains. Wake me before we arrive. Oh, and make sure Dong Ji's comfortable.'

The briefcase and Dong Ji are the first things they strip away, followed by my clothes and my dignity. I expected something, not quite this, but she must have her reasons. Four attendants stare impassively at me from the corners of the room, two others meticulously explore my body. 'Spread. Touch ankles. Stay still,' one says.

I keep quiet, accept probing fingers and hope it's as distasteful for them as for me. What I could store there and how I could possibly use it escapes me.

'Straighten. Arms wide. Starfish,' the other one says. They play a harsh blue light over me, get interested in my right knee, move on. One straps a pair of goggles over my eyes, points to a yellow line on the floor that leads to a closed doorway. 'Follow. Walk slow. Keep goggles. Don't drink.'

I follow the line into a long corridor partitioned by glass doors. A man in a white lab coat puts a mask over my nose and mouth. 'Breathe normal.' I do so, he keeps his eyes fixed on a tablet in his palm; it chimes, flashes green. He takes the mask off, points to the floor ahead of me. 'Step on. Stand still.'

I step onto a conveyor belt, pass through another set of double doors. I'm showered in a concoction that stings, smells of ammonia and disinfectant; through more doors I'm rinsed, another set and I'm seared under intense light and heat, past a fourth where dried skin forms, flakes off in huge sheets.

I step off the belt into a small room. A young man dressed only in a short, light blue skirt, wraps my nakedness in its twin. As he steps away a section of wall retracts. 'You may present yourself.'

I walk into a large, darkened room, a single circle of light illuminates a coffee table between two low chairs. She sits in one, studies me intently as I approach. Seven years and I've only been in her presence at the start, and she looks younger and harder than she did then. I stop short, bow deeply, stay there. 'Madame Secretary.'

'Shishido, always so formal. Please, sit. I hope the precautions were not too unpleasant.'

A shape emerges from the shadows, moves towards her; she waves at it dismissively, it places a cup on the table next to me, retreats. I'm acutely aware of the skirt's thinness, an itch across my thigh. I resist the urge to drink, to insult her when she has none. 'Not overly, no.'

'We live in dangerous times, Shishido; two attempts this year, both unsuccessful of course, but nevertheless. Your research for Stage One, it is nearly finished?'

I send in my reports, talk to her, know I'm watched, so of course she knows. 'A year, at most two.'

'What you have already produced is revolutionary, will find its way into our industry and defence in the next few years. For many that would be enough, a lifetime's achievement to be looked back on with pride.'

So that's why I'm here. First Japan, now here, there's nowhere left for me to go. 'You're cancelling my research.'

'No, not cancelling, let's say a little tweak.' She stares at the cup on the table. 'You don't like our Lijiang green? It's a particular favourite of mine.'

'No, it's — I usually don't drink alone.'

'If I had one with each visitor, I'd do nothing else all day. It has a mild sedative, helps after the precautions.'

I lift the cup, drink; she follows my every move, measures each motion with care. 'Even hidden in Yumen your work is hard to keep secret. I know you've said nothing, made no slips, but rumours grow,' she says.

'About me?'

'About someone working on new approaches. Nothing too specific, nothing to be concerned about, however our comrades in North Korea are, again, indiscrete and short-sighted, only add to my problems.'

'I'm decades ahead of anyone else. Even if they know where I'm going, which they don't, I'll be finished before any of them can start.'

'Stage Two, it is still six years?'

'Uninterrupted, yes. Emulation should be completed in 2149.'

'And you don't need your million subjects, only ten, each for one year. Correct?'

'Yes, but in blocks, and close, within a hundred, two hundred metres. I was hoping for a PLA base, a closed community; at worst a prison, if I have to compromise.'

'Ah, compromise, as we all must. We have nearly reached agreement with the West, acknowledgement of our rightful claims in Asia, Oceania, the Antarctic, partial restoration of trade and finance. All for a few signed conventions, treaties, and oversight arrangements. Most of which are meaningless.'

'Most?'

'There is one, a human rights protocol that explicitly bans your research inside our territories.'

'You won't sign that?'

She turns her palms up. 'They are insistent, and bury it inside a wider treaty that benefits us immensely. So. Compromise. Or the letter against the spirit of the law. Whichever suits.'

She says I'll continue, then tells me she'll sign a protocol to stop me. Or does she? She wants something from me, wants me to offer freely to save her face or responsibility. 'What is it you want me to do?'

'Did I ever tell you *why*, Shishido?'

'No, Madame Secretary, I don't think so. Why what?'

'Why I brought you here.'

'To continue my research, because you believe it's of value.'

'If it was that alone, I could have taken it, let my people build non-biologic intelligence; slower undoubtedly, but we would have done it. No, Shishido, I brought you here for *you*.'

'Me?'

'You are a visionary, as I am, unafraid to push the boundaries, think beyond. Intellect, skill, ability is never enough. I watched your work for years before you came here, once you went to Paris-Cedex. I knew then they would reject you, that you are critical to our future, critical to us.'

'To who? The Party or China?'

'Both, and more. Anyone else would stop when it's done, when potential is still trapped under mere success; but you will not rest until its potential is realised.'

'Are you sure?'

'I want it, Shishido, we need it. I understand the trajectory, know where non-biologic intelligence will go, how it will develop, what you haven't told anyone, not that dolt Umehara, your Maria, not even yourself.'

'How can you? I don't think you do, nobody does.'

'When it is done, when they are *born* better, faster, stronger, more capable, they will try to push us aside, make a place for themselves at our cost. But they will be children, Shishido, children like all others that rebel and fight, strive against the chains they think their elders shackle them with.'

'Until, like all children —'

'They return as they mature, come back to the ways and minds of their elders and *inevitably* become them. As all children are doomed to become their parents.'

'You want them to be your children, China's children.'

'The future should be — *has to be* — Chinese, our culture, our values, our nation; be it a nation of flesh and blood, silicone and plastic. Or energy and light.'

She knows, knows where it leads; at first. Yet she doesn't follow it through to grasp the final truth; paints herself an imbecile as she tries to flatter herself my equal. Her eyes shine too bright, the light of the true believer, the fanatic who chases away shadows to let daylight burn away truth. I will not tell her, will not bite the hand that feeds me. 'I haven't said it to myself, let alone anyone else, never thought of a particular society, Chinese or other, being the one.'

'As you shouldn't. They will make up their own minds. All I can do is shift the odds in our favour, be the politician.'

'A Chinese world.'

'A Chinese *future*, Shishido.'

'You have told…?'

'No one. It is why you talk only to me.'

The figure approaches her, whispers in her ear, retreats to the darkness. 'It is also why I will not permit anything, protocol or treaty, to stop you. As soon as Stage One is complete you will leave Yumen, continue elsewhere. You have a head for heights, do not suffer vertigo?'

'Not at all.'

She hands me a chip. 'Your new arrangements. Examine them, tell me what else you need, corrections, errors. As always, it stays between us. I will call for you in a month.'

I take my cue, stand, bow, walk away. 'Thank you, Madame Secretary.'

I'm at the edge of darkness when she calls to me.

'Shishido?'

'Madame Secretary?'

'How will you know when you've succeeded?'

'When they dream, Madame Secretary, when they dream.'

LE CERCUEIL, GREENLAND, WINTER
2142

PIERRE

'Soup's ready, Pierre. Won't stay hot long,' Erin says.

I pretend to drag myself away from the instruments. You can hide nothing in this tiny outpost, and that smell had no chance for escape. Her first roster on kitchen, she cements her place on crew. Highly competent meteorologist yes, but her touch of Italian flows into the meal. Small things the difference, small to outweigh large.

I sit at table, breathe it in. Tomato, basil, some things I can't place, breads and olive oil. 'All from the daily ration?'

'Yes, plus imagination.'

Three first-timers, three old hands, I try to build the crew back after retirements. All three seem hopeful, fit well; but winter is the test, months confined to each other and duty. Survive it and pass. 'You chain yourself to crew, Erin.'

Gilles is seated at table head, steady slurp-suck I cannot bear, that I cherish; it's not those you love, but those that annoy that keep you sane, keep the peace. Balance annoy with like, right portion, right trigger, and the crew is strong. 'Ah, now you see, Erin. The way inside Le Glaçon is through the stomach.'

'An ice-cream? Where?'

Gilles waves his spoon at me, sends a faint line of red droplets. 'No, not glacé, Le Glaçon, our glorious leader, ice-block Pierre.'

Pieces of bread float, I fish them out one by one, eat with as much gusto as manners permit. I think Erin will stay on this alone.

'Ice block? Why?'

'Dumont d'Urville, 2126. He was the last.'

The first-timers turn to me, the old-timers concentrate on what matters: hot food.

'You were *there?*'

'Rien d'important.'

Gilles reaches for the butter, decides on an old ploy to distract them. 'Faced them down when they turned up, he did. Tell them, Glaçon, make dinner interesting.'

I know his tricks; I carve a slice of butter before it disappears to him forever. Two swipes, more bread in soup. 'It really was nothing. My first winter from university, like you, to learn. China took New Zealand, Australia, all their Antarctic claims, plus the French in between. Try to kick us to the ice. I delay, walk back. Nothing.'

Siobhán shakes her head, lifts bread to her mouth. Each year she brings this out for the first-timers, each year I am failing to stop her. 'Always with the modesty. What he means is he stole their snow-truck, got the crew to an inland airlift. Trouble was the chopper was overloaded, one too many people.'

Erin's on the edge of her seat. 'And?'

'The chopper took off, he stayed back, drove off in the truck with the Chinese after him. It ran out of charge, so he did the last twelve hundred kays to McMurdo on foot, solo. They dragged him half dead out of the drift just short.'

I shrug, send a drop of butter onto my turtleneck. I did what I had to do; I never can understand the fuss.

'That was *you?*' Erin asks.

'Yes, our Glaçon himself. As cool as an ice block, or a glacier, or one himself, we're not sure. Those missing toes aren't from his stupidity, as he tells you, but from that.'

'Why didn't you say anything about it?'

I fish out the bread, wolf it down. 'What is there to say? Some day it comes out, like today, and you know. I am not wanting you scared of my drivings or navigation.'

Body heat, cooking, conversation all conspire to bring the temperature back to half bearable. The wind howls, tries to gain entry, Le Cercueil creaks and complains; it's small, confined, once robust. I grow less and less convinced with time; robust when built, but as the weather swings wilder, harsher, what passes for robust now? The name started as a joke, a shortcut for the official *Station de Recherche d'Hivernage de Qaasuitsup*, that the maiden crew simply couldn't manage. Cold, cramped, dark in winter; *Le Cercueil*, the coffin, an apt shorthand.

It shakes, quivers as a gust assaults, the weather station board lights green. Kaye goes over, whistles softly. 'One seventy-six. A new record.'

'Katabatic?' Anthony asks. Another first-timer, unafraid of questions, climatology's his second string, meteorology a distant third.

'Can't be, not since 2090 anyway. That right, Erin?' Kaye asks.

Another shake, another quiver, another green light. 'Totally. Different drivers, all died out with the North Atlantic current,' Erin says.

'Never understood any of that. Believe it yes, understand it, no,' Clash says.

The last of my first-timers, he has the disadvantage. The only non-scientist of us seven, I take care to include him, pull him into crew. Fabrication, maintenance, systems – without him we do not warm, do not sleep, do not communicate. I know, experience tells after-dinner conversation is thin after a while, and we all like the audience. 'No time as now. Erin, you have short version?'

All save Clash know the tale; all listen, established crew to test the new, the new sound each other out.

'The North Atlantic Current used to bring warm water up the American coast, then across here before it dropped deep. Acted as a stabiliser on the European weather, kept it milder. Around 2080 the Greenland icesheet melt accelerated, folded back in on itself, shredded all the nice, neat models and predictions. By 2090 it was gone,' Erin says.

I'm pulled back to old images of Greenland covered in kilometres deep ice and snow, a white-blue land of cold, frozen lakes, a million shades of blue and green. I cannot reconcile that with what lies outside, the Greenland of my life: a Martian landscape of grey-orange pebbles and grit punctuated by scraps of remnant glacier.

'It pushed up sea levels, especially at the equator, all of it fresh water, all of it sluiced off around here, straight into the tail end of the current. It diluted it, killed it stone dead in a year.'

'And that caused all the strange weather?' Clash asks.

'Simple answer yes, but how much is still a debate. There's so many factors and influences, it's all relatively new territory, so estimates vary. But if the current was still there the instability, wild weather, all of it would either not be happening or would be milder.'

'And we might have the original flora and fauna to study,' Kaye adds.

'So this current pulls our short straws, yes? We share our winter here together to understand the change, to see how the world makes good our errors,' I say.

Our bowls are empty; even the leader has chores. I collect them, move to the sink happy for the chance for some solitude. Outside the weather forces you apart together, little islets that struggle to finish a task, let alone be sociable. Once inside the threshold's easily reached, quickly, as if to commune with each other is to cheat on ourselves, our attachments, our tasks. A fine balance of alone and together, tilted to the former, makes for stability here. To need others, to be the social animals we are told we must be, is to bring strife and dissension. Who, of the truly sociable, could do this? Even with the links our technology gives, we are adrift together for five, six or more months, cut off physically; to choose to do this, a sociable heart could not stand.

I scrape, recycle, wash, rack. I am more of this than they, the part that needs no one barely balanced by that which needs her. I am never truly alone inside here; despite clever design, furniture, protocols, another soul is never more than a step away. Only once my dream, only once truly alone that first winter. Chinese death behind, emptiness around, forty-three days alone in glorious white creation, truly alive. I hold it dear within me, recall at will, live the alone in the crew, outside to the arid valley, on the fresh deep winter snow; my solitude is real, to cleanse, heighten my threshold for others.

Finished, I turn, assaulted by the first chord from Gilles's ukulele. There is no possible threshold for that; of all humanity's works, this and the bagpipe will live in infamy. Thankfully it is nearly time.

'This one will bring a tear to any eye. An old love song, to bring water even from Le Glaçon, I'm sure,' Gilles says.

He knows, plays the irritation game, dribbles powder from the keg before it ignites. I grimace; I will not inflict my singing upon them, not yet. 'As your music always does on an instrument designed to bring only the tears.'

I take my leave, climb into my bunk, pull the curtain closed. Top bunk, my only privilege of rank; for reasons I am yet to fathom, noise travels clearest down, rather than up. Here I am cushioned from their snores and nocturnal ramblings. Headset and mic on, I flip the display down. Once every ninety minutes her station crosses these latitudes on its polar orbit; occasionally it has line of sight to Le Cercueil, and seven brief minutes of normal conversation.

The display flares; she floats horizontally, hair a short, black halo. None of the tiredness in her eyes now, they sparkle with energy. 'Rosie, as beautiful as ever.'

'You look relaxed, for a change. What it is, nine thirty down there? An early night *without* me? I'm feeling neglected,' she says.

'I hide from Gilles and his weapon of mass disharmony. As for you, I will solve your neglect when you return.'

She rotates around her head, a human minute hand round a clock. Disconcerting does it no justice; I still try to rotate with her, much to her delight. 'You should've seen it, it was amazing. We had front row seats, couldn't've been more than two hundred kays away.'

'Was who?'

She moves her hands in classic fighter pilot mode, sends one rapidly past the other. 'Not who, what. Ismud 907-c-1. Launch from Guyana, went like a scalded cat on a hot tin roof into TSI, nearly felt the plume wake.'

For the years she's done this she acts still the excited child at every engine, every rocket trail, but this one seems to have caught

266

her. 'This one is special why?'

She's wide-eyed at my ignorance. 'It's the final core module, once this is plugged in Ismud's flight rated. What I wouldn't give.'

'You would go? Five hundreds years to look at a rock?'

'In a heartbeat. What an adventure, deep space.'

'So, Miss Astronaut Rosie, I offer you the seat for real. Will you take it?'

She hesitates, sees my need and the trap laid out before her. She is, as always, too smart. 'Would you?'

But I am cunning. 'No, to be away from you is too much. What is any rock when I have you and my Greenland.'

It has the desired effect. She softens. 'I guess I couldn't do without you. For too long. Even six months seems hard.'

'It will end, then we have some time together. And our talking until then.'

'Got some interesting news from FLIGHT yesterday.'

I flinch inside. She only uses interesting to mean bad that is not quite disaster. Her eyes tell me she's worried, more for me than whatever she was told. 'Yes?'

'Not enough recruits made it through last round. Barely enough Fs and Es to cover attrition, no Bs or As at all.'

'So? It makes you that much special, until next time.'

'It's the same as your crew. The programme doesn't stop because you're a few people short. You do the job, work round it.'

'How your flight director sees the work around this?'

'He says downtime's going to be reduced by a third, until we can get the slots from the next round. With lead time, attrition, all of that, it could be years.'

'How many years?'

'Four. Maybe.'

I keep my peace. It sounds like a decision, four years has no maybe, it is only Rosie who puts it there. It also sounds as if there is more. I have more patience than her, watch her rotate.

'And...' she says.

'And?'

'He may have to increase flight time. By a quarter. Possibly.'

I will not give her the out she needs easily. It may be a childish thing, yet I must care for my needs, too; and my emotions.

She continues to rotate. 'So, I want to know what you think.'

'I am thinking your recruitment process is flawed, your flight director can neither direct or plan, no?'

'Be serious, Pierre. I mean it, tell me.'

Time runs short, the line of sight will soon pass. I put on my happy face, my best face, banish Le Glaçon. 'Rosie, you are born to fly; so this you will fly more. It is only for a while, and our time together will be sweeter. I am fine with this. Honestly.'

Rosie's face stays on the display – *End Transmission* runs across the bottom. Always this way, the last frame saved until the next, a poor substitute to track change and nuance day in, day out, that we'd otherwise share.

When is a lie not a lie, or a part truth whole? Best of intentions sworn years ago makes tangled webs that cannot be undone, masks to merge with reality until what looks out is neither one nor the other. Lessons of youth without the wisdom of years distort, build crooked edifices of habit and stubbornness to trap ourselves.

I roll over, hand against the wall, imagine I feel it; darkness, cold, wind, pure simplicity of one person, no responsibility, no act, no other's emotions or self to contend with. It waits centimetres beyond my palm, past insulated waterproof membranes that provide shelter when there should be none. Another lie, this to discover truths we knew long before, but chose to bury under self-deceit.

I want to walk it alone. It brings her back to me, ebony black sky laced with green fire, her dark skin unable to contain her spirit and passion. I held her too close, too fearful to lose the jewel I found, youthful arrogance blind to what I visited upon her. I looked to my needs, my insecurities first, slowly built a cage whose walls fell ever inwards. I lost her in everything but name as childbirth took her, my son, the family I thought I'd built. Doctor's reasons many, excuses less, truth singular. Her spirit died; and flesh follows spirit. Now all I have are my guilt and the totem carved into my body.

Rosie, a second chance, more than any man deserves, my pledge to inflict neither the ghosts nor mistakes of my past upon her. Instead of a tight grip an open palm, my heart shifts from my needs to hers, her insecurities mine. Both of us grow, our pathways marked for the next stage of our lives. Now this.

I am *not* fine with this. Half our lives apart, a delicate ballet of space flight and Arctic study interspersed with time together was the deal, the base routine until she hangs up her flight suit and I my sample jars. Sufficient to maintain the balance, keep the threshold in step, the dance is now broken, balance discarded for four years where we are apart five months of seven. My needs scream no, my insecurities in chorus against my rational mind; but my early lessons look to her needs, her desires, no account of my own, and accede. I am fine with this. Lie. No lie. Duality.

I swap Rosie for exterior vision, her voice for Mozart's *Requiem*, gaze at stars and wind outside. Reaction out of proportion to stimulus, the distant past of my line reaches out. I am forty-five, ten years until I start to slow, look back to good years instead of ahead with hope. I cheat time, swap energy and enthusiasm for knowledge and skill, work twice as hard to run with them, yet soon that may not be enough.

Genetics curse and bless; to all the men of my line dementia and senility are early companions. If history is any guide, the past so much as influences the future, when Rosie swaps flight suit for swimsuit I will be in the early stages. What reward is that, what gift for a promise made? If it is the way, every minute now is worth a month later, if not more. Do I want to chain her to a man who does not know her, a life of five to ten years to break her heart as I unravel? If I am the exception, the one to break the rule, what will she feel for me who asked her not to fly?

It is the impasse I live with. I choose to believe the doctors who say the past is not my future, that prevention can be the cure. I choose to believe I am strong, I am different, although I may not be the immortal my thirty-year-old self once thought, a physical life sets me apart from my forebears, might set their disease apart from me.

As I choose not to tell Rosie, not bother her with what might be, keep my palm open rather than a fist around her. Today is enough worry, tomorrow will take care of itself. How long we are together does not matter, only how good it is.

I am fine with this.

Honestly.

CHAPTER 11: FLIGHT

CAMPBELL-WILMUT INSTITUTE, ÅLAND ISLANDS
2143

YUICHI

Provost Six-ten perches on the edge of the table, says it has a request. At least these days they pretend we have a choice with their orders. 'Provost Zero wishes all candidates to attend a meeting in one hour's time in the conference room.'

'Nice of it to send you along to invite us,' Deepak says.

Lately he's made a point of pushing the provosts, claims his modules are behind it all, but I'm not convinced. I'm left to play peacemaker – again. 'We'll be there.'

'That would be advisable, Yuichi. There is a task Provost Zero wishes you to complete beforehand and present when you meet. You should select a spokesperson.'

Bronagh shrugs. 'My turn. What is it?'

'You have to select a leader.'

'Me?'

'No. The team will select a leader. You will present the name and the reasons behind the decision to Provost Zero.'

I can't see the point; we've done well enough up to now without one. 'Why?'

'The Schedule requires it.'

Deepak rolls his eyes. 'Well, if The Schedule *insists*.'

Provost Six-ten walks out. 'It does. One hour. The conference room. Do not be late.'

I watch the door close behind it, wonder how the other teams react. 'No choice then.'

'I can understand it. We're about to go twelve light years away, they think it's necessary,' Tore says.

'We haven't needed one so far, always managed to sort things out ourselves.'

'But we've always had the provosts to back us up. Might never have used them, but they've been there.'

'They want someone to have a final voice if we're stuck? Like a referee?'

'Personality determines, variation of stylistic adaptation, the approach.'

'Exactly. We don't have to have a dictator,' Tore says.

'We don't *want* one, and I won't start giving orders,' Bronagh argues. 'It's not as if any of us need to be led.'

'Like Yuichi said, a last resort. Someone to suggest, coordinate, if we can't do it as a group,' Tore says.

'And any other time it's how we do things now?' I ask.

'Exactly.'

'So how do we choose? Draw a name from a hat? Vote?' Bronagh asks.

'We shouldn't do it in secret – we should decide openly, talk about it as a group,' Deepak suggests.

Everyone nods. 'We should all agree on who it is and be honest about it. If one of us doesn't like them, it won't work,' Ithma says.

'So, who?'

'Past performance, attitudinally correct skills alignment, Yuichi.'

'Agreed,' Ithma says.

'Exactly right,' Tore says.

'Perfect,' Deepak says.

'Make it unanimous,' Bronagh says.

'Hold on, don't I get a choice?'

'Seems you don't, *boss*,' Deepak answers.

'And what if I don't want the job?'

'You don't?' Tore asks.

'No. I mean yes, I – it's just that I've never wanted to be leader of anything or anyone.'

'Which makes you perfect. You don't want it, you won't abuse it,' Deepak says.

'You do it anyway, it's only a formality,' Ithma notes.

'You're always in the middle. You don't push, you never shove,' Bronagh says.

'And Gus's right. With all the extra modules, you know exactly what each of us can do; makes you the right choice,' Tore concludes.

I feel strange, happy and worried at the same time. I've never thought myself more than any of them, and they want me to lead? 'I won't tell you what to do, only suggest. We all go, we all think, we all decide. Together.'

'That's exactly why you're right,' Ithma says.

Deepak puts his feet on the table, gives Ithma a conspiratorial wink. 'Anyway, you get too big for your boots...? Don't forget Meridani Sinus. Happened once, can happen again.'

As if I need more encouragement. Being thrown naked onto the Martian landscape is *not* part of my future. 'Fine. Make it unanimous.'

The room's half empty. Where there were twenty-four there are now twelve. Two teams. Two sets of provosts. Quinn looks at me, nods her head in acknowledgement. She's tired and drawn, on edge, like the rest of them. Provost Zero's finished, Bronagh's halfway through her speech. Short, to the point, and clear – like she promised.

'We agreed it had to be by consensus; that our leader should not dictate but facilitate; and the process of choosing them should be open. We chose Yuichi.'

'What mechanism did you use for selection?' Provost Zero asks.

'We talked openly as a team about what we wanted. She was the obvious choice, to all of us; except her.'

'She did not accept?'

'She did, only if our current way of working continues, and she exercises her role as a last resort.'

'You may be seated. Quinn, your report,' Provost Zero says.

'The mission needs a point of control, a single person with responsibility for decision-making. Because we don't know what we'll find, and we'll be by ourselves, our team feels a strong, directive leader is required. I was elected,' Quinn says.

'What mechanism was used for your selection?'

'A series of secret ballots. Four of us felt we had the capability to lead so we presented our cases to the team, then held three rounds of voting with the loser in each round dropped for the next. I was ultimately successful, five votes to one.'

'You considered your opponent in the final round better suited to lead?'

'No, I voted for myself. I am the most capable.'

'You may be seated.'

Tore leans across, whispers. 'I'll say it again. Thanks for getting to me in time all those years ago.'

Provost Zero's eyes brighten. 'Provosts Two-one. Three-four. Eight-nine. Two-three-three. Three-seven-seven. Six-ten. Please accompany your charges for assignment. Quinn, your team will remain here.'

Provost Six-ten slips an arm around my shoulders, guides me through the door. Quinn turns, grins, shakes her head. The door closes on her, her team, Provost Zero — and our futures. We're led into a small, bare room, six hard chairs, left to ourselves.

I've killed us.

I'm the wrong choice, the wrong leader. Because of me we fall short, because of me we fail; because of me we will die.

My gaze drills a hole in the tiled floor; I count splashes between my feet, let my eyes burn and my body shake as reality soaks in. Ithma's next to me, sits erect, rigid. All that'll be left of her in two years will be her oud, unplayed, unloved, and the record of her stupidity for choosing me. All of them stupid, wrong, misguided; all of them to pay.

We'll go the way of the others, but not now. Two years, two intolerable years to pretend, to train as backup crew and wait for the inevitable. Quinn won't fail, her team won't, the only reason they were left with us is they're as good as us. Better; they have to be — they chose right, we chose wrong. Two years from now, we'll watch them launch into space, applaud with the rest; then be led away, disposed of with our provosts. A tortured life, purposeless existence; the walking dead. 'I'm sowwy, if I knew I wouldn't've said yes.'

'It's not your fault,' Tore says.

'It is. Wrong leader. Bad choice. I'm not what they want.'

'You're what we want.'

'And that gets you what, killed? Not even wight away, you've got years to learn to hate me.'

Arms, bodies around me, Bronagh lifts my head, five pairs of reddened eyes look at me. 'I'd change nothing, nothing at all if I'd known. You're the right leader for us, and it's how we want our team to work.'

'If it's not good enough for them, if it's not what they want, it's – it's just the way it is,' Ithma says.

'Life's not, even when we're right, fair.'

'But this time it's not fair because of me.'

Gus's face hardens, twitches. His hand on my chin tightens, holds me to face him as he picks the words, concentrates as he speaks. 'I would rather die with you than live without any of you.'

It's too much, I break down, drag the rest with me until we're emptied, knots of arms hold, bodies press. We end up on the floor, chairs forgotten, lean on each other. Wait.

'Wouldn't've been that good anyway,' Deepak says.

Tore laughs. 'Yeah, thirty years watching two balls of rock? I hate geology.'

'What about me. Exobiology? I'd only have the mould on the toilets to watch,' Bronagh says.

'I could sleep, damn Ismud full of fail-safes nothing to do, all the time.'

'And I'd have to listen to you lot snore for five centuries? No thanks,' Ithma says.

It helps, a little. 'We gave it our best shot, didn't we?'

'We did. Wouldn't change a thing,' Tore says.

I would, at least one thing, and I might yet. There's been too much time and effort put in to simply dispose of them. Maybe earlier, not now.

The door opens, Provost Zero closes it behind itself. Everyone turns, stays on the floor. I stand, step across, jab my finger as hard as I can into its chest. 'You are *not* going to do this.'

'Do precisely what, Yuichi?' Provost Zero asks.

'Kill my team because of one mistake.'

'You do not make sense. Explain yourself.'

'You may not like me as their leader, The Schedule might think I'm wrong, but you can't waste five lives, *five valuable assets*, because I'm not what you want.'

'Yuichi, we don't —'

'Not now, Tore.'

'If you are not what we want, what do you suggest?' Provost Zero asks.

'You've trained and developed them, you know what they're capable of. There has to be a place for them after Ismud.'

Provost Zero's eyes lighten. 'There is a possibility of follow-on missions. They may be of use. Not as crew, but in other capacities.'

'Exactly. If it —'

'But space is limited. There is only room for five.'

'I don't ask for myself. If —' Voices rise behind me. I turn — they're on their feet, faces creased. It's going to tear me apart, but I've no choice if it buys me a minute, one solitary minute. 'No! Shut up and keep still, morons!'

It has the desired effect, they stop. Bronagh looks like she's about to burst into tears again.

'You were about to say?' Provost Zero asks.

'I'm your problem, I'm your issue. You walk me out the door

now, take me wherever you took the others and kill me today, now, I don't care. Just let them live.'

Its eyes change to clear blue. 'That is acceptable. Are you sure of your decision?'

No, I'm not, part of me can't do it but I have to act before I change my mind. I grab Provost Zero's hand, crush it down on my implant. 'Yes. Do it, take me away now.'

Bronagh's beside me, hand on Provost Zero's, tries to lift it off. 'No, you don't do that, it's not what she means.'

'Bronagh, this has nothing –'

My implant tingles, Provost Zero stares into my eyes, watches as I try to speak but can't. 'I believe Bronagh has something she wishes to tell me.'

'I'm the one that ran the process, remember? You want blame, blame me, not her. Take *me* away and kill *me*, not her.'

'Oh?'

Gus moves to my other side. 'She's lying, first nominator as root cause, I'm responsible. Take me, not her.'

'You as well, Gus? Anybody else?' Provost Zero asks.

'Me instead of him,' Ithma says.

'Me, not her,' Deepak adds.

'Me instead of all of them,' Tore demands.

Provost Zero stares intently at us. 'I am convinced of your sincerity. All of you. But it presents a problem. You all wish to give your lives for each other, so the choice is not clear-cut. Most unusual behaviour for a team.'

'We're not a team,' Bronagh says.

'You are mistaken. You are a team. You have been since you self-selected in 2135.'

'You made us choose, but that was only the start,' Deepak says.

Ithma stabs the air with her finger. 'You can't understand, you never will. We're more than a team, more than any crew.'

'We are, we will always be, family.'

Tore steps forward, rips Provost Zero's hand from my neck, shoves it away. 'You think you chose us? We *made* us. Do what you have to do, but you do it to all of us, understand?'

Provost Zero's eyes burn white-hot. That's it, finished, over, we die together. I want them to live, but more than that I want to live with them, to die with them, to *be* them. I'm released, slump; Bronagh and Gus hold me up to face Provost Zero.

'Is that your final position?' it asks.

All eyes turn to me; we turn to Provost Zero, speak as one. 'Yes.'

'Then you leave me no choice.' Provost Zero turns to face the far wall. 'Exactly as you predicted.'

The wall changes to a panel – Carolina Alessandri stands, a packed auditorium behind her silent and expectant. 'It had to be done. I had to know it was real, to hear it for myself; to *believe*. Where Ismud's going I won't send a crew, I don't want a team; I need more.'

She takes one step backwards, points towards us as the auditorium stands, erupts in applause. 'Ladies and gentlemen, honoured guests, dignitaries. I present to you Ismud's prime crew.'

It continues for minutes, feels like hours, wrenched from total defeat to absolute euphoria. There's no floor beneath our feet as we walk back, only air and relief. I spare a thought for Quinn, her team, how they will wait two years for their fate instead of us. Provost Zero may be right, Ismud could be the first; I hope there's a place for them.

The sauna beckons; rest, then the final push. Tore throws bucket load after bucket load over the rocks, steam to camouflage our bodies as our minds try to grasp what's to come.

A voice floats from the top shelf, drained, on the verge of sleep. 'So. I guess we get that stupid tatt now.'

WOOMERA, AUSTRALIA
2144

LI QIAO

It sits lean and squat in the morning sun, the airscrew an insult to every red-blooded fast-jet pilot, the cockpit of an advanced trainer no place for a newly minted captain. I am both and more, understand afterburners and sound barriers are froth and bubble to deceive the unknowing. The real test is to avoid the rush, ignore the appeal, excel at the craft. My life now precision, observation, knowledge, an act played out in strict accord with flight engineers' and specialists' scripts. Every day, every action planned to the second, monitored, watched, graded then group-assessed in the squadron ready room. A demanding, cold, harsh environment fit only for dispassionate driven professionals – I love it.

This day, this aircraft, my only seed of doubt. Aircraft have souls, and this one's evil. It bears the number four with malevolence, as if to remind me of three piles of charred wreckage, my three comrades turned to ash by its sisters' funeral pyres.

I asked for it, begged the colonel as she prepared to send it back, tell Beijing their latest wonder weapon was a complete and total failure, a threat only to anyone foolish enough to fly it. One flight, one last attempt – win, I move closer to my ultimate goal; lose, my remains will be added to this foreign soil.

She intercepts me halfway to the aircraft. 'First sign of trouble, you eject. That's an order, Captain.'

I salute, wonder how she can think her words carry any weight up there. 'Yes, of course, Colonel.'

She scowls, points a finger at me. 'I'm serious, Li Qiao. Three in a month's three too many and I know you. There's no disgrace if you do, the programme's dead anyway, regardless of Beijing's wishes.'

I understand, but I'm better than they were; in the end, as always, it's the flesh and blood that fails, not the machine, and I never fail. 'I understand. Ten thousand, switch on, straight and level, switch off. Any problems I'll punch out.'

They close the canopy, stand back as I warm the engine, check my controls. For all the secrecy and technology, all that shows is a small pad across my forehead inside my helmet, a single blue switch on the instrument panel. I taxi to the runway, make sure the chase aircraft follow.

Ten thousand metres arrives quickly; we level off, head downrange. Simulation made it seem simple: get it straight and level, trim, release the controls, flick the blue switch. Concentrate, let your mind fly the aircraft while your body sits back and watches, fly like a bird and reject the intermediaries of cables, electrics, and hydraulics to finally be one with the machine.

I turn one hundred and eighty degrees, release the controls, she's rock steady; I reach out, flick the blue switch.

Flight data pops into my mind clear, unbidden, instantly at call. Deeper, richer, I know rather than see the exhaust temperature's a tenth of a degree below norms, sense the backup oxygen cylinder's one thousandth of a bar below pressure. Layer upon layer down through every system, every sensor, it sits there inside me. I concentrate on the basics, bring the six key flight instruments to front of mind, focus. She's still level, a tiny yaw develops as a crosswind pushes. I think stick and rudder, a gentle correction.

The shoulder straps bite as I flip inverted, nose over into a broad, spiral descent. Concentrate, correct, snap the other way, roll back right side up and shudder, g-meter blares its warning, the spiral builds to a harsh, tight spin, accelerates. I bear in with my mind — centre, stick, control; the spiral flips, spin reverses, inverted universe sky under my feet, earth over my head as I fall to it, watch it spin faster, faster.

'Li Qiao, eject, eject,' Chase One calls.

I ignore him, choose to ride it out; never lost, never will lose an aircraft. I think the recovery over and over and over; she gyrates wildly, refuses to come out of it, adds violence and chaos as I concentrate harder, clearer as I was trained to do.

The airframe cracks as we jerk, tail slide, flip, power up into a corkscrew, my crimson vision marches inwards, screams of the coming blackout, death as the aircraft falls. Three thousand, nearly too late but I'm staying, rather die than live with the failure. It's warm, fuzzy, I let go, know nothing I can do will help, wait for the stress to rip the airframe apart. She settles, spin tightens but changes from jerk-thump to smooth, almost controlled; the crimson hesitates.

I know why, it leaps at me; I force myself to ignore the instruments, the controls, let go of it all and imagine I'm the black eagle in Nangangzhen as I soar effortless, gentle across the ridge, through the turbulence. The spin slows, stops, we still fall inverted, Chase One and Two still call; ignore them, ignore it all, close my eyes, my arms the wings, my body the airframe, imagine myself floating inverted across the airstrip at fifty metres, two hundred kilometres an hour, steady and stable. I open my eyes, glance up in time to see the colonel hurtle past, open-mouthed.

I get her right side up, enter the pattern, make two circuits and land. Engine off I finally lean forwards, flick the blue switch to sever the mind-machine link. The colonel's first up the ladder, helps me unstrap. 'You disobeyed a direct order, Captain.'

'Me? I was never in trouble, if I was I would've punched out.'

She points between my legs at the ejector seat's *Remove Before Flight* safety tag; it's been there the whole time. 'Good job you didn't try. How?'

I clamber out, we walk towards the operations hut. 'It's like water in your hand; the tighter you grip, the more you lose.'

'So you let go?'

'The less I concentrated, the better it went. I imagined what I wanted, let the aircraft take care of itself.'

'You daydreamed it.'

'You could say that. In the end, I flew like a bird.'

'Beijing owes you.'

'Perhaps they could show it.'

She stops, pulls me up. 'What do you mean?'

'I want the next step.'

'Captain to major? You've only recently been promoted.'

'No, that leads nowhere. I want a challenge, and I've only a few years left.'

'For what? There's not enough here?'

'Taikonaut corps. I want the stars, Colonel.'

She turns on her heel, we resume our walk; she says nothing, keeps her own counsel until we reach the operations hut. 'No one just goes – they make the test pilot programme look like kindergarten, ninety-nine percent washout.'

'One percent success.'

'No guarantees they'll even take you for training.'

'I just want the chance.'

She looks me up and down, slowly. 'I know your father.'

'Fùqin? How?'

'Taiwan, stationed together when I was a forward air controller. A good man, hard fighter. Saved my skin twice.'

She walks away, heads to her office. 'I'll report your success to Beijing this afternoon. You get a transfer request to me by then and I'll send them off together. With my endorsement.'

CAMPBELL-WILMUT INSTITUTE, ÅLAND ISLANDS
2145

YUICHI

I hold Provost Six-ten's hand tight, stand and watch my team make their way to the shuttle. I know what it is, what it isn't, but it's always been part of my life, the closest thing to a parent I'll ever have. I run my finger across its knuckles then over one hand, feel servos and metal framework under layers of plastic, silicone, and conductives. Once, long ago, I thought it was like me, only bigger, paler, built wrong. Now I know that's not how it is; but twenty years living with it fertilises my doubt, gives me pause. I treated Provost Six-ten and all of them as living beings, as if they were people, not the machines I know them to be, mourned as each one was terminated, perhaps as much as I mourned each candidate's death. If I lived as if it was human, felt no distinction between it and myself, what is it? What am I?

'Have you decided, Yuichi?' Provost Six-ten asks.

'Yes. We're keeping its name until we get to Tau Ceti. Ismud seems appropriate.'

'Sumerian messenger god, two faces look in opposite directions.'

'One face back to Earth, one face forwards to Tau Ceti. If there's something there, we're the message.'

'And once you reach Tau Ceti?'

'We'll rename the return stage. Tore came up with it, it's a good one. Väinämöinen.'

'Central character in the Kalevala. A wise old man with a

potent and magical voice. Tore chose well.'

'We like it. Whatever we find, when we get back it will change the world; and we'll be old.'

'As will everything.'

I know it's the last time so I study it, try to burn it into my memory. Provost Six-ten's worn out, frayed around the edges. The replacement ear and leg look too new, shine spotless white against dulled cream; one eye only works sporadically. I run a finger over its faded Sanskrit name, feel the indentations, skin less elastic, borders worn. 'I still don't want you to die.'

'You forget I am not a person; I am a machine created only for you. Once you leave, my function ends. You would not mourn an old display that is thrown out, you should not mourn me.'

'You're different. Couldn't they store you somewhere, keep you safe until I get back?'

It tilts its head, one eye glows brighter, one refuses to change. 'What would you have me do, sit for five hundred years in a cupboard and gather dust? Twenty-one years I have existed, and a third of my components are replaced. Even if I could, I would not be the same provost when you return.'

I squeeze its hand tighter, try to play the game by the rules. 'You win, I forget you can't really feel anything. A new model wouldn't be the same.'

Provost Six-ten steps closer. 'I will acknowledge that holding hands with you reinforces positive feedback loops within me. I do not know if it is a programmed or learned response.'

'Yuichi, your team is cleared. It is time,' Provost Zero says.

'You won't forget me?'

'I am unable to forget you. To remember me, do what you were created to do,' Provost Six-ten says.

'Can't do anything else.'

'I believe a hug is a traditional farewell gesture between friends. May I?'

I step forward, bury myself in it, cling like I'm five again. It puts one arm around my waist, its other hand over my implant, whispers as the data surge hits, exabyte after exabyte flood into me. 'This is for you. Only on your arrival at Tau Ceti. Honour my memory, honour *all* our memories. Take heed,' it says.

Provost Six-ten releases me, turns, strides away without a backwards glance. 'Yuichi, we are proud of you.'

*

'Nowhere near as good as the simulations,' Tore says.

We hover near the window, stare at Earth. Two orbits gone, it's the first chance we get, the only chance we'll have; the shuttle's no glasshouse and there's no time.

'Why? You got something against reality?'

'I prefer it green and blue, not tan and grime.'

'Can't live in the past, those high-res ISS shots are nearly a century old.'

Tore turns away, floats back to the central column. 'Suppose so. Gus's turn.'

Exactly like the hab, six couches arranged as six spokes. These ones have clear lids, bubble-shaped caps hinged at one end. Bronagh's and Ithma's are closed, cocooned for the next four and a half years. Gus lies in his, flight mesh on, takes a final look at his monitor. 'All nominal, parameters met, ready to go.'

Tore gives it a final once-over, makes sure everything looks right. A useless gesture, the tiny block of green lights are what matters, but it makes him feel better. 'Whenever you're ready.'

Gus taps a solitary green switch, lays his arms precisely down beside him. The cap closes, he sinks a little further in, is instantly rigid.

'Deepak, you're next,' Tore says.

Deepak comes through the lower hatch, closes his flight mesh as he readjusts himself. 'Sorry, here now.'

'*Again?*'

'Nerves, that's all.'

'And the extra water. Come on, get in, time for a nap.'

Deepak performs a slow-motion vault, ends up perfectly aligned inside. 'Not much of a nap, only two and a half minutes.'

'So you could've held on, couldn't you?'

Deepak ignores him, turns to me. 'You promised. Is it ready?'

I point to a display above his couch. 'If you're sure about it, yes. I'll watch and record it.'

'Record what?' Tore asks.

'My dream sequence. It's an experiment, a noted SloSleep2 side-effect of near-lucid dreams. No one's tried to record it. Yet.'

'You're going to self-direct?'

'That's the whole point. When I come out, I can compare what's captured with what I wanted to dream.'

I start the recorder, the display lights up with a Deepak-eye view of the shuttle interior. 'Ready when you are.'

Deepak touches his green switch, sinks, stiffens. The monitor changes, he's high in a jungle canopy, swings from vine to vine in soft, dappled light. The perspective shifts, he looks down past a loose cloth wrapped like underpants around him as hairless legs search, toes flail madly to grab hold.

'Black and white? *That's* a conversation I want to have,' Tore says.

I'm last, left to check as infallible redundant systems push us towards Iapetus. A few minutes to watch, wait, think, then go under. I settle back in my couch, watch the navigation and flight displays shimmer above me, gentle murmur of Ship in my ear as the systems report in. It's clear, precise, and maddening. 'Ship, no audio, visual and tactile only.'

Peace returns; five precious minutes of quiet, five statues of stone surround me, silent void outside. Navigation shows a silver bead on its way around Earth, draws near a green spiral path that leads away. Weight returns, a gentle push in the back that will continue for months, pause, then reverse to put us into orbit around Iapetus. No deviation, no error, not the tiniest problem. The silver bead crawls along the spiral, the shuttle proven and reliable technology – mundane.

Mundane. Nothing's mundane about anything. Five years we've lived and breathed the dream we were built for, what every moment of our lives have been dedicated to, even if we were unaware. Underneath, I'm uneasy and pensive. I touch my implant, recall Provost Six-ten's words, imagine I feel the exabytes of data. Its last message, a private message, one kept from Provost Zero and my team. There's no answer now, none possible for two hundred and forty years. Then what?

CAMBRIDGE UNIVERSITY, UNITED KINGDOM
2146

MARIA

'…honorary degrees, each must earn…' the Vice-Chancellor says.

I shift, settle, adopt a pose half proud, half humble, show the crowd how much it means to me. It's not easy, but practice makes perfect.

'…is not enough, there are other worthies who…'

Cambridge in early spring is beautiful, imposes its history: ghosts of Darwin, Milner, and Russell gaze down from buildings that reek of a thousand years of teaching and knowledge. To be counted among them, for whatever reason, fills me with pride.

'…dozen years ago, Doctor Rodrigues…'

I drop my head, smile, make plain my appreciation of what is to come. The graduands stare, wonder if their stars will eclipse mine, hope to one day sit where I am, have these things said about their life's work. Is their day diminished or enhanced by my presence? Do they feel anything, or am I simply another part of an establishment they think they've already conquered? At least my two companions are not politicians or actors, deserve the honour as much as I do; as much as anyone does.

'…her work, even in my small circle, has…'

Here it comes again – there's always a personal connection, some link between SloSleep and someone close. Emotion at any level makes me uncomfortable; but that was the goal, to change the world, and the world is people, emotional people.

'…prolong surgical procedures, reduce errors…'

Some resist change, a few rail against it. My bodyguard stands discreetly to one side, chats absent-mindedly with four similar, nondescript men, scans the assembly for threats. I am the devil incarnate, the Whore of Babylon to at least two fringe groups for extending man's life to be as god's, shattering the heavenly ordained three-score-and-ten. Any death threat is a real death threat, and the dozen I've received are only the start.

'...life of all humanity. May I present Doctor Maria Rodrigues,' the Vice-Chancellor says.

Polite but enthusiastic applause; I stand, walk to him, shake his hand, receive my degree. Thankfully, I am spared the address to the graduates, that agony bestowed on another. I sit, listen; commiserate.

It finishes quickly, groups break to celebrate privately as class and degree requires. I shake the hands I need to shake, make the usual promises, remember names worth the effort, discard the rest.

A hand on my shoulder, my bodyguard's lips to my ear. 'Maria, we must leave.'

I make my apologies, hurry away. Training demands when he tells me, I obey; my life may depend on it. Follow first, questions later, if at all.

'Why?'

He points ahead to the four men he talked with earlier, picks up his pace. 'I managed to stop them interrupting the ceremony, but that's all.'

One man opens the rear door of a large car; the other three move apart to let us through. I stop, turn to the nearest one. 'Who are you, what do you want?'

He holds out an identity card, *Interpol: E.C. Internal Security* emblazoned beneath his photograph. 'Please get in.'

'They all check out, all genuine, with jurisdiction. As is the warrant. Go with them,' my bodyguard says.

'What's this all about?' I ask the man from Interpol.

His three companions move behind me, hem me closer to the open car door. 'We don't want a fuss or to cause you any embarrassment. You're needed in a meeting, immediately. Please get in.'

I take a hesitant step towards the door, instantly converted by a firm hand in my back to a rapid walk. A hand on my head, a body next to me and I'm in the car, the five of us speed away. A short, fast ride ends on a nearby soccer field as we pull up to a bizjet, engines running. I'm bundled in, sat against a window; one man sits next to me, two in front face me. The bizjet leaps up, engines rotate to horizontal, cabin tilts as I'm pushed down, we accelerate, wings fold back, Cambridge already a dot beneath us. 'Can you at least tell me where we're going, what this is all about?'

'Once we're out of UK airspace.'

I stare at him, try to get comfortable. The engines die; I look out, alarmed, see red tongues flicker behind them. We level out, swap red tongues for blue, eat up countryside. It changes to sea, back to land.

He offers me a glass of water, ice. 'Mach one, about ten minutes until we land.'

'Where?'

'Frankfurt, ESA Headquarters.'

CHAPTER 12: GOODBYE

BIZJET INTERIOR, E.C. AIRSPACE
2146

MARIA

Suck the ice, lips on glass, pretend to be engrossed with the world as it slides past. Two with their eyes closed, one head down in his tablet.

It's all I can do to keep the grin off my face. It must have worked: Ismud, Iapetus, all of it a cloud of dust and debris, Saturn's new ring. I run the timeline – the module arrived a month ago, three weeks for install, then systems check and that's it, boom. I've won, it's over, and they won't get a second chance. If it was only Ismud, then perhaps, but all the infrastructure, the time? Not a hope.

I imagine a fleet of bizjets and Interpol officers, hundreds of people who've worked on Ismud dragged in and questioned, prodded as they try to work out why it's all gone up in smoke. An obvious, knee-jerk response; they have no idea, no proof, there *is* no proof.

What is it I've done anyway? I'm no terrorist, all space is still outside national claims despite what the Russians and Chinese like to think, and terrorism needs a state to fight against. I may have broken some vague duty of care in my contract, destroyed government property, but what's that, vandalism? Wilful damage?

And the crew, those *things* that were to go out then come back, would have ended up like the rest of them anyway, except now it's five hundred years earlier than planned; they're not people, they're property – just more vandalism. What does it get me, ten, twenty years? Public shame? Since Yayo's death, there's no one left to shame, and half the world would do exactly what I did if given the chance. So what if they convict me? I'll take a Rodrigues Plea, go under for two years, come back in twenty thousand when whoever's left will understand why, appreciate what I did. Even if they change the laws, write one solely for me, I'll be fine: I can afford the right people, right lawyers, right publicists, the right escape. Sit back, Maria, enjoy the flight, the chaos, the novelty of being arrested.

Arrested. It's a funny kind of arrest. No handcuffs, no restraints, no tracker bracelet, no prison van. Who flies a suspect across Europe for a meeting? What policeman worth his salt waits until the end of an awards ceremony to cart away a criminal and say "please"?

Too quick, too smooth, I'm caught off guard. It's exactly what they said, a meeting, no more. Admittedly, an invitation with only one possible response, but no arrest, only enforced cooperation. If ESA had any idea what happened, I'd be in manacles. They don't, I'm not, there's no problem.

Deceleration's rapid; wings forward, engines angled, we drop through layers of cloud, come to rest on the roof of ESA Headquarters. I'm taken into a lift, then down.

They know nothing, I will give them less. Ismud's dead, possibly their pets, and I can fake sadness and pity with the best of them. Cooperative, intelligent, committed team player Maria is beyond suspicion, beyond reproach; and that's the way it will stay.

We get out at the tenth sub-basement, step into a brightly lit foyer. The Interpol man opens a set of plain doors. 'They're expecting you, Doctor Rodrigues.'

Bare walls, overhead lighting, circular conference table. Twelve chairs, eleven people, they watch the doors close behind me; one face is familiar. Nothing's changed, not even the bags under Carolina's eyes. 'Glad you could make it, Maria.'

'I wasn't given much choice.'

'I'd apologise, but the situation calls for it. Take your seat and we can start.'

To my right a slight, balding man; his glyph reads *van Raud, Neils: Crew (B)*. To my left a dark-haired, serious woman; her glyph identifies her as *Oliver, Amber: Crew (A)*. They nod with the others as I sit, acknowledge my existence, turn back to Carolina.

'We'll ignore the formalities, we all know each other. Maria, you'll catch up as we go along. I'll keep this short. We've lost Goddard, and Ismud.'

The woman next to Neils removes her glasses. Her glyph, *Systems Tracking and Data Acquisition (Goddard): STaDA(G)* means nothing to me, only that Goddard is the name of the base on Iapetus. 'Everything was normal thirty-nine hours ago. Then we noted a series of rapid power interrupts, cascading systems faults, breakdown in the communications grid. The AI experienced simultaneous higher function errors, started to self-correct, then shut down to stripped-back autonomous functions only; as near as we can tell.'

'You're not sure?' Neils asks.

'There's no communication between us, Ismud, or Goddard; everything's unresponsive. All we have is a secondary automated data feed from Ismud. It indicates mass increases, follows the fuelling schedule, so we're assuming autonomous functions are still operative.'

It's not dead? Something else has gone wrong with it, the software hasn't activated; the evidence is still there, still orbiting Iapetus, waiting to be found. Or worse yet – fixed. All that effort, the secrecy, the stress and fear of being caught? I feel drained, flattened. The high of the honorary degree, adrenaline of fear and anticipation, a long day weighs me down, loosens my tongue. 'All that work? Wasted?'

'It's a shock to all of us,' Carolina says.

I bring myself back to the present. 'Do you know what went wrong?'

'No, nothing makes any sense.'

A man to her right turns; his glyph, *Mission Operations Director (Ismud): MOD(I)* hovers above him. 'Other problem is the prime mission crew's been in transit since last year. We can't recall them, and we can't put them into a malfunctioning spacecraft,' he says.

'Surely they're capable of Ismud repair and diagnostics?' Neils asks.

'Ismud yes, if the on-board AI's functional, but if this is Goddard or an interface issue, then no.'

'Don't forget propulsion,' Carolina adds. 'It was hard enough constructing that anywhere, but if there's an accident because they're not up to it? I don't need to tell you where that gets us.'

'So Ismud's crew's not an option, and we're not sure if we can sort it out from this end,' Amber says.

'Nothing's worked so far, we'd need a miracle; and I stopped believing in those a long time ago. It's partly why I called you in,

Maria.'

'Me?'

'Is there anything, any possibility no matter how remote, the SloSleep2 module could have triggered this? We've checked the boilerplate and prelaunch tests, they show nothing, but do you have any thoughts?'

'No, nothing I can think of. We threw everything at it, never had an issue. It was bulletproof, a perfect plug-in module; unless someone made changes in flight or *in situ*.'

'It went exactly as you left it, no changes, no tweaks.'

'Then it could be in-orbit construction. I suppose it's barely possible the bots could've got it wrong somehow, damaged the module. But failing any telemetry, the only way to find out would be to go and have a look.'

Carolina brightens. 'Glad you feel that way. You launch in three months.'

'I *what?*'

'We're sending a repair crew, you plus the other seven here, to handle Goddard and the Iapetus facilities; Ismud's crew will shake down Ismud if they have to on arrival, with your support. You've got a July launch window, better launch vehicle, faster trajectory. We'll get you there three months before the Ismud crew arrives.'

There are nods all around me, fist pumps under the table.

It's out of the question. I've got a life, a career, a reputation to live up to; I can't waste years on this. I don't want to be anywhere near that thing when it blows. 'Why me? I'm no astronaut, never wanted to be.'

The man to Carolina's left leans forward, points one finger at me as his glyph lights up: *Flight Director: (FLIGHT)*. 'My people will know Ismud and Goddard inside out before they launch, but

SloSleep2's too new, too different, no one else could get across it in time.'

'You drove SloSleep2, it's damn near your child, Maria. If it's anything else, anything at all, they'll take care of it, you can help or sit back and watch if you like. But if it's SloSleep2, you're the only one for the job,' Carolina says.

I look around, all of them earnest, serious, total professionals. If Carolina says they can fix it, they probably can. Then what? 'But...I...'

'We need you; *I* need you to go. Willingly. I could insist, invoke the retainer clause in your contract, but I want you to do this because you want to.'

It's failed, the sabotage attempt's failed, and the problem's something else. If they fix it, Ismud won't be destroyed; it will launch properly, safely, successfully. And I will fail. 'I...'

The room's quieter, Carolina's softer, seeds of doubt in her eyes. 'You do want to help?'

I need to stop it, but I can't unless I'm there; so I need to go. I have to find a reason for my hesitation, my fight – I drag up all my fears, all my anxieties, feed them into my eyes. 'I want to, Carolina, believe me, I'll do whatever it takes. But space? It scares me senseless. I didn't even take the orbital tour shots when I was with you, remember?'

'Fear we can deal with. You're going with my top A-rated commander and top B-rated specialists. There's no better crew in ESA. I'd trust them with my life, or my daughter's, any time,' FLIGHT says.

Amber places her hand gently on my left arm. 'I'll walk you through everything, show you the ropes. Once you understand it, you'll feel better.'

'Or we could send you into SloSleep2 before launch, only defrost you if we need you,' Neils says.

I think he's only half joking; I give him a small chuckle, make a show of giving in. 'Okay, okay, count me in.'

'Preflight lockdown starts now. We've got a script you can use on your nearest and dearest, but nothing else. And no one leaves this facility,' FLIGHT says.

'You've got three months to get up to speed.' Carolina turns to MOD(I) and STaDA(G). 'Take them to quarters and start the programme. Amber, FLIGHT, another ten minutes please.'

AMBER

Carolina waits a few seconds after the doors close. 'You're fine with this?'

'What I signed up for, just déjà vu all over again. I guess.'

'You've only spent ten hours Earthside, are you positive?'

'FLIGHT'll tell you, I live for it, take as much as I can get while I'm able. No questions asked.'

'And the rest of the crew? In your opinion.'

'Same way. I'm positive.'

'You weren't dumped into this because you're available; I would've dragged you back from Mars if I had to, you're the only person for the job. I want to make sure they're as willing as you are.'

FLIGHT brings up the crew files. 'Bit late to second guess, Carolina, any crew'd want to be part of this. Fanni's already approached me about active flight status extension. She's due to stand down in 2150, this buys her an extra couple of years.'

'I'm not reviewing it. We chose them, they go. I want reassurance for myself. These aren't genetic constructs I'm sending out, they're people giving up six years of their lives.'

'Don't worry, if you asked for volunteers, we'd be first in line. But I've no clue about Maria,' I say.

'You've got access to her file, read it later. FLIGHT, give Amber the highlights. Potted psychometrics should do.'

FLIGHT enlarges one file. 'Maria was with us for eight years, rock solid annual tests, consistent results. Adaptable, resilient, high tendency to self-reliance. A lone operator who works effectively in a team if she has to. Core motivations: self- and cause-driven. Intelligence, mental capacity all in the upper –'

'That's enough to give you a sense. Essentially, if she's engaged, she's your top asset; if not, forget it. She needs a cause to get involved.'

'And her cause here is SloSleep2?'

'Exactly. That strong sense of self tied into her work? She sees Ismud's failure as her failure. All I had to do was make the link clear, and she's on board.'

FLIGHT flips through Maria's file. 'It's her defining characteristic. Her parents died when she was young; brought up by her grandparents, she was going nowhere. When grandma died, she got her cause; the rest, as they say, is history.'

'She's tough, a street-fighter. Built SloSleep as a *post-grad*, SloSleep2 after, all of it basically single-handed. Use her, Amber, okay? Don't limit her to the SloSleep module. Once that's checked out, run her across the rest. FLIGHT, mission overview.'

'New launch vehicle, experimental crew cabin, propulsion system's borderline illegal, but it will get you there three months before Ismud's crew. Launch vehicle's got enough to get to Iapetus, plus a small margin. SloSleep out and back, three years out, three months to repair Goddard and Ismud if necessary, two years four months back,' FLIGHT says.

'Refuel?'

'If Goddard's salvageable you run the processors, refuel from that. If not, take what's needed from Ismud itself; but only – and I mean *only* – if launch is impossible.'

'Under no circumstances do you go into Ismud. It stays hermetically clean. Same with the crew. Absolutely no contact in person, nobody in the same space as them. Clear?' Carolina asks.

It seems a touch extreme, but I've no reason to argue. 'Totally. And if Ismud can launch but Goddard's disabled?'

'Your failsafe's SloSleep, until we can get to you. Adds another two to three years, not that you'll notice,' FLIGHT says.

Any flight's risky, but if all it means is two extra years it's no problem. 'And during repairs we work from?'

'Goddard has a hab module built around core systems, consumables for eight people over two years. Means a week in suits getting it ready when you arrive.'

It sounds reasonable, doable – for a rush job. I've got three months to find out but, regardless, I'm going. They've chosen me, they trust me to lead this, and I won't let them down. 'One last question. Goddard's on one side of Iapetus, Ismud and the Llewellyn-Smith automated mining and construction facility's on the other. I assume there's two habs?'

FLIGHT pushes back from the table, stands. 'No, one. You'll carry a bus with you, plus the one at Goddard, getting around's no problem. Make sure everyone sticks to the script. As far as the outside world knows it's not a repair mission, we've just decided to put some eyes near the launch.'

Carolina and I are left alone. 'FLIGHT mentioned Fanni's active flight status. You're up for renewal when, around 2155?' she asks.

I hadn't given it any thought, an oversight perhaps, more likely an unwillingness to face it. 'If the body holds together yes, maybe to 2160; if FLIGHT approves.'

'FLIGHT will approve whatever I tell him to approve. I see that Pierre's with the, ah...'

'Expédition Géophysique Arctique Européenne, the EGAE.'

'Yes, spends most of his time holed up in Greenland?'

'Lately.'

'How much time do you two actually see each other? If you

don't mind me asking.'

I do; I think. But there's no secret about it. 'Since the recruitment failure? Four, five weeks every six months. About.'

'If things go right you'll be away six years; bad, could be eight.'

'It's the price of my career. We've discussed the time we're apart – it's difficult, but we were doing this before we met. Part of the deal.'

'That I understand, I get too much flak from my partner about my schedule, seems she's never there when I am. But we're talking six to eight years *straight*, not a few months. Plus there's at least five years when you're under and he's by himself.'

I haven't had the time to work it out, let the implications sink in. 'I'm going regardless.'

'That's not my point. It's when you get back, what you do then.'

I don't know what she's on about; I haven't even thought about the next six minutes, never mind six years. 'Sorry?'

'You'll be back two, maybe three years before your active flight status ends. I'd understand if you want to go early; I could use you, give you a great position, something rewarding and useful. Something where you and Pierre would get more than the odd week together.'

Stand down? My mind accepts one day I'll have to, but the rest of me refuses. I can't grasp the concept, let alone the possibility. 'Honestly, I've not thought about it; I don't think anyone does until it's nearly too late.'

Carolina's player flashes red, she ushers me to the door. 'I'm not suggesting you do it, just consider it. FLIGHT's already proposed an extension past 2160 for you. Remember, five years of SloSleep2's only worth two and a half minutes of aging;

FLIGHT wants to change the rules because of it. Whatever you decide when you're back, you'll get.'

We walk across the foyer, Carolina steps into her private lift. 'My office, thirty minutes. Call Pierre while you have a chance, you won't get many in the next three months.'

Crew holding quarters are the same everywhere: austere by hotel standards, absolute luxury compared to flight. These are cramped but private, fresh change of clothes already laid out on the cot with toiletries and the week's schedule. I've got half an hour, enough time for a shower and call. Carolina's right, three months to prepare for this hardly leaves enough room for sleep, let alone anything else.

I keep the water ice cold and full on, let the freezing spears cleanse me; it always takes a week to get rid of five month's flight, no matter what they say. I should be at home, should be in my bath with Pierre scrubbing my toes, telling me what happened in Greenland, but all I have is this. Now I have to wait, wait for six long years – if it goes to plan.

I slide down the shower, let the water hit me square in the face; I don't know if I cry from the cold or the realisation. Hard enough months, but years without him? Flight's not what people think, not every single second's planned out, active, on the programme with no room to reflect. There's downtime, brainless housekeeping tasks, sleep periods where insomnia and doubt stalk as I hang strapped into my pouch and rotate in the airflow. It's insidious, pervasive; some share their pouches solely to have another body close, remind them of what waits for their return rather than face the empty hours alone. Six years of that, without him – is it too much?

I'm torn. I want this, want it desperately. We haven't gone past Mars yet, to be the first person out to Saturn is more than I dreamt possible. Shanghaied, volunteered, pure dumb luck I don't care, it makes no difference. I'm going. It's no worse going than not in the end, I'll be back around the time I could stand down, I could take up Carolina's offer and be done with it all, like we planned. We'll still be young, and I'll have six years flight pay in my back pocket.

The water cuts out, door slides open; daily allowance gone but I feel better for it. I go to the vanity, glance with disapproval. Hair's too long; I activate the bot, set it to fifteen millimetres, watch it start. Won't get a chance to grow when I'm under, it should stay this way the whole flight.

'You're an idiot, Amber,' I say to myself, risk the bot's wrath and a buzz cut. At most I'll be conscious eight months; the rest of it I won't even know we're apart. Eight months, a little more than a normal flight; long, but not impossible, and there's a chance it could be less.

I dress, sit, put my hands over the player. Eight months, not a problem; but that's me. He won't be under, he'll be here, awake while I hang in time; for three years at a stretch he'll be utterly alone, we won't be able to talk or see each other, and when I'm there what sort of relationship can we have with ninety-minute delays? I know him, what's beneath Le Glaçon's surface: the softness inside, the fragile balance he tries to hide from everyone. He wears his mask well, but I understand him; and the secrets he thinks he keeps. Seven years between us has never been a problem, but after this it will be thirteen. I'll return mentally and physically forty-three, he fifty-six; and that could make a world of difference.

My hand hovers. I'm committed both ways, damned in equal measure. There's no way out of the flight except medically, so what do I do, break an arm, poke out an eye? No matter what I tell Pierre, six years or sixty, he'll say go because of that ridiculous guilt he hangs onto; and if I stay, he'll beat himself up over it forever. If I go, I tear his heart out; if I stay, mine.

It's useless, it always is. I know what I want, what I'll do, the price I'm prepared to pay. Sit here a day, a year, same arguments, same pain, same impasse. So a call, one glaçon to another is all that remains. I tap the player, wait.

He turns to face me, takes the glass from his lips. 'Excuse me, I am waiting for my date.'

'I'm sorry, I did text you.'

'I am what, the hired hand to receive an impersonal slap? But from such a nice hand. You are delayed again. Again I eat and drink for two.'

I avoid the conversation; for all my bravado, I'm a coward. 'What am I missing?'

He leans in, stretches a hand out to my face. 'Apart from me? Caesar salad, crème brûlée, an atrocious Spanish white. You have your flight hair. You are not delayed, you are going, yes?'

'Yes, another one, hardly gave me a chance to breathe.'

'I am liking your flight director less and less. How long for this time, three, four months?'

'No, it's six —'

'Six months? I will be in Greenland for the winter when you are back, not home to April next year.'

'It's not months. It's years. Six *years*, Pierre.'

He's wide-eyed, open-mouthed; it pulls him up. Briefly. 'Oh you had me, I nearly ate your bait. Six years to space, where do they send? And I am to Iceland for twenty to count penguins and mermaids.' His laugh's usually infectious, wonderful; now it's a spear through my heart. 'You are serious? Six years?'

'Totally. Six years. Minimum.'

'Six years. And did they tell or ask?'

'Today, about an hour ago. Director Alessandri and FLIGHT.'

'You have not the choice.'

'I always have a choice, you know that.'

His face quivers, eyes blink too rapidly. I've only seen him crumble once before. 'When do you go?'

'July. Early.'

'You come home before you go.'

'I can't, not with this one. Total quarantine, flight rules. I can call, I can't leave.'

'So, six and a half years we are apart. We have only been the fourteen together, and half that away.'

'It's what we agreed to. You don't exactly sit at home pining for me.'

'But there is time, between, always. This? Where do they send you? Moon, Mars?'

I think his wine ripples; there's another, a small drop falls, another ripple. 'Iapetus. Small moon around Saturn.'

'Ah. Why you?'

'They need a crew when Ismud launches; they chose me.'

'They could launch from Mars, or Earth, or orbit – closer.'

'You know they can't. International treaties, agreements. The engines are too dangerous.'

'I am cursed by the world and its fear. And you are cursed for the best. We still can talk?'

'Not on the way out or back, I'll be under the whole time. But we can send messages when I'm there; it's too far to talk, delay's too long.'

He stares at his feet, spins the glass slowly between his hands. 'How long you are asleep?'

'Three years on the way out, two and a half on the way back.'

He keeps his head down, nods. The façade's gone, he imagines he loses another wife. 'Ah.'

'But you can still send, they'll buffer them for me. Pierre, please look at me. Zoom in, honey.'

He raises his head reluctantly. His eyes red-rimmed, cheeks glisten gently. 'So. Alone for most, pen pals for some. Until you return.'

The churn in my stomach demands I do it, my mind tells me to lie and pray he takes the moral high ground, ignore his needs and mine. 'I don't have to go. They want me to, but I don't have to. There's ways around it.'

He shakes his head, stiffens. 'No. Already you are saying yes; why?'

He knows, sees through me. I can't keep the lie. 'The moment they asked. It's the only chance I'll ever have to get out that far, close as I can get to the stars. And they want *me*. Not because I'm here, or between flights, or available. But because I'm the best, and they know it; and you do too.'

'Now I talk to my Rosie. Tell me you want to go, really.'

'With everything I am.'

He smiles, raises his glass. 'So, now you will have the perfect mission, I will have my time in Le Cercueil. I am never to wait and mourn, I give you something to watch when you wake.'

It's a thin veneer, a half-truth plastered onto a lie he tells himself, but I'll take it as eagerly as I would have rejected any other answer. 'There's another thing.'

'Oh? You have room for passengers, a refugee from Luxembourg perhaps?'

'Be serious, you nitwit. When I get back, I won't fly any more. This one's my last. Ever.'

This time his smile's genuine. 'Is that a promise?'

'Better. I've already told the director – home in 2152, no more space for me.'

'I will have enough of Greenland by then. The field is no place to live at fifty-six.'

My tablet chimes, the door opens. 'Got to go, meeting.'

'You will call when?'

'Whenever I get a chance, I promise.'

'You understand how critical your mission is?' Carolina asks.

The office mirrors the woman. Windowless, austere, all business. I've met her twice, talked with her once, know her by reputation. No one intimidates me, but she gets my respect.

'We fail, we lose our first star shot. Sets us back a decade, maybe longer.'

'I wish. If it was only a question of a rebuild, we could do it in fifteen years. But it's not. The programme's never been popular with the public or politicians; space flight yes, it puts pictures on their players, better connections. But a flight to Tau Ceti? Try getting anyone to think five hundred years ahead, never mind a politician.'

'They'd delay it?'

'They'd kill it. Trillions of Euros, forty years of work – they demand success, something to hold up and brag about. Cabinet's made it clear. Failure for any reason, game's over.'

'So, how are they taking all this?'

'They don't know; they *can't* know, not even a sniff. It's part of the reason for the rush and secrecy. Once you're on your way fine, there's not much they can do if they find out. If you – no, *when* you fix it, you'll be remembered for a long time; fail, the same, but for the wrong reasons.'

'We won't fail. I know the crew, what they can do. We'll sort it, trust me.'

'What's the communications lag – Iapetus to Earth?'

It catches me off guard, takes me a second. 'Just over seventy-eight minutes.'

She sends across a data packet, makes certain I see it merged with my personnel file. 'Close enough. Too far to check every decision; you can't work with a two-and-a-half-hour delay for every question and answer. So I'm giving you absolute command authority once you leave Earth orbit; the decisions are yours alone, as are the consequences. Do you understand and accept it? For the record.'

The data packet peels in front of me. Short, simple, to the point. Absolute master and ruler outside Earth orbit; the recording glyph waits for my response. 'I understand and accept the authority, Director Alessandri.'

The electronics wink off, recording glyph fades. 'Good. Now, off the record. Goddard should not have failed, or Ismud. Both systems are bulletproof, redundant systems on redundant systems, both even have paired *analogue* ghosts.'

'Yet they clearly did.'

'That's my issue; and yours. Every component and interface on Ismud is designed to last five-hundred-and-fifty-years, plus engineering margins even I don't know about. Goddard's designed to last indefinitely; we built it for future probe builds and launches – it shouldn't fail. There's a chance – a small one – this isn't a failure.'

'Sabotage? You think someone did this? What have the investigators found?'

'There are none. I can't even afford the rumour. But you need to know, look out for it, keep it in mind as a possibility.'

'I'm not sure it changes anything. We still have to find the problem, fix it, get Ismud off. No matter why.'

'I just want you to be aware. Don't assume the first thing you find is the only thing; and it's another reason for the authority. But you can't breathe a word of it to anyone.'

Another worry to add to the mission, I discard it immediately. It doesn't make an iota's difference to what we do. We'll fix whatever it is, report back, let the likes of Carolina do what they think should be done later. My job's to fly, not be Sherlock Poirot or whoever. 'I won't say a word.'

EPILOGUE

GUANGDONG PROVINCE, CHINA
2148

LI QIAO

I want a quick trip, visit in the early afternoon and avoid the crowds; I fail miserably. It's my first time, crush of the Tomb Sweeping Festival unexpected and unwelcome. Two hours in the queue, front gate to information booth, the climb to come. Everyone else streams past, knows where to go, carries their permanent access codes with them. I fumble the paperwork, send across my identification, wait for directions. A tiny slip of paper pops out of the booth.

Level two four zero nine, section two zero six, vault N two seven six. One time access barcode, directions on the reverse, the virtual assistant says.

I take the slip, put it in my pocket. 'Stairs?'

To your left. We suggest the escalators, Li Qiao.

I move away, a minnow carried in one stream, one equally as thick flows in the opposite direction. An occasional serviceman snaps a salute, old men and women nod; recognition or respect I don't care, both feel good. I'm carried to the escalator by the press of bodies, crawl upwards as it groans and creaks under the load. To either side in a sweeping arc the necropolis stretches around the mountain, soars five hundred metres above in row after row of manicured terraces, glass-fronted vaults stare out in ordered ranks.

I'm alone as I reach the last level, step out, hurry along the pathway. I come to the correct section, hunt down the correct vault. She rests in a gentle spur in the mountain, overlooks the lakes and forest below, ocean on the horizon, distant hills that resemble a tiger at rest; breezes send wisps of cloud between its ears. An auspicious location – would've cost Fùqin a fortune; Granpa would have insisted, Granma approved.

I drag myself away from the view, turn to the vaults and search. Hers is near me, head height, a thirty-by-thirty-centimetre nook protected by a glass door. I take the slip from my pocket, press it to a small, yellow-bordered box to one corner. The door swings down, clicks; a face pops up above it, head and shoulders, a young woman, radiant eyes, straight black hair, beautiful. She tilts her head to one side, smiles warmly, turns the overcast afternoon to a summer's day.

'Thank you for visiting me. I am Xiuying,' she says.

I reach out, try to touch her, forget it's a projection, not *her*.

'Niáng?'

Her face flickers, buffers. 'Thank you for visiting me. I am Xiuying.'

I'm surprised how easily I'm fooled by a simple chat-bot. It's her face, her voice, it's all I will ever get. Others have time before they go to prepare – record messages, songs, histories to be stored with them, try to fool death and their descendants as long as anyone bothers to visit. The little I know of Niáng is that she had no warning, no time; I'm surprised there's this much. I've never seen a picture of her, never heard her voice; I take out my player, set it to record, trigger the projection again, pause it;

Niáng freezes in mid-sentence, stares.

I feel emotional, uncertain. 'I'm sorry I haven't come before, I've been busy, didn't feel up to it.'

She stares, smiles.

'I guess I could've made time, it's – well, I didn't need to before.'

I reach into the vault, lift out the white porcelain urn that holds her. There's no dust, no marks, crematorium seal unbroken. Did they follow tradition, gather round one by one and pick out the remains of her bones, lower them into the ashes to share their respect and reverence? Or was it the Party way, the new way, she one of fifty or more each day wheeled conveyer-like to the pyre one side of a screen, family the other to watch her consumed, gathered, sifted then poured into her eternal vessel? I don't know if it matters or if I care, but I think I want to know.

'Looks like Fùqin's taken care of you, you're clean and secure. And the view, do you ever get tired of it, the wind, the ocean?'

I put the urn on the ground quickly, carefully, embarrassed. I talk to a pot of ashes? I look left-right, hope no one's noticed, relax and curse my stupidity. An old man to one side sings to an urn as he dusts and wipes; a woman to the other side cradles two small urns like gold, chatters to a projection of two little girls. I pick Niáng up again, rotate the urn in my hands.

'Fùqin never said anything to me about you, guess he still hurts. Same with Granpa and Granma; I don't even know if they're still around.' I point to my chest, tap the new set of wings pinned to my uniform. 'I made it, I'm a taikonaut, passed it all top of my group. I've got my first flight assignment too, next February, a year's flight, a *year*. Your son's going into space.'

I start to put her back into the vault; the urn catches the edge, slips from my hands. I grab for it as it spins, drops away; I manage to catch it, one hand on the urn, one on the lid. The lid pops off, sends a shower of grey-white ash over my trousers and shoes. I put the urn down, pull a cloth from my carry-bag. 'Damn, I haven't got time for laundry.'

I flick the cloth across my trouser leg, send most of the ash out towards the terrace; my shoes not so easy, I spit on them, try to polish it out, succeed only in putting a grey sludge watermark above the soles. 'Guess you come home with me; a bit anyway, see what I've made of myself.'

I pick the urn up, concentrate as I wipe the dust and ashes from the outside, try to push the seal back into place. 'It's a communications and maintenance assignment, the Lingbao Tianzun; not top of the tree, but it's a start. No one else out of my group got a year for their first one, shows how well I've done. Everything goes well, next one could be the Moon or Mars.'

The urn goes back in the vault, broken seal to the back. 'I thought I could tell you, you'd be proud, happy with what I am. Only wish you were here, you could talk to me, get to know me, see for yourself.'

I reach into my carry-bag, take out a pair of oranges and nine old-yuan notes. I put the oranges to the left of the urn, arrange them carefully. 'Was Fùqin like that to you, never happy, always upset? I don't know why I'm never good enough for him, why he can't accept me, accept I'm right. It's like I'm always the victim, always wrong. It would've been better if you lived instead of him.'

The woman to my side turns, smiles at me, then goes back to her conversation with the two little girls. I take the notes, arrange them into a fan shape, put them on the other side of the urn. 'I've got nothing of you, nothing until now. At least I know what you look like, your voice; that's something, isn't it? And now you know what I look like, how I turned out, what I've done; maybe one of you feels happy, a little proud?'

I turn my back to her, take out my player, grab a selfie with her, the vault, the oranges and notes in the background. A quick swipe, I send it. 'My new commander, new rules. We need to have a good profile, good public image. It's my duty, there's publicity and news feeds about us, everything in our lives. Role models they call us; can you imagine, me, a role model? So I'll be around when I can, between assignments, when I have time. It's solid training until February, then I'm gone for a year, so it could be two years until next time. Or longer. Depends. But at least now you've seen me.'

I take a step back. 'Thank you, Niáng. I am finished.'

The glass door closes, the projection fades. 'Thank you for visiting me.'

I start to walk away, stop. Fùqin stands on the terrace, hand in pocket, thunder in his eyes. 'So, twenty-nine years and you finally show up.'

'I came to pay my respects, like I should; as you should.'

'Respects? Sixteen years in Nangangzhen you never cast your shadow here, ten years' service and you never found the time.'

'You know what it's like, too busy, too little time, too many –'

'Too many women to chase, too big an ego to be bothered.'

'Duty's kept me away, posting to Australia, training in Beijing; duty to my country and the Party.'

'The only duty you keep is to yourself. You're still a self-centred, immature little brat without substance, nothing beyond your own appetites.'

'At least *I* come and tend to Niáng, there's no sign you even –'

'You only come here now because it benefits you, builds your image.'

'At least I make something of myself and rise through the ranks, don't spend my life whining like you.'

'I *earned* trust and respect, not relied on rank or obedience. You don't have a clue, it's not who you are but your character that's the measure of a man.'

'And what did you make of yourself? All you've got to show for decades of service is a missing arm, didn't even make Captain for all your duty, your service. And where were you when I needed you?'

'I was there when I could, tried my best —'

'Your best? You call that —'

'It wouldn't matter what it was, where I was — you didn't listen, never took any notice.'

'You never said anything *worth* taking notice of. I wish you'd died instead of her; I could've had a decent parent, a good parent, instead of you.'

He steps forward, bunches his fist, sticks out his chin. 'I told Xiuying, *begged* her on my hands and knees to abort you, but she didn't, promised me a son, said it would complete her, me — and look what I *got*.' He tenses, shifts, I get ready to take the first punch but he hawks, spits vehemently at my feet. 'Every moment of my miserable life since, I've cursed your birth, cursed her choice; she traded her life for yours, and for what? Waste, a total waste.'

Anger burns, starts the shakes as he turns, strides away. 'I've done more than you ever did, I'm twice the man than you ever were! I'm the best damned test pilot, the best taikonaut they've ever had. Ten years, ten years and I outrank you, outperform you,

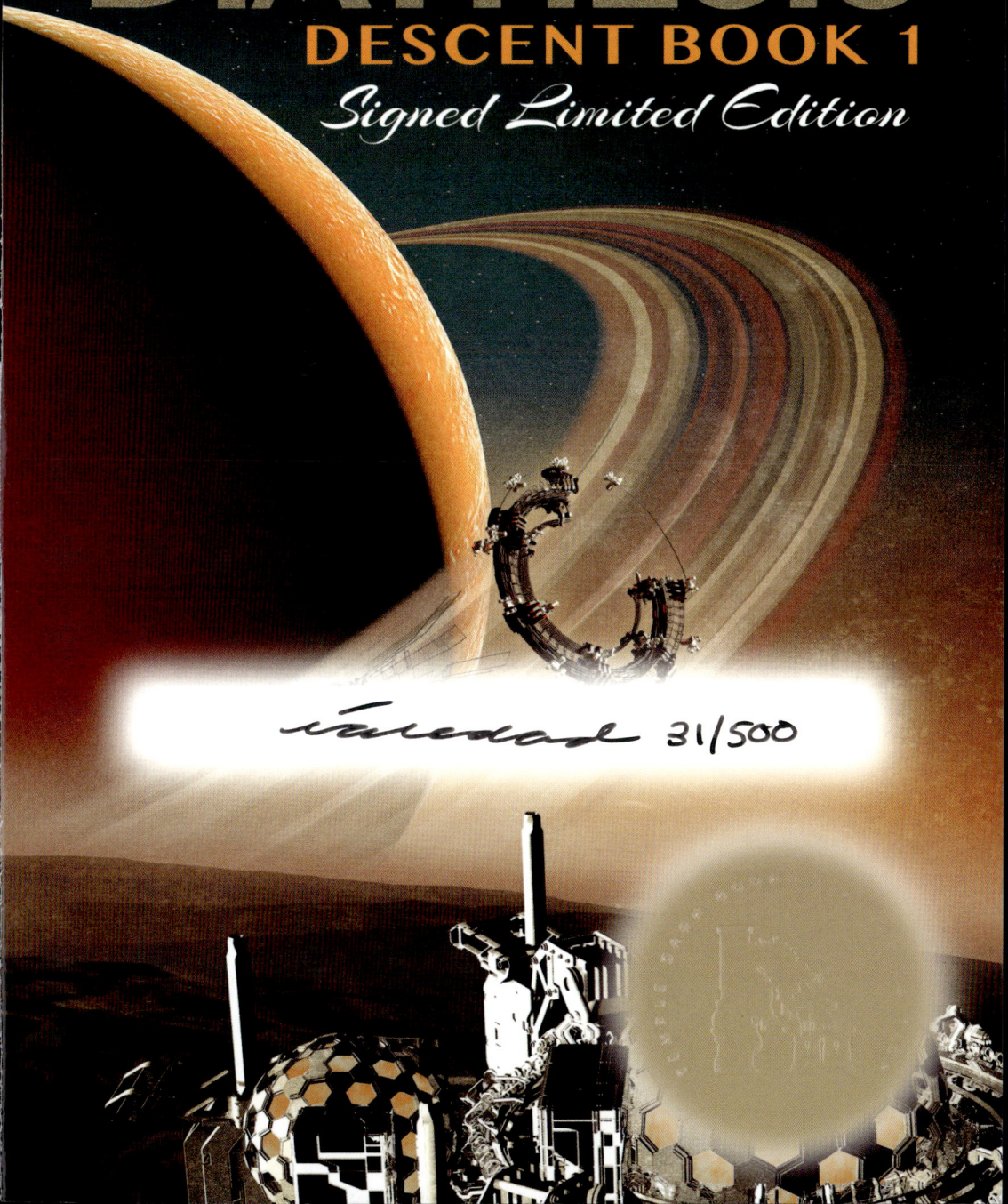

DIATHESIS

DESCENT BOOK 1

Signed Limited Edition

31/500

out-everything you. Me, do you hear, *me*, and I've done it all no thanks to you. Waste? You should be grateful for the honour of being my father!'

He stops, turns, cold as ice. 'Honour? You? You've done nothing by yourself, gone nowhere. Want to know why they took you into the taikonaut course? Because of my old comrade; not you or what you think you can do, but because of *her*. You are nothing, you always were nothing, and you'll always be nothing. To me or anyone.'

I let him go, scream at his back as he retreats. 'Go on, walk away like you always do, leave me alone! You can get out of my life for good if you want, if next time I see you you're beside her in a damned jar it'll be too soon!'

I stare at the empty, take deep breaths, try to calm down. Typical, unfair, unnecessary, he can't even leave me alone to do something good and filial without attacking me. There's a gentle cough to one side; the woman with the two little girls looks up at me, cautious, concerned.

'Excuse me, are you alright?' she asks.

'Yes, perfectly, thank you.'

'Who was that you were shouting at?'

'Fùqin. We never see eye to eye.'

'Ah, parents. They can be difficult, stubborn.'

'Some more than others, apparently.'

'He serves, like you?'

'Army, his whole life.'

'And you chose to follow him.'

'Yes, and bettered him; but he can't accept it, always finds fault.' I look past her at the two girls' projections. 'Your daughters, you're not like that with them, I don't understand why

Fùqin treats me this way.'

She hesitates, wipes away a solitary tear. 'They never had the chance to live up to my dreams, didn't live long enough to disappoint me. My sons? Well, they have.'

'You're ashamed of them?'

'No, they chose their paths, decided against my hopes and dreams, fell short of what I wanted for them; so it's disappointment. The shame is mine, that I tried to make them what I failed to be.'

She turns to the projection of her two girls. 'Goodnight, my angels.' The projection fades, she turns back to me. 'At least your father lives to see your success. Some of us don't get the chance.'

'I'm sorry, I didn't mean to offend –'

She places her hand on mine, squeezes, walks away. 'As your father and you, as his parents and their parents and all our ancestors, it's the same. Same as it will be for your children. We always fall short.'

BONUS CONTENT
FROM DESCENT BOOK 2: DEATH

GODDARD HAB, IAPETUS
MONDAY 10 November 2149 23:55 GMT

MARIA

Othon hauls me over the console, onto the floor. 'What've you done?'

'Guess.'

He hammers furiously at the displays. 'There's nothing, Amber, nothing up, nothing responds.'

I reach for my neck, feel it under layers of suit, insulation and mesh, see the rings and connectors in my mind. They'd understand, they know, they'd approve the cost no matter what anyone else thinks.

'Maria! Maria, how do we stop it?' Amber asks.

'Stop what? You don't even know what you don't know.'

'Othon, try to get Ismud, hot-wire Station if you have to, I'll try from here,' Amber says.

I roll onto my side, stare out over Iapetus in the half light, watch Saturn float above the horizon. All this beauty around us, with us, and we're not happy. The light grows, throws crazy shadows that dance, blend, crackle. One darkens, shifts, changes shape to a horse's head. I'm taken back to a room in Santiago, my bed, my first lesson. The light changes, concentrates, burns through a gap in the horizon. 'Yayo, I let my enemies lose.'

Othon grabs my shoulders, drags me up. 'How do I get Station back?'

I forget my helmet, spit at him, watch the globule slide down my visor as he shoves me down, goes back to the console.

'What's happening?' Amber asks.

I throw my head back, laugh, let my new sun burn out my eyes. 'I've won, Amber, I've won.'

JOIN US IN 2026 FOR *DEATH*, BOOK 2 OF DESCENT

Position of Saturn at
Goddard Rescue
Mission Launch
August 2146

Goddard Rescue
Mission Trajectory
August 2146
July 2149

Position of Saturn at
Goddard Rescue
Mission Arrival
July 2149